MIRAGE

ALSO BY KRISTI COOK

Haven

KRISTI COOK

Simon Pulse

NEW YORK LONDON TORONTO SYDNEY NEW DELHI

SIMON PULSE

An imprint of Simon & Schuster Children's Publishing Division

1230 Avenue of the Americas, New York, NY 10020

First Simon Pulse hardcover edition June 2012

Copyright © 2012 by Kristina Cook Hort

All rights reserved, including the right of reproduction in whole or in part in any form.

SIMON PULSE and colophon are registered trademarks of Simon & Schuster, Inc.

For information about special discounts for bulk purchases, please contact Simon & Schuster Special Sales at 1-866-506-1949 or business@simonandschuster.com.

The Simon & Schuster Speakers Bureau can bring authors to your live event. For more information or to book an event contact the Simon & Schuster Speakers Bureau at 1-866-248-3049 or visit our website at www.simonspeakers.com.

Designed by Mike Rosamilia

The text of this book was set in Berling LT Std.

Manufactured in the United States of America

2 4 6 8 10 9 7 5 3 1

Library of Congress Cataloging-in-Publication Data

Cook, Kristi.

Mirage / Kristi Cook.

p. cm.

Sequel to: Haven.

Summary: Seventeen-year-old Violet McKenna, back for her senior year at Winterhaven, finds her friends in danger, a mysterious new teacher as her psychic coach, and her *Sâbbat* tendencies threatening her relationship with Aidan.

ISBN 978-1-4424-4299-3 (hardcover)

[1. Psychic ability—Fiction. 2. Supernatural—Fiction. 3. Boarding schools—Fiction. 4. Schools—Fiction. 5. Orphans—Fiction. 6. New York (State)—Fiction.] I. Title.

PZ7.C76984Hav 2011   [Fic]—dc23   2011041952

ISBN 978-1-4424-4301-3 (eBook)

For my mom, Laurie,
my number one fan all these years

MIRAGE

1 ~ There's No Place like Home

I'd never thought too much about friendship before I came to Winterhaven, mostly because I hadn't had many friends. Not because I didn't want to, but because I couldn't. The more people I got close to, the more people I saw in my visions, which were harbingers of awful things to come. Besides, the more friends I had, the more people I had to hide my secret from, the more I had to pretend that I didn't know about things before they happened.

But now . . . now I had friends. Friends I didn't have to pretend with. I looked around the classroom at them, their heads bent over their desks—Marissa, her dark hair falling across one pale cheek; Kate, her chin propped in one hand as she stared dreamily out the window; Sophie, pushing her strawberry-blond curls off her forehead, her brow furrowed in concentration. Jack and Joshua, sitting side by side, as if there were nothing weird about a telekinetic football star and a shape-shifter outcast being friends. And Cece—wonderful, amazing Cece—my roommate, my best friend.

Together, they had risked their lives for me. And for Aidan.

I glanced over one shoulder at the tall girl sitting two rows back, her model-perfect face pale and taut. Jenna Holley. Jenna *hadn't* been a friend—not even close—and yet she'd saved us all.

Why? I still didn't know. I wanted answers, and now that we were back at Winterhaven—

"Five more minutes," a voice called out, startling me. I looked up and saw Dr. Byrne pointing to the clock on the wall.

I glanced down at the page on my desk, blinking hard. There were still a half-dozen little circles that I hadn't filled in. Good thing this was just the SAT practice test, and not the real thing. There was no way I could concentrate right now, not with all of us back together again. All I could think about was that horrible day in May—a day I'd never forget, as long as I lived.

On the plus side, my friends knew the truth now—that Aidan was a vampire and that I was some supposedly rare kind of vampire slayer. A *Sâbbat*. I was finally getting used to it, and even coming to terms with the fact that I'd actually slain not one but *three* vampires with my trusty little hawthorne stake. The *Sâbbat's* weapon of choice, apparently. Ironically, mine was lovingly crafted by a vampire, which had to be a totally new one in the *Sâbbat* world—not that I'd know, as I'd never met another *Sâbbat*. Chances were pretty slim that I ever would, since there were only three in the world at any given time. At least, according to the legend.

"Two minutes," came Dr. Byrne's voice, interrupting my wandering thoughts. Dr. Hottie, the girls at Winterhaven liked to call him, and I had to admit it was a fitting nickname. I briefly wondered what his talent was, since everyone here at Winterhaven had one. Maybe he was an empath, like my friend Marissa, I mused. That would make him ideal for teaching the SAT prep course—he could make us all feel relaxed and confident, if he chose to.

"One minute," he intoned, and I began to hastily fill in the remaining circles. If I marked them all C, chances were I'd get some right. At least, I hoped so.

It was the first day of orientation, that weird transition time at Winterhaven when the upperclassmen had to hide their gifts and talents from the freshmen till they all caught on. And while the other upperclassmen were busy finalizing their schedules and signing up for extracurriculars, my friends and I were all stuck making up the final SAT prep class, the one we'd missed last spring after the whole showdown thing. None of us had been in any condition then to finish the class, much less take the actual SATs.

So here we were, stuck inside this stuffy classroom, trying to remember everything we'd learned three months ago. Everyone except Aidan, that is. He was still at home in Manhattan, but he'd promised he would be here tomorrow. I could barely wait to see him—the minutes were dragging by. It had been too long. *Way* too long.

After all, my summer hadn't exactly gone as planned. Instead of spending a few weeks in Atlanta, I had spent the entire break there. I hadn't really had a choice. On the last day of finals, Gran had had a stroke—a fairly serious one—and so I'd packed up my trunks and flown down there to help out the moment classes were over.

Not that I was complaining. Sure, I missed my friends. And I missed Aidan, especially since our telepathy didn't seem to have a long-distance channel and we were forced to use more conventional methods of communication to keep in touch. But Gran and her companion/housekeeper, Lupe, needed me, and family comes first. Besides, it had given me a chance to catch up with Whitney, my best friend since kindergarten, even if we *had* grown apart lately. How could we not, with all the secrets I was forced to keep from her?

Anyway, my Winterhaven friends had mostly scattered over the summer, and Aidan had remained at school, working obsessively in the chemistry lab on his cure for vampirism. And since the only way we could ever really be together was if he *did* manage to find a cure, let's just say I'm *very* supportive of his work.

And so summer had come and gone. Whitney and I had successfully rekindled our friendship. Gran had gotten stronger and fully regained her speech, and I'd helped Lupe hire a full-time home health aide who moved in with them just last week. The aide, Melanie, seemed great, and that alleviated my guilt about leaving them. I knew they were in good hands, and I was excited to get back to school and start my senior year.

"Time!" Dr. Byrne called out, and I realized that he'd given us way more than the one minute he'd promised. With a sigh, I set down my pencil and followed the chattering crowd up to Dr. Byrne's desk to drop off my answer sheet.

"Don't forget the senior meeting in the auditorium," he yelled over the din. "We'll be talking about college applications."

Great. I glanced over at Cece, who rolled her eyes. It seemed like we were never going to get any time to just hang out and catch up. Cece and I reached his desk together, slapping our answer sheets onto the top of the pile.

"Oh, and Miss McKenna?"

I glanced up in surprise at the sound of my name.

"Can I see you for just a few moments, after we're all done here?"

The whole room seemed to go silent at once, everyone glancing from me to Dr. Byrne and back to me again. "Sure," I said, feeling the heat rise in my cheeks. What in the world did he want with me?

"Do you want us to wait?" Cece asked, tipping her head toward Sophie, Marissa, and Kate, who stood by the door, goggling.

"No, it's okay. Just save me a seat, okay?" I stood there awkwardly by his desk as the room emptied. Jenna was the last out, glancing back curiously over her shoulder as she stepped into the hall.

Dr. Byrne picked up the answer sheets, adjusting them into a neat stack before he shoved them into a manila folder. Finally his gaze met mine, and he smiled. Which, embarrassingly enough, caused my heart to do a little flip-flop. Since I had no idea what his gift was, I kept my thoughts locked up good and tight—a preventive measure. At Winterhaven you never knew who might be listening in.

"Do you want to sit?" He gestured toward the seat in the front row, right across from his desk.

"Sure," I murmured, slipping into the seat he'd indicated

while he leaned back against the desk, his arms folded across his chest.

"Don't worry," he said with a laugh. "You're not in trouble or anything. I didn't mean to scare you."

I looked scared? Well, I guess that was better than looking flustered.

"I was just speaking with Mrs. Girard, and she tells me you were getting some psychic coaching from Sandra Wilkinson last year. She's a mind reader, right?"

"Yeah," I answered, wondering where this was going. "At first she was just teaching me to block. But then we started working on my visions. It's not really her thing, but she tried to help as best she could."

"Well, you're in luck. I've got a little extra time this semester, and I told Mrs. Girard that I'd be willing to help out. I've never really coached before, but I'm willing to give it a try if you are."

I wasn't quite following him. Give it a try? He was offering to coach me?

"I'm a precog," he clarified, noting my confusion. "Visions. Pretty much just like yours, from what I understand. Generally bad stuff, and almost exclusively about people I'm close to. Sound familiar?"

"Yes," I said breathlessly, leaning forward in my chair. "Are you able to control them? You know, summon a replay, or anything like that?"

He nodded. "Pretty much. It's not an exact science, but I know a few tricks. Anyway, if you're interested, I'm willing to share what I know."

"Definitely," I said, nodding. The idea of working with someone with the same gift as me, someone who actually understood what it was like and who might even be able to help me—well, it gave me a new kind of hope.

"Great," Dr. Byrne said with a smile, and I couldn't help but wonder how old he was. Rumor put him right around twenty-five or so, but that seemed awfully young, considering he had a PhD and had been teaching at Winterhaven for a year already. "How are Saturday mornings for you?" he asked, drawing me from my thoughts. "I'm living on campus this year. Assistant West Hall dorm master."

Marissa had said as much, just this morning. The school was abuzz with the news that we'd now have Dr. Hottie around seven days a week, instead of five.

"Sandra and I always met on Saturdays at eleven," I offered. We'd met in my dorm room, which I supposed wasn't an option with Dr. Byrne, considering the "no guys on the girls' floor and vice versa" rule—even if he *was* a teacher.

"Okay, then. Eleven on Saturdays it is. We can meet in my

office. It's in the science wing, corridor C. I'm on the fifth floor. Probably more comfortable than a classroom."

"Sure," I said with a shrug, going for nonchalance. But oh my God, my friends were going to *die*. Truly, I was never going to hear the end of this one. Because they all had crushes on Dr. Byrne—pretty much the school's entire female population did.

Unaware of my current train of thought, Dr. Byrne nodded, pushing off from his desk. "Great. We'll start this Saturday, then."

I nodded, a little too stunned to do much else.

After a pause, he glanced down at his watch. "You should probably get over to the auditorium. The senior meeting's just about to begin."

"Sure, thanks," I managed to mumble, my cheeks burning with embarrassment. I reached for my bag and slung it over one shoulder, suddenly anxious to get out of there, and fast.

I hurried out, my sneakers squeaking against the tiles as I made my way through the now empty hall toward the auditorium. For the, oh, perhaps fiftieth time that day, I wished Aidan was there beside me. The anticipation was driving me nuts. I could feel it—a living, breathing thing pulsing through my veins, making my heart beat faster. After an entire summer apart, Aidan had never felt so close yet so far away.

He should have been there at LaGuardia to meet my plane;

he should be at school with me now, suffering through orientation like the rest of us. Instead, he was out hunting murderers and rapists, drinking their blood to slake his thirst so that he could come to me completely sated and not at all tempted to drink *my* blood. Not that he'd ever really had the urge to do so, except when we were making out.

Of course, he had no idea about *my* urges—the ever-increasing desire I had to feel his teeth against my neck. I couldn't understand it—it went against all my natural *Sâbbat* tendencies. And I'd certainly never admit to it, especially to Aidan. It would only alarm him, and probably rightfully so. It definitely alarmed *me*.

Increasing my pace, I made a sharp right turn and hurried down the corridor till I came to the last set of doors on the right. I stepped into the auditorium, scanning the crowd for my friends. I saw them near the back, a row of familiar heads all bent toward each other in conversation. As if she sensed my presence, Cece turned. Spying me just inside the door, she waved me over.

A slow smile spread across my face. Aidan or no, it was awfully good to be back home at the 'Haven.

2 ~ England and Scotland and France, Oh My!

Hey, the Sorbonne is on this list!" Kate exclaimed, plopping down on the little loveseat next to Sophie.

I glanced down at the sheet of paper I held in my hands. "Yeah, there's a couple of schools in France listed. England and Scotland, too."

Kate kicked off her shoes and tucked her feet beneath her. "Cool. Can you even imagine going to school in Europe?"

Marissa perched on the edge of my bed beside me. "Nope. My parents would never let me."

"Yeah, mine either," Sophie agreed glumly. "But hey, at least they've got most of the Ivies covered. Harvard, Princeton,

Brown, Columbia, Dartmouth, Cornell. No Yale or Penn, though. Interesting."

I flipped the page over and scanned the back. "I'm surprised there's so many." The two-page sheet included all major universities with faculty members who were "sympathetic to our situation," as they'd termed it in the senior meeting. An asterisk by the school's name meant a significant psychically gifted population. A cross meant psychically gifted faculty members on the admissions committee. Schools with both an asterisk *and* a cross would be a best-case scenario. Still, Dr. Ackerman, the senior adviser, reminded us that we were free to apply anywhere we chose. The list was just a helpful guide, she said.

I was kind of leaning toward Columbia or maybe NYU— both on the list—thinking I'd like to stay in New York City, close to Aidan. I was hoping to convince him to apply too, though I knew that if he hadn't gotten any closer to finding his cure, he'd think it was pointless.

Still, I harbored this crazy little vision of the two of us living cozily together in Aidan's town house on the Upper East Side while studying at Columbia. Of course, my stepmom, Patsy, would never in a million years allow it—but still.

Once the happy glow of the daydream wore off and I

was faced with reality, I had no idea what our future together held. If Aidan didn't find his cure, he would remain a perpetual boy—like Peter Pan—while I'd continue to age, to mature into an adult. I knew he'd never stick around if that were the case. Or worse, he'd try to convince me to destroy him. I didn't want it to come to that. *Ever.*

"Well, we don't have much time left to decide, do we?" Kate said, then let out a sigh. "I wish we could just freeze time and stay here at Winterhaven forever."

"Me too," I murmured. That way, I'd never have to worry about the future—about my developing *Sâbbat* tendencies or anything like that.

"Anyway," Kate continued, setting aside the list, "did the rest of you see how fast Jenna got out of there when the meeting ended? I was trying to get her attention, but she totally blew me off."

Sophie nodded. "Yeah, she definitely doesn't want to talk to us. I don't get it—it's not like we're going to spill her secret. I mean, c'mon. If it wasn't for her . . ." She allowed that thought to trail off, and we were all silent. I'm sure we were all picturing it—that bloody scene beside the chapel where we'd fought Julius, the rogue vampire who'd tried to force me to kill Aidan.

"She's got to talk to us at some point," Marissa said. "You

don't just save someone's life"—she swallowed hard—"and then refuse to tell them why you did it."

Because it had been Marissa's lifeblood staining the grass when Jenna had appeared in wolf form and started ripping out the vampire's throat. It had been that action that had set off a new chain of events, events I hadn't foreseen in my gruesome vision. Jenna's unexpected appearance had been the catalyst, the turning point that had allowed us to change what I'd seen. Because of her we'd won and Aidan was still alive.

Finally Marissa spoke again. "Hey, where's Cece?"

"Student council meeting," I said, my voice thick now. "Declaring her candidacy for senior class president. She thinks Stacy Dalton is going to run against her."

Kate raised her brows. "That should be interesting. I guess Stacy'll lock in all the clairsentient votes."

"Except for mine," Sophie put in cheerfully.

"Well, we've got the tellies," Kate said. The telekinetics, she meant. "More of us."

"And I assume the shifters are in too, thanks to Joshua," Sophie added. "Which way do you think the empaths will go?" she asked Marissa.

Marissa shrugged. "Dunno. Either way, I guess."

It still amazed me the way kids grouped into cliques according to their psychic abilities. As far as I could tell, my group of mixed-ability friends was the exception rather than the rule. And what a diverse bunch we were, especially when you counted a vampire in the mix.

I glanced down at my watch, willing away the hours till tomorrow. When I looked up again, Marissa was watching me closely, her brow furrowed in concentration.

"What?" I asked her.

"Just trying to figure out if you're counting down the hours till you see Aidan again or until your first training session with Dr. Hottie."

I shot her a scowl. "Ha-ha. Very funny. What do you think?"

"I just can't believe your luck. I mean, c'mon. Why couldn't he have been an empath? You've *got* a boyfriend."

"You *do* realize he's a teacher, don't you?" Sophie asked. "First off, that's, like, totally illegal. And even if it wasn't . . . ewww."

Marissa looked mortally offended. "What do you mean, ewww? You were drooling over him last year, just like the rest of us."

"Yeah, well." Sophie's cheeks pinkened. "Still. He *is* a teacher. It's one thing to lust after him in secret, but he's definitely not boyfriend material."

"Well, duh. Thanks for enlightening me."

I was happy to see that Marissa hadn't changed much, despite her near-death experience.

"Okay, Marissa, take it down a notch," Kate said. "You're starting to suck all the happy out of the room."

Marissa's emotional state could affect us all. It apparently worked in reverse, too. Pretty interesting, but sometimes it could be a drag.

"Sorry," she said, though she didn't sound it. Still, I felt the tension in the air dissipate. "Hey, did anyone notice the new guy? Brown-haired surfer dude sitting in the front row during the senior meeting?"

Sophie nodded. "Yes! Transfer student from Summerhaven. I heard his name is Tyler something or other."

I'd only recently learned that Summerhaven was our "sister school" in California—in Malibu, right on the coast. Turns out there's an entire network of schools like ours scattered across the country.

"Poor guy, transferring his senior year," I said. "That's gotta suck."

Kate shrugged. "I dunno. Did you get a good look at him? People will be falling all over each other trying to cozy up to him."

"Yeah, the really shallow people," Marissa said with a scowl.

"I prefer the term 'aesthetically inclined,' if you don't

mind." Kate stuck her tongue out at Marissa before continuing. "Anyway, since he's coming from Summerhaven, he knows exactly what's going on here. It's not like you last year, Violet."

I winced, remembering my first day. To say that I had been caught completely off guard by Winterhaven's secrets would be a gross understatement. At first I'd thought they were lying to me. Then, once I realized they were telling the truth, I'd cried like a baby. I'd kinda hoped they'd forgotten— I know I wish *I* had.

"I should finish unpacking," I said, tilting my head toward the open duffel bag in the room's corner, the contents spilling out haphazardly.

Kate rose with a yawn, stretching her arms toward the ceiling. "Yeah, I'm supposed to meet up with Jack in a little bit, anyway."

"Will you tell Cece to call me when she gets in?" Marissa asked, getting up from the bed and moving toward the door. "I want to make sure we're signed up for the same English section."

"Sure," I said. "Soph, you've got third period with Ackerman too, don't you?"

Sophie nodded. "Yep. Looks like we're starting with the gothic novel, then doing the romantics second semester. Fun, huh?"

"Maybe we'll read Bram Stoker's *Dracula*," I said, raising my brows for emphasis.

Sophie laughed. "Now, wouldn't that be ironic? You think Ackerman knows?"

I shook my head. "I have no idea who knows what anymore."

"Yeah, it seems weird around here without Dr. Blackwell, doesn't it? Sometimes I almost forget . . . well . . ." Sophie trailed off with a shrug. She didn't need to finish the sentence; we all knew exactly what she meant.

Dr. Blackwell had been Winterhaven's headmaster, and we'd all been involved in the events that had led to his demise. But it had been Mrs. Girard, together with the vampire Tribunal, who'd ultimately destroyed him. I didn't know the details—didn't want to know them. All that mattered was that he'd betrayed Aidan and paid the price.

"Anyway," Sophie continued, "see you tomorrow."

"Yeah, later," Kate called out, opening the door—without using her hands, of course—and stepping out into the hall, Sophie and Marissa following behind.

"Hey, you awake?" Cece whispered as she tiptoed across the floor toward her dresser.

"Yeah," I said, rubbing my eyes as I sat up. "You can turn on the overhead light."

"Nah, I'm fine," she answered, rummaging around in her drawers. "Sorry I'm so late. Todd and I were having the 'maybe we should see other people' talk, and time just got away from me."

"Uh-oh. How'd it go?" I propped my pillows behind my head, watching Cece as she pulled out an old, ratty T-shirt and boxers, her usual sleep attire.

"A lot better than I expected." She headed into the closet, where she stripped off her clothes and deposited them into her hamper. "Sounds like he was having some doubts too," she called out, her voice muffled as she pulled the T-shirt over her head. "I mean, being apart all summer really gives you some perspective, you know?"

"Yeah, I know." I missed Aidan like crazy. *That* was the perspective I'd gained over the summer.

Cece strode back in and started gathering up toiletries. "I bet you do. Speaking of which, when is Aidan planning on gracing us with his vampiric presence?"

"Tomorrow around lunchtime," I answered, butterflies fluttering in my stomach at the mention of his name.

"Ah, now I get it." There was a wicked twinkle in Cece's dark eyes. "Why you're in bed way before curfew, I mean. The faster you fall asleep, the faster tomorrow comes, right?"

I couldn't help but laugh—she knew me *so* well. "I swear

it feels like Christmas Eve. I've just been lying here, staring at the ceiling."

"Awww, that's so cute," Cece teased, sliding on her bunny slippers before heading toward the door. "I'm going to wash my face. Be right back."

"Okay. But when you get back, you've got to give me the play-by-play of your talk with Todd."

"Deal," she said.

"Oh, and Marissa wants you to call her!" I shouted toward Cece's back just as the door slammed shut.

With a yawn, I reached for the clock radio beside my bed and flipped on the switch. Clearly the station dial had been moved in transit, and some weird new-age music droned out. Actually, it wasn't too bad, I decided. It reminded me of the time that Patsy had taken me to a spa in Buckhead for a massage and facial—a girls' day out, she'd called it. The music was supposed to be relaxing, and I guess it was, considering how heavy my eyelids suddenly felt.

Breathing deeply, I closed my eyes. My limbs felt weightless, somehow disconnected from my body, as I allowed the music to wash over me, soothing me.

An elevator. Glass panels and shiny, dark wood. It was the elevator in Patsy's building, I realized. Someone was pushing the L button, stabbing it repeatedly—a girl wearing a pink sweater and jeans, her nails painted a metallic blue. I could hear her breathing loudly, nearly panting. She turned, looking around wildly, her pale blond hair slipping from a ponytail. Whitney! I could sense her fear. The elevator pinged, and the doors slid open. Whitney ran out, stumbling through the lobby, past the doorman's empty desk and out through the building's double doors. It was nighttime. Whitney looked back over her shoulder, as if she were trying to see if anyone was following her, and then she took off running.

Soon she was darting into Central Park, where the trees were bare, the grass a dull, brittle brown. She headed toward a covered tunnel lit with a yellowish light, but then veered off, down a narrow footpath to the left. And then someone popped into my vision directly behind her, as if he'd simply materialized there out of thin air. I saw Whitney turn, saw her eyes widen when she saw him there behind her.

"No!" she cried out. I saw him then—Aidan. I saw the way he looked at her, his eyes rimmed in red and full of bloodlust. He reached for her just as she tripped, falling to her knees on the path with a look of pure terror on her face.

I sat up with a gasp, my fingernails digging into the mattress. I blinked several times, trying to get my bearings, fighting off the hysteria that was bubbling up inside me.

Oh. My. God. There was no mistaking what I'd just seen—

Aidan was going after Whitney, fully intending to . . . to . . . attack her.

Only it didn't make sense; none of it made any sense. What was Whitney doing in New York, at Patsy's apartment? And more important, what was wrong with Aidan? Because something would have to be *seriously* wrong with him if this was going to occur. He didn't hunt innocents, didn't feed from people who weren't evil to the core. And Whitney was *not* evil. In fact, she was about as far from evil as they came.

What the hell?

I shook my head, attempting to clear it, to rid my brain of those awful images. Was it possible that I'd just fallen asleep and dreamed it? Just before the vision, my eyelids had felt heavy. The spa music had definitely made me sleepy. That had to be it—I'd dozed off and had a weird dream, maybe even a dream masquerading as a vision. That made way more sense.

Besides, I hadn't experienced my usual prevision aura— my sight hadn't tunneled, my ears hadn't buzzed. There hadn't been any warning signs at all. One minute I was lying there, all relaxed and sleepy, and the next minute the images had appeared in my mind.

The door opened and Cece shuffled in, setting down her toiletries on her desk. As soon as she looked in my direction, her eyes went wide. "Uh-oh, you've got that look. A vision?"

"No, a dream. A nightmare," I corrected, praying it was the truth.

"Whew." Cece's eyes narrowed. "You look terrified, though. You okay?"

I licked my lips before I could reply. "Yeah, I . . . I guess so. It's just that I fell asleep for a second there, and when I woke up I thought maybe it had been a vision, but . . ." I trailed off, shaking my head, still trying to clear it. "But I was definitely asleep," I said, more to convince myself than Cece.

Because my visions didn't work that way—they never happened when I was lying in bed, relaxing, floating off to sleep. No, they were way more inconvenient than that. I'd never had a dream that I mistook for a vision, or the other way around. Maybe because I wasn't prone to nightmares? And why should I be, when I saw horrific enough things while wide awake?

The memory of my father's kidnapping and murder came flooding back, and a shudder racked my body. Hot tears burned behind my eyelids, and I blinked them away. I'd never be able to banish those images—ever. They'd continue to haunt me the rest of my life, no matter how hard I tried to erase them from my mind. I mean, how could a nightmare possibly compete with *that*?

It couldn't, I realized. Not even the one I'd just had.

"You want to talk about it?" Cece offered, climbing into her own bed and turning onto her side to face me.

I shook my head. "Definitely not. Anyway, you promised to tell me about the breakup."

"Yeah, I did, didn't I?"

With that, I pushed aside all thoughts of the dream—the nightmare—and concentrated on Cece's voice instead.

3 ~ Love Bites

I was walking across campus to fencing practice when I first felt it—that familiar little buzzing in my head. And then Aidan's voice, as loud and clear as if he were standing right there beside me.

Violet?

Excitement flooded my veins, made my heart accelerate.

You're here? I glanced around, hoping that nobody was watching me as I stood there smiling giddily to myself.

I'm here, he confirmed. *Where are you?*

On my way to the gym for practice. I'll be done in an hour. Where are you?

I'll meet you at the chapel after practice, came his reply.

Okay, see you then.

Oh, man. This was going to be a *long* hour. I hurried my step, walking on air now. The anticipation was nearly killing me, like a sharp, searing burn beneath my skin.

I slowed as I neared the gym, allowing myself to remember the last time he'd kissed me, just before I'd boarded the plane to Atlanta back in June. It had taken every ounce of strength I possessed to finally step away from him, to turn and walk toward that plane.

I only hoped the reality of our reunion could live up to my imaginings. Which, I realized, seemed unlikely, given the enormity of the buildup in my mind. It was probably a good thing that I had to get through an hour's worth of practice first, to focus my mind elsewhere.

"Hey, Violet!" a voice called out, and I turned to see one of my teammates headed toward me, one hand raised in a wave.

I waved back. "Hey, Suzanne." She was a telepath, but since my own telepathy only seemed to work with vampires, I had to call out to her. "How was your summer?"

She glanced down at her watch. "Great, but we better hurry or we'll be late."

With a nod, I fell into a jog beside her.

"So glad you could join us, ladies," Coach Gibson called

out as soon as we stepped inside, just two minutes late. "I was just introducing the newest member of the boys' varsity team, Tyler Bennett."

I stood on my tiptoes and saw the new guy standing there looking slightly uncomfortable. Shaggy brown hair streaked with gold fell almost to his shoulders. He looked like he belonged on the beach beside a surfboard, not here on the piste.

"McKenna, I think you might have finally met your match," the coach added with a smile, clapping Tyler on the shoulder. "Finally, a boys' top seed as strong as our girls'."

Great. Way to start him off on the right foot, I thought. The other guys on the team looked almost mutinous.

"Okay, grab your foils and pair up," Coach Gibson barked. "McKenna, I want you with Bennett." Of course he did. "We'll start with some warm-ups."

"Hey," Tyler said with an easy smile as I approached. "So *you're* McKenna?"

"Afraid so." I nodded as I took my place beside him. "But you can call me Violet."

Before raising his foil, he brushed his hair out of his eyes— pale green eyes that reminded me of sea glass, particularly striking in his tanned face. I might have been in love with someone else, but I wasn't blind. He was cute.

And he's the competition, I reminded myself as Coach began to call out commands.

As soon as warm-ups were finished, we broke from the line, donned our protective masks, and turned to face our opponents. Coach moved among the pairs, his voice a muted rumble as foils began to slash through the air and feet shuffled across the rubber mats.

"C'mon, McKenna," Coach called out from somewhere to my right. "Be more aggressive. Show him what you've got."

Beneath my mask, sweat dripped down the side of my face, my breath coming faster now.

"That's it, McKenna," came the coach's voice. "You've got to move more quickly, Bennett. Anticipate her every move."

It was immediately obvious that we were well matched, just as Coach had said. I sharpened my focus, pushing every extraneous thought from my mind as my foil whipped toward his, my feet moving faster, my thighs beginning to feel the burn.

Several minutes later, Coach called out the command for us to stop. I pulled off my mask and wiped my forehead with the back of one hand.

Tyler did the same. "You're good," he said with a drawl that didn't sound very California-like. "But I'm better," he added with a smirk.

"Oh yeah?" I challenged. Too bad he couldn't see me in action with my stake. "We'll see about that."

His mouth widened into a smile, the corners of his eyes crinkling with the effort. "I like a challenge."

I couldn't help but roll my eyes. "I bet you do."

"Cut the chatter," Coach Gibson barked. "I'm going to call you up in pairs. Everyone else watch, and then we'll critique. Got it?"

We all nodded in unison.

"Okay, first up, McKenna and Bennett. Let's show 'em how it's done."

A half hour later, Tyler and I sat side by side on the dusty gym floor, stuffing our equipment back into our bags with matching scowls. Our technique had been deemed "sloppy" and "careless" by our teammates, which seemed a little harsh, all things considered.

But it was par for the course, considering the competitive nature of the team. After all, fencing scholarships were plum deals, especially at top-tier universities. Everyone wanted to be the best. Attempting to rattle your competitor's confidence was just part of the game. I assumed that Tyler had experienced the same at his previous school.

"So, you transferred here from Summerhaven, huh?" I asked, just trying to make conversation.

"Yeah," he muttered, apparently not quite over the insults that had been tossed our way.

"How'd you guys do at state?"

"We came in second," was all he offered.

"Huh. And what is it that you do? You know, your gift?"

He zipped up his bag and glanced up at me with a mischievous grin. "Yeah, I knew what you meant."

I shrugged. "It's not like I care, but it *is* against the COPA not to tell." The Code of Paranormal Activity basically outlined the school's rules about using your psychic gift.

"I'm telekinetic," he said, reaching down to adjust the braided bracelets he wore around one wrist. There must have been a dozen of them, a rainbow of colors against his skin. "Micro," he clarified.

Ah, like Jack. "I'm a precog," I offered, zipping up my bag.

"A precog, huh? How's that workin' out for you?"

"I'm still not sure," I answered with a shrug. "So where are you from, Tyler Bennett? Because that drawl is definitely not from California."

"Nah, I'm from Texas. Austin. What about you? That ain't no New Yawk accent you got there," he teased.

I shook my head. "Atlanta. So . . . Texas? That's pretty far away. Why'd you transfer here?"

"Why so many questions?" he countered, catching me off guard.

I wasn't sure if he was teasing me, or if he was serious. "Sheesh, I was just trying to be friendly. Forget it," I said, clambering to my feet.

"My dad died," he said quickly, rising to stand beside me. His steady green gaze met mine, all traces of humor gone now. "And my mom wanted to move back east, to Connecticut, where she has family. So . . . I came east too."

I swallowed hard. God, I felt terrible—such a careless question. If only I'd known, I never would have prodded him like that. I knew exactly how he felt. I wanted to tell him that my dad had died too. But I didn't. I couldn't. "I'm sorry," I mumbled instead.

He shook his head, looking contrite. "No, *I'm* sorry. I'm such an ass. It's just . . . kinda . . . habit, I guess."

"What, being an ass?"

He winced. "Yeah, pretty much." He glanced up at the clock on the wall. "Anyway, I better go. I'm supposed to meet with the headmistress in a few minutes."

"Okay. I guess I'll see you. You know, around," I added lamely.

"That you will," he said with a salute, then slung his bag over his shoulder. He took several steps toward the door, then stopped and turned back to face me. "Oh, and McKenna? There's one more thing you should know about me," he said, the wicked gleam back in his eye now. "You know, since we're on the accelerated 'getting to know you' track and all that."

Again, I rolled my eyes. "I'm sure you're going to tell me."

"Just this: I *hate* to lose." With a wink, he turned and jogged out.

I stood there staring at his back, shaking my head in amazement.

Suzanne sidled up beside me. "Hey, were you two flirting?" she asked. "Because I thought you and Aidan—"

"Trust me, we were *not* flirting."

"You sure? Because it looked an awful lot like flirting," she insisted, her eyebrows raised quizzically.

"Just some competitive banter. And yeah, me and Aidan . . ." I trailed off, glancing down at my watch.

He was waiting.

As soon as I stepped inside the chapel, my heart sank. I heard voices—we weren't alone. I hadn't expected that. This had always been our special place—mine and Aidan's—the place we'd come to be alone, away from prying eyes. Until I'd brought my friends here to train to fight Julius, that is. Then it had become our meeting place, our group training ground.

I loved the chapel, loved the cozy loft with the window to the sky. So many memories had been made there. But they were my memories. *Our* memories. Call me selfish, but I didn't want to share the space, not even with my best friends. Julius was gone, the imminent threat of danger gone with him. I wanted things back the way they used to be—was that too much to ask?

Taking a deep breath, I hurried through the vestibule and made my way into the chapel itself, anxious to see who was there, invading our space.

Turned out it was only Jack. He and Aidan were leaning against the rearmost pew, near the wall. "I think I can work with the molecules some more, but you're right, he's definitely on to something," Jack was saying.

I took two steps toward them, my fatigued legs trembling.

At once, they both looked over to where I stood. "Oh hey, Violet," Jack called out, but it was Aidan's face that my gaze sought.

He didn't say anything—he didn't have to. It was there, written all over his face. If I thought my legs were weak before, they were now near total collapse. *Oh, man.*

I swallowed hard, barely able to believe that he was finally there, just a few feet away from me. My gaze skimmed over him from head to toe, taking in all the details I'd pressed to memory—his face, as pale as always; his nose still slightly crooked; his golden hair tousled as if he'd just raked his fingers through it; his eyes, the one bright spot of color in his face, the same blue-gray as I remembered, not yet faded as a vampire's were wont to do over time but darkly shadowed from ignoring his nocturnal instincts for far too long.

He hadn't changed, not one bit. And my heart still leapt at the sight of him.

I realized that Jack was speaking and pried my hungry gaze away from Aidan long enough to glance his way. "Maybe tomorrow afternoon, if he has some free time," he was saying, carrying on their conversation as if I weren't standing there. I couldn't help but feel slightly resentful.

But then, Jack probably didn't realize that this was the first time that Aidan and I had laid eyes on each other since June.

"That sounds great," Aidan said absently, looking past Jack, his gaze still locked on me.

Jack, still oblivious, nodded. "Okay, I'll check with him before football practice tonight. Anything else I should do?"

Aidan didn't reply.

"Aidan?" Jack tried again. With a shrug, he followed Aidan's gaze toward me. "I guess this is my cue to leave," he muttered.

Yes, go find Kate or something, I silently urged, even though he couldn't hear me.

"I'll catch you later," Aidan said as Jack strode by me, headed toward the vestibule. "Let me know what Byrne says."

Byrne? As in Dr. Byrne? I wondered what he had to do with whatever they were talking about. Probably something to do with their work, since Dr. Byrne was a science teacher.

I didn't turn to watch Jack go; I just continued to stand there looking at Aidan. Jack's footsteps faded away and, at last, the door clanged shut.

We were alone.

Oh, Vi . . . His voice was like a sigh inside my head.

I launched myself into his arms. That connection we shared, an electrical current that seemed to flow between us, was there in full force. He wrapped his arms around me, lifting me off my feet as he hugged me tight.

How had I ever doubted it? How had I let myself believe that our feelings might ever change?

"God, I've missed you!" I said. I breathed in his familiar scent, burying my face in his neck as his fingers tangled in my hair.

"As I've missed you," he said gruffly, sounding more like his Viscount Brompton self than my Aidan.

He set me back on my feet, and for a moment we simply stood there. And then, inch by inch, his head bent toward mine. I rose up on my tiptoes, meeting him halfway as his lips found mine. I heard him groan as I pressed myself fully against him, every cell in my body igniting, firing at once.

His kiss was gentle at first, almost tentative. Once, twice, his lips brushed mine, soft and featherlight, his tongue sliding across my lower lip as his hands pressed against the small of my back. I parted my lips, wanting more. *Needing* more.

I must have dropped the barrier around my thoughts then, because I heard the sharp intake of his breath, felt his fingers dig into my hips as he dragged me backward, pinning me against the wall in the blink of an eye.

His kiss was urgent now, his hands sliding up my body. I clutched at the back of his head as his mouth moved lower, toward my neck. With a sigh, he murmured my name, his teeth scraping against the sensitive skin beneath my ear where my pulse fluttered wildly.

Do it! I cried out in my mind. I knew it was wrong, completely irrational, and yet at that moment, I wanted it more than anything—his teeth, buried in my neck.

Mercifully, he didn't obey my silent command. Instead he went entirely still, his body rigid and taut against mine. I knew without looking what was happening, but I opened my eyes anyway. His were squeezed shut, his jaw clenched. A vein at his temple throbbed. For several seconds he stood just like that, unmoving.

And then, at last, he opened his eyes.

Just as I expected, they were rimmed in red—a terrifying sight, even now. I knew that his canine teeth would be slightly elongated, as they always were when he fought against the bloodlust.

I swallowed hard, erecting the wall around my thoughts, guarding them tightly. I was a little bit scared, and I didn't want him to know it. It was something I'd never get used to, his transformation.

Still, I'd wanted him to bite me. I'd *asked* him to bite me. He'd refused, of course, but what if he hadn't? What if he wasn't always stronger than me?

"I'm sorry, Violet," he murmured.

Guilt washed over me. He couldn't help what he was, and I'd been the one to push. "You didn't do anything, Aidan."

"Not this time. And maybe not the next time, either. But someday . . ." He trailed off, leaning his forehead against mine. We stayed that way for a while, till our breathing slowed to normal.

Finally he stepped away. "How's your gran?" he asked, suddenly unable to meet my eyes.

I reached for his hand, lacing my fingers through his. "She's good. Much better. Melanie's all settled in, and she and Lupe seem to get along, so I think it's going to be okay."

"That's great. And what about Whitney? I bet she was sad to see you go."

My blood ran cold. *Whitney.* The dream began to replay in my mind. Instinctively, I dropped his hand and took a step away from him, wanting to increase the distance between us.

At once his brows drew together over troubled eyes. "What's wrong?"

"N-nothing," I stammered, my mouth suddenly dry, my throat tight. "She's still really mad at her parents—you know, for making her miss the summer dance program she was supposed to go to—and I just . . . I'm going to miss her, that's all."

His eyes narrowed with suspicion; he knew me too well. "You're sure that's it?"

I nodded, biting my lower lip as I did so.

"Come here, then." He reached for my hand, drawing me back toward him.

I hesitated, forced to remember the way Whitney cowered in fear—or at least the way I'd seen her cower in my dream—while Aidan advanced on her with bloodlust in his eyes.

"Violet?" Again, he tugged me toward him. Reluctantly, I let him. Releasing my hand, he cupped my face with his palms, staring down at me with troubled eyes. "About before . . . I had hoped I could control it better, after all this time apart." He shook his head. "I'm so sorry, Vi. You know I don't want to hurt you. I would *never* hurt you," he corrected.

"I know." It was better to let him think that his vampire reaction had made me skittish than to tell him the truth—that I'd had some stupid dream about him going after Whitney. I didn't want to examine it any further, didn't want to risk wavering in my certainty that it *was* a dream, and not a vision.

"But I heard you. In my head, willing me to bite you," he clarified, as if I didn't know exactly what he was talking about. "God only knows it's hard enough . . ." He trailed off, shaking his head. "I would never forgive myself," he said at last, his voice barely above a whisper. "You understand that, right?"

I swallowed hard, unable to speak. But I *did* understand, I really did. I knew Aidan well enough to know that if he lost control and bit me, I'd lose him. He'd leave Winterhaven and never look back. Who knows where he'd go or what he'd do—but whatever it was, it wouldn't include me.

Finally I nodded. "How's the work on the cure coming?" I asked, desperate to change the subject.

His eyes brightened at once. "We've made a breakthrough. Some cellular changes, though they're minor. Still, we're definitely on the right track now."

I let out my breath in a rush. "Thank God. Was Jack around at all this summer to help you out?"

He shook his head. "Not much. I've been working with Dr. Byrne, though. Turns out he focused his doctoral research on malaria—go figure."

"How much does he know?" I asked. Because it would be pretty hard to explain Aidan's work to someone without, well . . . raising questions.

"I'm pretty sure he knows a lot more than he's letting on. It's okay, though. I guess Mrs. Girard figures she can control the situation if need be."

"It's just weird that it's Dr. Byrne." I shook my head, an uncomfortable feeling settling in the pit of my stomach. "Just yesterday he offered to become my new psychic coach. He has visions, like me," I explained.

"Yeah, I know. About the precognition, I mean. He didn't mention anything about the coaching." His eyes seemed to darken. "You and Dr. Hottie, huh?"

I decided to ignore that comment. "Yeah, he said Mrs. Girard suggested it. I don't know, I guess it's just a coincidence."

"That, or Mrs. G. wants him to keep an eye on us. On what you see." He seemed to consider it, then shrugged. "But even if that's the case, I can't really see any harm in it. It might even prove useful. You know, in case you have any more visions involving me."

And they usually did involve him.

"Anyway," he continued, "I have to admit he's brilliant. Byrne, I mean. Graduated from high school at sixteen and got his PhD at twenty-four. From MIT, no less. He's been extremely helpful, and now with Jack back on campus and the three of us working together, I'm more confident than ever. That's what we were talking about just now, Jack and I—an idea that Dr. Byrne suggested. I think it just might work."

The excitement in his voice was contagious, and I couldn't help but smile. "You really think so?"

"I do. I want this, Violet. It's the only way."

I nodded. "I know. I want it, too." I meant it, with all my heart.

So then why did a cold knot of fear lodge in my stomach when his lips moved toward mine this time?

4 ~ . . . And Vampires Suck

You're not hanging out with Aidan tonight?"
Sophie asked, setting down her steaming mug on
the glossy tabletop in front of us. The café was
crowded tonight; you had to yell to be heard over the din.

I shook my head—I'd spent all afternoon with Aidan, and truthfully I was glad for a little a space, a little time to get my head on straight. "It's girls' night, remember?" I shouted. We'd made a pact that this was going to be our new Friday night tradition. "Anyway, I think Aidan's with Jack, working in the lab tonight."

Kate let out a long sigh. "Yeah, what else is new?"

Marissa reached across the table to pat her hand. "Aww, poor Kate. You'll live."

Kate wrinkled her nose at Marissa. "I swear, it's all he can talk about lately—the work in the lab. It's like he's totally obsessed now or something."

I shrugged. "It sounds like he and Aidan have become pretty good friends."

"It *is* kind of a life-or-death situation," Sophie said. "For Aidan, I mean. Well, maybe 'life or eternal life.'" She shook her head. "Or something like that."

The big group of underclassmen milling around near the counter finally made their way out the front door, and the noise level dropped considerably.

"Isn't it kind of weird for you, though?" Sophie continued, lowering her voice a decibel. "I mean, knowing that he's been alive all these years, pretty much invincible, and yet *you* have the power to destroy him?"

I shifted uncomfortably in my seat, my face flushing hotly. Because yeah, of course it was weird. Really weird, and totally unsettling. I mostly tried not to think about it, tried to forget the satisfaction I'd felt when my stake had done its duty—not once, but three times. Julius, and the two females he'd brought with him.

Sucking in a sharp breath, I squeezed my eyes shut, willing away the horrifying memories, but it was no use. They came back in a flood, raising goose bumps across my skin in their wake.

The initial resistance as the stake first pierced vampire flesh; the ear-splitting shriek as the sharpened wood found its mark; terrifying convulsions as dark, nearly black blood pooled around the protruding shaft; and then . . . total stillness, vampire eyes staring at the sky, unseeing.

It could have been Aidan.

I tried to swallow, but my mouth was too dry. I reached for my steaming mocha with shaking hands, draining it in one long gulp, the hot liquid burning a path down to my stomach.

As I set the mug back on the table, Cece put one arm around my shoulders, drawing me close. "Hey, it's okay," she murmured. "Just take a deep breath."

I nodded, doing just that.

Cece turned on Sophie, her dark eyes flashing. "What's wrong with you? I can't believe you just said that to her."

"No, I—it's okay," I stammered. "Really." Sophie's eyes had filled with tears, and I reached across the table for her hand and gave it a squeeze. "Seriously, Soph."

I glanced over at Marissa, who'd remained silent, watching us with wide eyes. She looked pale and just as shaken as I felt, and I realized that she was probably absorbing some of my discomfort. I wasn't quite sure if it was intentional or not—I still didn't know exactly how her gift worked.

"Yeah," I said at last. "It *is* weird. But . . . well, he could kill *me* pretty easily if he wanted to. So I guess we're even. A balance of power, right?"

"I can't believe we're having this conversation," Cece said, shaking her head.

"Can you guys just . . . lighten up?" Marissa said at last. "God, you're all killing me here."

Kate nodded. "Okay, okay. New topic. Um . . . hot new guy. Violet, you had fencing practice with him. Dish."

I relaxed slightly, leaning back into the booth's tufted vinyl. "Tyler Bennett, from Texas. Overconfident and *very* competitive. Oh, and he said he was telekinetic. Micro, actually."

"Interesting," Kate drawled. "Not a lot of micros around. Anything else?"

"Not much else to tell. He was kind of funny, I guess." I shrugged, trying to remember what we'd talked about, exactly, but came up blank.

"Funny ha-ha, or funny weird?" Cece pressed.

"Funny like he seemed to have an okay sense of humor," I clarified "I don't know. Mostly we were practicing. It's not like we had that much time to talk. He's definitely going to be top seed on the boys' team. I kinda felt bad for him—the other guys weren't too happy with the way Coach was going on and on about him."

"Hey, speak of the devil," Cece murmured, elbowing me in my side.

I glanced up and saw Tyler step inside, Max Armstrong trailing behind him. His gaze found mine, and he nodded and headed our way.

"Hey, Tyler," I called out with a wave. Might as well get this over with.

He stopped, even with our table now. "Well, if it isn't the competition."

"In case you didn't notice, I'm on the girls' team. So it's not like we'll ever be competing against each other."

He shrugged. "Maybe not, but you're still the best here at Winterhaven. At least, you *were* the best," he challenged with an easy laugh.

I groaned. "Yeah, whatever. Um, these are my friends Cece, Marissa, Kate, and Sophie." I gestured toward each in turn. "Guys, this is Tyler."

"Hi," Tyler said with a nod, repeating each name back with surprising accuracy. "Do y'all know Max? Lucky dude is my roommate."

Everyone knew Max—the spiky-haired guy wearing eyeliner who liked to sit in the quad strumming his guitar.

Kate nodded. "Yeah, we know Max. Don't we, Marissa?" She shot a knowing look in Marissa's direction. Clearly, Kate knew something that I didn't.

"Yeah, um . . . hi, Max," Marissa murmured, her cheeks

scarlet. I was pretty sure I'd never seen her so embarrassed before.

"A new roommate senior year?" Cece asked Max. "What'd you do—scare away the old one?"

Max shrugged, looking vaguely amused. "I had a single last year, but it was way too quiet. Thought I could use some company."

Kate looked at Marissa, and then back at Max. "You were a singleton last year like Marissa? Wow, who knew the two of you had so much in common?"

Marissa shot her a deadly glare.

After an uncomfortable pause, Tyler shrugged. "Well, good to meet y'all. Violet, I'll see you at practice tomorrow."

"Sure will," I chirped, watching as he and Max turned and walked away from our table.

"Thanks a lot, Kate," Marissa muttered once they were out of earshot. "Way to be Captain Obvious."

Kate's blue eyes danced with mischief. "Oh, c'mon! Did you see the way he blushed? He's totally into you. You just gotta let him know you're interested."

Marissa folded her arms across her chest. "*Some* of us appreciate the fine art of subtlety."

"Obviously some of us appreciate guyliner, too," Cece murmured under her breath. "Who knew?"

"Subtlety isn't going to get you a date for the Halloween dance," Kate said with a smirk.

Marissa rolled her eyes. "Oh my God, I hate you."

"No you don't. You love me—admit it! I just helped you out." Kate glanced back over her shoulder toward where Tyler and Max stood by the door, talking to a group of guys I didn't recognize. "Trust me, he'll ask you out before the week's over."

"You're lucky I *do* love you," Marissa conceded. "Anyway, he's an empath like me. I'm pretty sure he knows exactly what I'm feeling whenever he's around."

Sophie's brows shot up at once. "What exactly *are* you feeling when he's around, Marissa?"

"Just shut up," she muttered in reply. "All of you."

"Ooh, is there a Max effect going on?" Kate teased, refer-ring to what we liked to call the "Aidan effect"—that woozy, tongue-tied feeling we got around Aidan. Which, it turns out, was just an effect of his vampirism.

Marissa shook her head. "It's nothing like that, thank God."

"Okay, not to change the subject or anything," Cece said, her dark eyes glowing, "but am I the only one here who thinks Tyler is seriously smoking?"

"Didn't you and Todd break up, like, just last night?" Marissa asked with a frown.

"So I'm a wee bit fickle," Cece answered with a shrug. "But c'mon, can you blame me?"

"He *is* pretty cute," I conceded.

"Agreed," Sophie said with a nod.

Just then, the clear plastic container holding the packets of sugar slid down the table, coming to rest in front of Kate.

"Oopsie," she said with a grin.

"You are *such* a show-off." Marissa tapped Kate's empty mug. "You don't even need the sugar."

Kate let out a long sigh. "I know. It's just so nice to be able to do stuff like that in public again."

"Technically, that was probably against the COPA," Cece warned with a grin. "As a candidate for student body president, I feel compelled to mention that."

Cece was probably right. I was pretty sure that "frivolous use" constituted a violation, albeit a minor one. Not in the same league as "using to harm a fellow student or faculty member," or "using for academic advantage," of course. Those infractions carried some pretty stiff penalties.

"Yeah, I guess you're right," Kate said with a shrug. "Still, it felt good."

Sophie looked pensive. "Have you ever thought about telling your parents? I mean, is it really that weird?"

"Are you kidding me? After what happened to Allison?"

Kate replied. Allison had been Cece's first roommate at Winterhaven, and she'd been pulled from school and briefly institutionalized when she'd tried to tell her parents about her clairvoyance. "Anyway, *your* gift could probably be explained away as intuition or something like that. But mine? My parents would freak if they saw what I can do. I mean, the sugar thing? That's nothing. But remember how I took down those beams in the chapel last year?"

"I guess you're right," Sophie said, then cleared her throat uncomfortably. "Hey, we should probably think about heading back. It's getting late."

The café had mostly emptied. Only one other table of students remained, and they were standing now, gathering their things.

Cece glanced down at her watch. "Yup, it's about that time."

As I reached for my bag, I felt the familiar tickle in my brain.

Hey, you still out with your friends?

I tried to look nonchalant, hiking up my bag on my shoulder as I answered him in my head. *Yeah, we're on our way back to the dorm now.*

Want me to come walk with you?

A battle raged in my mind. I *did* want to see him—I really

did. And yet . . . I still couldn't banish that image of him going after Whitney from my mind. Tomorrow morning was my first coaching session with Dr. Byrne, and hopefully he could help me learn to summon a vision. If it *had* been a vision and not a dream—a big if—then I'd work at replaying it. And if I couldn't, then maybe that would confirm that it *was* a dream after all. I hoped to have some answers by this time tomorrow, and then maybe—

Vi? You still there?

I needed to give him an answer, and fast. *I'm pretty tired. Do you mind if I just go to bed?*

Of course not, he said, but I could hear the disappointment in his voice. *I'll see you tomorrow, then.*

Definitely. After my coaching session, I offered, hoping that would give me enough time to figure things out.

It's a date, then. Good night, love.

"Hey, you coming?" Cece reached for my hand. "You were off in space for a minute there. Oh, wait . . . you were talking to Aidan, weren't you?"

I winced, feeling the heat rise in my cheeks. "Is it that obvious?"

"You should see your face! That must have been some reunion today."

She had *no* idea.

5 ~ Tick, Tock

Okay, close your eyes and take a deep breath—in through your nose, out through your mouth," Dr. Byrne said. "And then concentrate on one specific thing. A sound, for instance, or a sensation. Do you hear the clock on my desk?"

I closed my eyes and nodded. The ticking was loud, like Gran's old mantel clock. I took a deep breath, just like he said—in through my nose, out through my mouth.

"Now picture one specific image from the vision you want to replay." His voice was almost hypnotic. "It can be anything that stood out vividly." He paused for a moment. "Do you have it?"

"Yes," I whispered, my mind's eye conjuring up the image of Whitney stabbing at the elevator button. I have no idea why that particular image popped into my head, but it was definitely vivid. She was wearing jeans and a pink sweater; I could see her blond hair slipping from its ponytail, a sheen of sweat on the back of her neck. Her nails were painted a deep metallic blue, contrasting sharply with her ivory skin, and she was pressing the *L* button over and over again.

"Empty your mind of everything, Violet. Everything but that image and the sound of the clock. Make the room around you disappear. Make my voice disappear."

But it didn't. For several minutes we sat there in total silence, but nothing happened. None of the weird sensations came that heralded an oncoming vision.

I felt a breeze blow against my calves, and I shifted in my seat.

"You're not focused," Dr. Byrne scolded.

"I'm trying," I countered. Taking another deep breath—in and out—I chose another image from the vision, this one of Aidan. My breath hitched in my chest as the image flooded my consciousness: his eyes rimmed in red and full of thirst as he reached for Whitney.

I kept it there, holding on to it as best I could as I listened for the clock's rhythmic *tick, tock, tick, tock.*

I sharpened my focus, trying not to physically flinch at what I saw in my mind.

Aidan, looking dangerous. Going after my childhood friend . . .

A whimper escaped my lips, and I opened my eyes, forcing away the image.

"Nothing?" Dr. Byrne asked, and I shook my head.

"That's all it takes for you?" I asked, my voice a little shaky as I regarded him sitting across the desk from me. Weirdly enough, we'd shown up at the coaching session dressed alike—khaki shorts, Converse sneakers, and a plaid shirt.

He had that "just rolled out of bed" look, like he'd forgotten to shave or brush his hair. Even so, he looked like he belonged on the cover of one of those outdoorsy catalogs, the ones that sold everything from cargo pants to canoes.

He studied me back, his dark gaze steady. "Yeah, that's all it takes," he said at last. "But I really had to work on my focus for a while before I got the hang of it, so don't give up just yet. The clock helps—that's why I keep this one in my office."

I rose and took a couple of steps toward his desk, reaching out to run one finger along the clock's smooth, curved frame. "It's nice," I said.

"Thanks. It was my grandma's, actually. She collected clocks." He was still studying me strangely, his brows slightly drawn. "So, you and Aidan Gray . . ." He trailed off expectantly.

I swallowed hard, not quite sure where this was going. Or how much he knew. "What about us?"

"I was just wondering if you're a hundred percent comfortable with the risks."

"I don't know what you mean," I lied. My heart was pounding in my chest, thumping against my rib cage.

His expression relaxed a bit. "I'm pretty sure you do."

He had me there. I decided to try a different tactic. "He says you've been working with him in the lab. Are *you* a hundred percent comfortable with the risks?"

He shook his head. "It's not the same."

"It is," I argued, sliding back into the chair behind me.

"It's not, and you know it. Look, I'm fully supportive of Aidan's work. I want to help him. This is . . . well, probably the most exciting work I've done in a long time. But I think someone here needs to be looking out for you."

He obviously had no idea about the *Sâbbat* thing—and I wanted to keep it that way. "Mrs. Girard is looking out for me," I offered. He must know *that* much.

He stood and came around the desk, leaning against it, just inches away now. I could smell him—soap and aftershave. He smelled . . . nice. Clean, kind of like the ocean.

"Obviously I'm screwing this up," he said, shaking his head. "So let me start over. I'm trying to say that I've got your back. That if you ever need to talk to someone—to an adult— about the . . . situation . . . I'm here. That's all."

"Just how much do you know about the . . . situation?" I asked, unable to stanch my curiosity.

"Not much, beyond the scientific details I've managed to put together. I get the feeling that he's not really at liberty to share."

"Not without . . . consequences." Oh my God, we were talking in code, like spies or something.

"Hmm. Interesting." He folded his arms across his chest, causing the rolled-up sleeves of his shirt to ride up, expos- ing the bottom of edge of a tattoo—something that looked vaguely like a dagger. Whoa, Dr. Hottie had a tattoo. Now *that* was interesting.

"Will you promise me one thing, Violet?" he continued. "Just this one thing, and then we can stop talking about it. For now, at least."

"Depends on what you want me to promise," I said with a shrug. Because some things weren't negotiable, especially where Aidan was concerned.

"Just that you'll come to me if things start seeming danger- ous, that's all. I'm not sure how much help I'll be, but I'll do whatever I can."

I sucked in my breath, surprised by his offer. "You don't even *know* me."

"You're a student here at Winterhaven. A precog, like me. That's all I need to know."

I needed to stall for time, to think this through before I made any promises. "That's very . . . generous of you."

"Then you'll promise?"

I searched my instincts, wanting to make sure that his intentions were on the up-and-up, that he wasn't trying to manipulate me for some unknown, nefarious reason. Because if there's one thing I'd learned in the past year, it's that you just never know.

My gaze met his unflinching one, and I felt nothing but a surprising kinship. He seemed sincere, I decided. Earnest. Whatever his reasons were for wanting to protect me, they were good ones—ones I could trust.

I nodded. "You've got yourself a deal."

"So, how'd it go?" Aidan asked, lowering himself to the grass beside me. The late afternoon sun shone down on his head, turning his hair a deep, fiery gold. I resisted the urge to reach out and run my fingers through it.

"The sun really doesn't bother you?" I asked instead.

Shading his eyes with one hand, he glanced up at the

bright orb in question, high in the clear blue sky. "Nope. Took the elixir yesterday. I'm good for a while."

My gaze was drawn toward his calves, bare below his olive-colored cargo shorts. He was definitely pale, his skin fairer than mine—but not pale in the "I haven't seen the sun for a hundred years" sense.

"Do you ever tan?" I asked.

"Nah, my skin stays the same exact same shade as it was when I was turned. Just think, if I'd been a laborer instead of a viscount's son, I'd have been stuck with a farmer's tan forever. Anyway, you didn't answer my question."

"What, you mean with Dr. Hot—Dr. Byrne?" I stammered, distracted by the mental image of Aidan wearing a nineteenth-century suit and cravat. "It went fine, I guess."

Aidan rolled his eyes. "Do you *really* have to call him that?"

"Are you jealous?" I teased, plucking a blade of grass and tossing it at him.

"Of course I am." He shrugged.

For a moment, I just stared at him, stunned. Was he serious? "He's a teacher," I finally said.

"A very young, very good-looking teacher." He reached for my hand, his thumb brushing across my knuckles. "You just spent two hours with him, locked away in his office on a Saturday."

I let out my breath in a huff. "Okay, let me repeat myself in case you missed this the first time. He's a teacher. Secondly, he's a teacher. And lastly, he's—"

"Yeah, I know," he interrupted. "A teacher. Allow me to repeat *myself*. He's a very young, very good-looking teacher."

"And for the record," I continued, as if I hadn't heard him, "the door was not locked." At least, I was pretty sure it wasn't. Why would it have been? "And he's *way* older than me, besides."

"And I'm . . . what? A hundred and something years older than you? Help me out with the math; I'm afraid I've lost count."

"You're seventeen, Aidan," I said with a sigh. "You'll always be seventeen."

"Not always, not if I can help it," he said sharply. The edge of desperation in his voice was unmistakable. As always, it made my heart break. I couldn't imagine what it must be like to be him—to be the same age forever and ever.

The very idea that some people actually yearned for immortality baffled me beyond reason. I wondered if they had any idea what it would be like to watch everyone you know grow old and die, to find yourself alone time after time. And even worse, to be a vampire, at the mercy of your cravings— cravings that meant you had to hurt people, even kill them.

Why would people glorify such an existence? The toll it took on Aidan was obvious—and yet the Propagators seemed to revel in it, wanting to spread vampirism far and wide.

Aidan pulled me closer, wrapping one arm around my shoulders. I could smell him now, his scent totally different from Dr. Byrne's—and far more familiar. "You cold?" he asked. "I can go get you a jacket. Rather quickly, if you want," he added.

And he could, in an instant, if he wanted to. He could teleport—or whatever it was he did—to his room and back again in a matter of seconds.

I shook my head. "I'm fine. People would see you, anyway."

"I would go the normal way, until I was out of sight. I'm not that reckless, Vi. There are still secrets to keep."

"Not from me," I said vehemently.

"Not from you," he agreed. "Never again." His mouth dipped down toward my neck, beneath my ear. My heart began to gallop as I felt his lips press against my skin. His teeth could pierce that fragile skin in an instant, I realized.

"Do you want to go to the chapel?" he asked, his voice hoarse against my neck.

Dangerous. The word popped into my mind, insistent and firm.

"Not now," I managed to choke out.

He sat up sharply. "What's going on, Violet?"

I shook my head, trying to catch my breath. "Nothing's going on. I'm just . . . it's just . . ." I couldn't even finish the sentence.

His brows drew together sharply. "You're afraid of me, aren't you? Because of yesterday. Or is it something more, something to do with your *Sâbbat* —"

"It's not that—nothing like that. God, I don't know what's going on," I said in exasperation. Tears flooded my eyes, my vision swimming.

"Please don't cry," he said, his voice soft as he cupped my face with his hands.

"I'm not crying," I said, even as he wiped away the evidence to the contrary with one thumb. "I don't know what's wrong with me. I missed you so much, and now you're here and I'm acting all weird."

He leaned forward and kissed my forehead. "I missed you, too. Just give yourself some time—we've got the whole year ahead of us."

"True." I took a deep, fortifying breath. "Speaking of which, what's your schedule like this year? I hope we've got some classes together."

"I haven't really looked at mine yet," he said with a shrug. "What are you taking?"

"I'm taking calculus, believe it or not. I have *no* idea what I was thinking. Please tell me you're good at calculus."

"Good enough, and I probably signed up for a section myself. What about history?"

"The senior-level British history class, whatever it is. Something about politics and foreign relations, maybe?" Winterhaven didn't offer normal high school classes like AP US history or western civ. The classes were *way* more sophisticated than that.

"So, you're really into British history now, are you?" he asked teasingly.

"Maybe," I said, laughing. I hadn't really thought about it, but of course I was. Because of Aidan. I wanted to know as much as possible about the world he'd come from.

He was grinning at me now. "What else are you taking?"

"Let's see. . . . I've got Ackerman's senior-level English class, and fourth-year French. Oh, and I'm taking art history—"

"Hey, me too."

"Yeah?"

"Yeah, I thought it might be interesting—field trips to the Met and all that. Looks like we're going to be spending a lot of time together this semester."

"I'm going to hold you to that." I hoped he wasn't going to be disappearing for days on end, like he did last year. But he probably was, considering he was redoubling his efforts to find his cure.

The sound of laughter drifted across the quad, and I looked up and saw Jenna surrounded by a group of her friends. Our eyes met and held for the briefest of moments, and then she turned away.

"She doesn't want to talk to us," I said, shaking my head. "I just don't get it."

"What does it matter?" he asked.

"Because she saved us, that's why. Why is she blowing us off now?"

He shook his head. "I don't think Jenna and I will ever be friends, Vi. It's against our nature."

"Why, because you're natural-born enemies?" I pressed. "Kind of like you and a *Sâbbat*?"

"Touché," he said quietly, giving my hand a squeeze.

"We deserve an explanation. Can't you do something? You obviously know each other well enough. Cece's seen you together, you know. Off in the woods, after curfew." I tried to keep the edge out of my voice, but it was no use. Jealousy was a two-way street, I guessed.

"What was Cece doing out after—"

"Not regular Cece. *Astral* Cece," I explained. "You know, out for a virtual stroll."

He cleared his throat, looking slightly uncomfortable. "As I've said before, I can't speak for Jenna."

"Well, then, get her to talk to us. Use your mind powers on her or something. Go." I tipped my head toward where she still stood, across the quad from us. "I'm serious," I prodded when he didn't move from his spot beside me.

He shook his head with a laugh. "Are you really suggesting that I manipulate her with my mind? Isn't that a serious COPA violation?"

It was my turn to roll my eyes. "As if those rules mean anything to you. What was it that Mrs. Girard called you that day in her office? Her 'greatest creation'?" I made air quotes with my fingers. "Yeah, I'm pretty sure you've got a free pass with her."

"Don't be so sure of that. But I *will* go talk to Jenna."

"Thank you," I said with a sigh.

"Talk," he repeated sternly. "Not manipulate. I'm not a hundred percent sure I could, anyway," he muttered, rising lithely to his feet.

With nervous anticipation, I watched him jog across the quad. As he approached, Jenna moved away from her friends, meeting Aidan under the branches of an enormous old oak. I watched the pantomime of their conversation—lips moving, hands gesturing. I could only imagine what he was saying to her. Finally I saw him nod, and then he started back in my direction. Again, Jenna's gaze caught mine across the distance that separated us. For the life of me, I couldn't read her expression.

When Aidan finally reached my side, he stretched out a hand toward me. I took it, rising to my feet beside him. "Well?" I prompted, brushing the grass from my butt with my free hand.

"She'll meet with us after dinner tonight and explain everything. You might as well go find your friends and tell them— dinner's in an hour. I'll tell Jack and Joshua. Seven o'clock, in the chapel."

I dropped his hand and threw my arms around his neck. "Thank you," I murmured, breathing in his scent, allowing myself to experience the full brunt of the Aidan effect. "God, you smell *so* good." Sunshine and spice and something that smelled almost like . . . bergamot, I realized. Like Gran's favorite hot tea, Earl Grey. Which, now that I thought about it, was kind of funny. Earl Grey, Viscount Gray.

"Better than Dr. Hottie?" Aidan asked huskily, one hand pressed into the small of my back, steadying me.

"*Way* better," I shot back, before I'd thought better of it.

"That was a test, and you just failed it. Quite spectacularly, I might add."

"Oh, please." *That stupid Aidan effect.* He'd caught me totally off guard. Truthfully, though, I kind of liked that he was jealous—or at least pretending to be jealous. It made me feel . . . powerful. And maybe a little bit naughty.

I reached up and tangled my fingers in the hair at the back of his neck, drawing his head back toward mine. "Dr. who?" I whispered against his lips. A jolt of electricity raced down my spine as I opened my mouth against his.

"I dunno," he murmured in reply, kissing me softly but thoroughly, careful to keep some space between our bodies. For the second time that day, his lips trailed down my jaw, toward my neck. That same thrill made my heart race and my palms dampen.

"Whoa there, cowboy," came a voice behind me. Aidan released me at once, and I spun around to find Cece and Sophie standing there, gaping.

"Sorry, but his, uh . . . yeah . . . his teeth were just a little too close to your neck for comfort, if you know what I mean," Cece finally managed. Sophie just continued to stare, her eyes wide.

Aidan laughed, his eyes bright with a level of amusement that I wasn't quite feeling myself. "You really thought I was going to bite her, right here in the quad, in broad daylight?"

Cece held up two hands, palms out. "Hey, I was just making sure, that's all."

"And your intentions are fully appreciated," Aidan said with a grin. "Why don't you tell them the news," he said to me. "I'll see you at seven?"

I nodded. "Sounds good."

Not as good as continuing to make out, but whatever.

6 ~ The Wolf's Tale

Jenna sat in the frontmost pew, Aidan beside her, both of them facing backward toward the rest of us in the pews behind them. I sensed then that perhaps Aidan was a bigger part of her story than I realized, and I wasn't quite sure how I felt about that.

Beside me, Cece turned and gave me a questioning look. I just shrugged. I had no idea what to expect from this little get-together.

"I'm pretty sure the coast is clear," Jenna said to Aidan, her nose lifted as if she were sniffing the air—and maybe she was, given that she was part wolf. Or something like that.

Aidan paused, his head tipped to one side. "Yeah, there's no one around. We're good. "

Jenna nodded. "First off, I just want to say that I've got my own group of friends," she began, her voice hard. "They don't know what I am, and I want to keep it that way."

There were assorted mumbles of "of course" and "yeah, whatever" around me. I just nodded, still a little disconcerted by the fact that Aidan was sitting there with *her*—possibly the most beautiful girl at Winterhaven. Tall, willowy, with wide blue eyes and perfect cheekbones. I got that they were mortal enemies—vampire and werewolf—but they seemed connected in some way, despite Aidan's claim that they weren't even friends.

"So don't expect me to start hanging out with you guys or anything," she continued, her churlish tone a stark contrast to her serene beauty.

"Yeah, I think they've got that, Jenna," Aidan said sharply. "Why don't you just start at the beginning, okay?"

"Fine," she said with a shrug. "I'm a lycanthrope. I was born one, in case you're wondering—it's not transmissible or anything like that. I can shift to wolf form any time I like, but it's easiest during the full moon.

"And yes, we usually live in packs," she went on. "You know, our families clustered together, living in small, isolated communities, mostly homeschooled. I hated pack life—everything about it. I just wanted to go to a normal school and live a normal life."

She paused, as if gauging our reaction. I felt a sense of déjà vu, remembering the day that Aidan had told me *his* story. It would seem that this one was just as unbelievably bizarre.

"I'd sent some pictures to a modeling agency in New York City, and they wanted to represent me. They offered to help me find a roommate, an apartment with some other models, whatever. But my parents wouldn't allow it—wouldn't let me leave the pack. They told me then that they'd promised me to the alpha's oldest son. Who is a total moronic brute, I might add." Her voice was filled with disgust. "It was supposed to be some honor—very prestigious for my family.

"I told them I wasn't interested in being their little pack princess, but they didn't care. Sixteen is the normal age for a pack female to marry, maybe seventeen, because lycanthropes have a pretty short life span," she explained. "That's why they want us to start popping out puppies as young as possible. That's all my parents cared about—the pack's breeding program."

On my right, I heard Cece's sharp intake of breath. "But that's—that's crazy!" she stammered. "They were going to force you to marry him at sixteen?"

Jenna shrugged, brushing a stray lock of perfectly high-lighted hair from her forehead. "That's just the way it's always been. All about bloodlines and lineage, breeding for strength and smarts. Anyway, I ran away when I was fourteen. They found me before I'd gotten very far and dragged me back. The alpha threatened to kill me if I tried it again. I ran anyway."

Everyone remained silent, digesting that. She was brave, I'd give her that. Brave, or reckless. Maybe equal measures of both.

"They caught up with me again. Thanks to a lycan's collective consciousness, it's almost impossible to hide your thoughts from the rest of your pack. It was my oldest brother who found me, and he turned me right over to the alpha, who was leading the hunt.

"Long story short, they left me for dead. Aidan found me." She glanced over at him. "He had no idea what I was—I'd shifted back to human form. So there I was—a naked, bloody, half-dead mess. I *would* have been dead, given another hour or two. Anyway, Aidan took me to Dr. Blackwell, who let Nurse Campbell treat me, and voilà, here I am."

"That doesn't explain what you were doing here at the chapel that day," I said, shaking my head. Try as I might, I couldn't seem to get the word *naked* out of my brain. "Or why you saved us. Or even why you gave me that miniature—the picture of Aidan's ex."

"I wasn't done with the story," she snapped. "So, Blackwell

agreed to let me stay here at Winterhaven, to enroll me as a scholarship student, and to offer me his full protection. I didn't have much of a choice—it was that or risk having the pack finish me off the moment I stepped off campus."

"The pack can't come on campus?" Joshua asked.

She shook her head. "Nope. Not with vampires here, protecting me. They wouldn't dare. It's a turf thing, and lycans are all about turf. It would start a full-blown war, and the pack can't risk that."

Jack shook his head. "But why would Blackwell have wanted to protect you? Aren't vampires and werewolves supposed to be enemies?"

"I think Blackwell just wanted to keep me around to learn as much as possible about lycanthropy. We're normally a pretty secretive bunch, but I was happy to trade pack information for a chance at a normal life."

Her gaze slid to each of us, one by one, silently daring us to criticize her for what could surely be interpreted as a betrayal of her kind.

No one said a word.

"So I accepted his offer," she continued. "Blackwell appointed Aidan my babysitter to keep a watch on me when I shift. You know, to keep the humans safe from the big, bad wolf." Which I had to admit was kind of funny, when you thought about it. A vampire assigned to keep people "safe." Of course, if that vampire was Aidan, then people *were* safe.

"And in case you're curious, it *is* biologically necessary for me to shift, at least occasionally. Anyway"—she waved one hand in dismissal—"everything was fine, until last year. Blackwell started setting these conditions for me—things I had to do, or else he'd turn me out. Giving that picture to Violet was one of the conditions. I had no idea what it meant—it seemed pretty harmless. It wasn't like Blackwell gave me much choice."

"It's okay," I found myself saying. "You did what you had to do." Besides, if Aidan hadn't lied about the miniature to begin with—

I said I was sorry about that, Vi, came Aidan's voice in my mind. *A million times over, and I meant it every time.*

How did you know what I was thinking? I asked, startled. I'd had the wall around my thoughts; I always did when he was around. He'd said that wall was impenetrable.

It was easy enough to figure out, he said. *I knew your thoughts would go there the minute she mentioned it.*

For the first time in a very long time, I wondered if he was lying to me. Had he figured out a way around the wall?

"What about that night here at the chapel, with Julius— how did you know what was going on?" Marissa asked.

Jenna shrugged. "I didn't. Blackwell sent me."

I was sure I had misheard her. Everyone started whispering at once.

Only Jack spoke up. "The acoustics must be really weird in here. Because it sounded like you said Blackwell sent you."

Jenna folded her arms across her chest. "That's exactly what I said."

All the air left my lungs in a whoosh. *What the hell?*

"Go on," Aidan urged, his eyes troubled, more gray now than blue.

I saw her swallow hard. "He said . . . he said it was his last condition, that he wouldn't ask anything more of me after that night. He didn't tell me why, didn't tell me what I was going to find. Just that I should shift and go to the chapel. So I did."

"You're lying," Kate called out. She turned toward Jack. "She has to be lying."

Sophie shook her head. "It doesn't make any sense."

Jenna shrugged. "Look, I don't care if you guys believe me or not—it makes no difference to me, one way or the other. You wanted to know why I was there; I told you. End of story."

Suddenly everyone was talking at once—everyone but Aidan. He was silent, his expression stony, entirely unreadable. I just sat there watching him, wondering what was going on his head, wondering if I dared attempt to breach his mind and listen in.

"Okay, let's say Blackwell *did* send you," Joshua shouted above the din, and everyone finally quieted down. "So you got here, you saw what was going on. You could have just turned around and left. Why did you decide to help us?"

She regarded him coolly, her jaw set firm. "Regardless of what you might have heard, I'm not a total bitch. I wasn't going to just sit there on my haunches and watch you all die. Besides, I owed it to Aidan." She glanced over to where he sat stiffly beside her. "He saved me, that day in the woods. And now we're even."

"I suppose we are," Aidan said softly.

"But . . . but what happens when you graduate, when you leave Winterhaven?" Cece sounded genuinely alarmed. "Won't they come after you then?"

Jenna's eyes glittered. "I'll move away, change my name. I *dare* them to come looking for me."

Whoa. I had to give the girl credit—she obviously had some serious cojones.

Jenna rose, gripping the back of the pew. I noticed a ring on her right hand, polished onyx with some sort of design etched into it. "So, are we done here?" she asked, sounding bored now.

Aidan rose to stand beside her. "I might be able to help you out with a cure. I've been studying up on it, reading about the effects of wolfsbane—"

"Why don't you just concentrate on finding your own cure," she interrupted, sounding a lot like the bitch she claimed she wasn't. "At least I'm not really a danger to anyone—"

"I'm not a danger to anyone either, Jenna. You'd do well to remember that."

"Oh, yeah? I saw you and your little girlfriend this afternoon in the quad. Your teeth were awfully close to her neck, don't you think?"

Little girlfriend? Okay, she was seriously starting to piss me off. "Aidan isn't going to hurt me," I said, rising. "And maybe you should consider minding your own business, besides."

"It *is* my business," she shot back. "It's everyone's business here at Winterhaven. Because if he hurts you, it's going to get out. It's going to bring attention to this school, and we'll all be exposed. Not everyone here has a luxury apartment on the Upper East Side to go back to. Did you ever think of that?"

I guess I hadn't. Still, it didn't change anything. "He's not going to hurt me," I repeated as resolutely as before.

"You're pretty confident about that, huh?"

"Yeah, I am," I said, moving closer, putting myself between her and Aidan. "And you of all people should understand that better than anyone."

The color rose in her cheeks, staining them scarlet. "Are you suggesting that I'm *anything* like a vampire?"

"Those lycans you described—your own family, even— sounded pretty murderous to me," I challenged.

Jenna's gaze met mine, her blue eyes flashing dangerously. She clenched one hand into a fist by her side, the hand wearing the onyx ring. For a second there, I thought she might actually take a swing at me.

Cece stepped up beside me, laying one hand on my wrist. "Um, yeah . . . we should probably call it a night, don't you think?"

I nodded. "Definitely. Aidan?"

"Aidan?" Jenna called out at the exact same time.

His head shot up, his gaze traveling from Jenna to me, and back again.

"I'm going to need your babysitting services tonight," she told him. "I could use a good, hard run."

Of course she had to make it sound dirty.

He sighed resignedly. "Fine, but I've got to go to the lab first." He turned to me. "Dr. Byrne's meeting us there in a half hour. We're going to start working on that new idea of his."

"Just be there," Jenna snapped. "Usual time and place." With that, she turned and strode toward the vestibule without a backward glance.

Hmm, so they had a usual rendezvous routine. That ember of jealousy stirred in my breast, newly stoked.

"Don't let her get to you," Aidan said as the doors closed behind her. "It's not personal—she dislikes you by association, that's all."

But my mind was already elsewhere. "So, when she shifts . . . what happens to her clothes?"

"What do you mean?" he asked, a faint smile tipping the corners of his mouth. He knew I was jealous—and he was *enjoying* it. Payback for the whole Dr. Hottie thing, I guessed.

"They just . . . what? Burst at the seams?" I made an exploding motion with my hands. "Pop off her, just like that?"

His lips twitched—yeah, he was enjoying this, all right. "I'm pretty sure she takes them off before she shifts."

"*Pretty* sure?" I pressed.

"Okay, I'm sure of it. There's a little outbuilding at the edge of the woods, down near—"

"Forget I asked." The last thing I wanted was the details. "Don't you have to go to the lab?"

"I do." He nodded in Jack's direction. "Hey, you ready?" he called out to him.

"Yup," Jack answered, leaning over to kiss Kate on the lips. "Later, okay?"

There wouldn't be a "later" for me and Aidan—not tonight. He'd be out with his werewolf instead. His *naked* werewolf.

Ugh.

7 ~ You Lie like a Rug

I set aside the stack of textbooks with a sigh. If these books were any indication, this semester was going to be tough. What ever happened to taking it easy senior year, having some fun? And why had I ever thought that taking calculus was a good idea?

The only consolation was that seniors weren't required to attend study hour in the East Hall lounge every night like everyone else it was one of the very few privileges afforded us, and I was grateful for it. It was so much easier for me to concentrate in my room, my radio set to a classical station.

My cell began to ring, and I hurried over to pick it up.

Whitney. I smiled as I touched the screen to take the call.

"So?" she drawled in my ear.

"Just shoot me now," I replied, readjusting the phone against my ear. Over the summer I'd traded in my old flip phone for a smartphone, which still felt clunky to me, despite its obvious advantages.

"That bad, huh?"

"It's definitely going to be a challenge. Anyway, ask me again at the end of the day tomorrow." I sank back down on my bed, tucking my bare feet beneath myself.

"I'm sure you'll do just fine," Whitney said, the rhythmic drone of a lawn mower in the background nearly drowning her out. "Can you hear me? I swear, my dad picks the worst times to mow the lawn. Here, let me go into the bathroom." I heard a shuffling noise and then the sound of a door slamming. "How's that?" she asked.

"Way better," I said. "So how's it going? With the parents, I mean?"

I heard her sigh. "Terrible. They're making me see a dietician *and* a shrink now." Because they thought she had an eating dis-order. She'd lost so much weight last spring that they'd refused to let her go to the summer dance program she'd gotten into in New York, and they'd even threatened to pull her out of the performing arts high school she attended during the school year. They'd finally given in on the latter—she'd started back a few weeks ago—but I knew things had been tense at home.

Over the summer I'd asked her point-blank if her parents might be right, if she might be suffering from anorexia or bulimia. Because frankly I'd been worried; I'd never seen her that thin before. She'd sworn to me that she was fine, that she'd been eating, just watching her calories a bit more than usual. I wanted to believe her, to think that we were close enough that she'd tell me if something serious was going on.

Then again, look at all the secrets *I* was keeping from *her*.

"A dietician?" I asked.

"Yeah, I have to keep a food diary, and I'm doing weekly weigh-ins. It totally sucks."

"But they're letting you stay at Performing Arts," I reminded her. "That's better than the alternative, right?"

"Yeah, but I swear they want me to get fat and give up dancing. God forbid I do anything artistic. I should go to law school, like they did, and spend my days cooped up in a stuffy office." I could hear the frustration in her voice. "Anyway, when are you coming back down here?"

"Thanksgiving, probably."

"Seriously? That's forever away." She sighed dramatically. "So, how are things going with Aidan? Everything still all rainbows and butterflies?"

"Pretty much." I couldn't help but smile. "But make that Technicolor rainbows and ginormous, sparkly butterflies."

"Wow. I cannot *wait* to meet this guy. Hey, bring him for Thanksgiving!"

"I don't know. Maybe. I'm not sure how Gran would feel about that." Or worse, Lupe. I could just imagine her barring the front door as she tried to ward him off with garlic and a crucifix.

Instinctively, I reached down for the delicate silver cross I wore on a chain around my neck—a gift from Lupe last fall.

"Speaking of your gran, I went by and saw her yesterday."

My heart swelled with gratitude. "Really? That was so nice of you!"

"No problem—you know I love her. She seemed stronger. Better. And I really like Melanie."

"Me too. I hope it works out." I looked up as the door swung open and Cece came bounding in.

"Hey," she called out.

"Hey," I called back. "I'll be off in a sec."

"Is that your roommate?" Whitney asked.

"Yeah, it's almost time for dinner."

"I should let you go, then," Whitney said.

"I guess." I turned toward the window, watching dark clouds move across the sky. "I'm glad you called, though. I miss you."

"I miss you, too." She sounded like she was going to cry.

"Hey, Whit . . . just promise me you're eating, okay?"

"I *am* eating. Do you really think I'd lie to you?"

Something in my gut told me that she would—and that she was. "Of course not," I said, despite my misgivings. "I'll call you tomorrow, okay?"

"Yep. Bye!"

My heart suddenly heavy, I touched the screen to end the call.

"Uh-oh, I spy a sad face." Cece sat down across from me.

I set aside my phone with a shrug. "I just hope she's okay."

"Me too," Cece said, and I knew she meant it, even though she'd never even met Whitney. "Hey, I told Sophie I'd go to the school store with her after dinner. Want to come? Maybe some retail therapy will cheer you up."

"Sure, why not?" I smoothed out the quilt on my bed, trailing my fingers across the colorful squares that Lupe had so lovingly crafted. "Marissa told me they've got a new boutique section."

"Yeah, really nice stuff. Expensive, but nice."

"Well, Patsy felt so guilty about not being able to spend any time with me before school started that she dumped a small fortune into my school account. Might as well start spending it, right?"

Cece laughed. "Yeah, you gotta love parental guilt. Hey, how was fencing practice? Seems like you were gone all afternoon."

"It was long, and I sucked. I was so distracted thinking about this whole Blackwell thing. I still don't get it."

"Yeah, I don't think any of us do. Have you had a chance to talk to Aidan, see what he thinks?"

I shrugged. "Not really. I was at practice all day, and he's going to be working in the lab again tonight on that thing with Dr. Byrne. Sounds like it was going well last night, but he had to stop early and go deal with Jenna."

"Hey, at least now you know what they're doing out in the woods together, right? Anyway, back to practice—any new Tyler deets to share?"

"Not really. He was just his usual annoying, overconfident self. I think maybe it's just an act or something. No one can be that arrogant."

"I like guys with a bit of swagger," Cece said with a smirk. "Todd had no swagger."

I shook my head. "Poor Todd."

She waved one hand. "He'll survive."

"Stone cold," I teased.

"Whatever." Cece was literally bouncing on the bed. "Any idea if Tyler's got a girlfriend? Back at Summerhaven or something?"

"I have no idea—seriously, we don't talk about stuff like that. Our conversation mostly consists of him telling me how awesome he is just before I kick his butt."

Cece stood and walked over to the room's little sitting area. "Well, if he ever needs anyone to soothe his wounded ego, feel free to offer my services."

"Will do," I said with a laugh. "Hey, you got any more of those peanut-butter cookies?" Cece's mom had dropped her off at school with a Tupperware tub full of homemade cookies, and I'd been craving one all day.

"Uh, uh, uh," she chastised, laying a hand protectively over the tub's lid. "Dinner's in fifteen minutes."

I stood, reaching for my shoes. "Well, it better be something good, because I'm starved."

I slid into a desk in the second row, Aidan beside me. I'd made it to fifth period, my last academic class of the day. All I had left was sixth-period fencing.

I glanced over at Aidan and smiled, watching as he slapped a notebook down on his desk and uncapped his pen. It had been a pretty good day so far. First-period calculus had been far less painful than I'd anticipated, especially with Aidan on one side of me and Sophie on the other. Second-period English seemed promising, and Sophie shared that class with me too.

Cece and I had third-period French together, and then after lunch I met back up with Aidan for fourth-period British history followed by art history. All in all, it was a pretty good schedule.

I looked up as Joshua entered the classroom, smiling as he made his way toward the empty seat beside Aidan. Joshua and Aidan seemed to have developed a particularly tight bond since last year—probably because Aidan had been responsible for making idiots like Scott Jackson leave the shape-shifters alone, once and for all. We'd passed Scott in the courtyard on our way to fourth period, and he'd given us a *wide* berth. Last fall he'd seen Aidan's red-rimmed eyes and elongated canine teeth, and then peed his pants in fright. No *way* would he want that last bit to get out. Nope, he hadn't picked on a shape-shifter since.

"Is this seat taken?" someone asked, startling me.

I looked up as Tyler dropped his bag to the floor and slid into the seat on my right without waiting for my reply.

I shook my head. "It is now."

"Fancy meeting you here," he said with a grin.

"Yeah, you don't exactly strike me as the art history type."

"No?" he asked. "Interesting."

By now Aidan was sitting forward in his seat, watching the exchange with obvious interest. "I'm Aidan Gray," he interjected, leaning toward me and draping one arm across my shoulders. "You must be the new guy. Tyler, right?"

Tyler looked at Aidan curiously, clearly taking note of the possessive gesture, which was totally un-Aidan-like. "Uh, yeah," he drawled. "I see you two know each other. Hmm, you never mentioned a boyfriend."

I narrowed my eyes at him—what, did he think he was going to get me in trouble or something? "That's because it never came up."

"Now, I find *that* interesting," Aidan said.

What was this, some sort of male pissing contest? Luckily, the teacher strode in just then, interrupting all the fun.

"And here I was worried about Byrne," Aidan whispered. He dropped his arm and leaned back into his chair, his gaze focused on the teacher who was settling his things on the desk at the front of the room.

He's on the fencing team with me, I answered in my head as the teacher scrawled the name "Dr. Charles Michael Andrulis" across the blackboard. I noticed that he wore a pair of thin tan gloves, which I knew by now meant that he was probably some form of clairsentient, able to sense information psychically through touch. "Psychometry," some called it. I wondered briefly if the gloves were to protect himself from information overload or to protect us from his psychic invasion as he handled things we'd touched. Maybe both.

"Don't let these put you off," he called out, almost as if he could read my thoughts. He held up his hands, palms facing out. "I just prefer a barrier between myself and your teenage angst. Not that I don't appreciate a little romance." He laughed, and the class joined in. I glanced over at Aidan, but his gaze was fixed on Tyler, who was drumming a pencil on his desk, a scowl on his face as he stared straight ahead.

"But occasionally my gift comes in handy," the teacher continued, mercifully oblivious to our little drama in the second row. "What I wouldn't give to get my hands on the *Mona Lisa*. Literally," he added wistfully. "Perhaps someday. Anyway . . ." He trailed off, reaching for a piece of paper on his desk. "Let me start with attendance. Then we'll talk about art."

Fifty minutes later the bells began to peal, signaling the end of the period. I closed my notebook and stuffed it in my backpack, trying to ignore the tension I felt crackling between the guys on either side of me. Did Aidan really feel threatened by Tyler, or was it all just posturing? Either way, it seemed pretty stupid.

"So, fencing's next period," Tyler said, rising to stand beside my desk. He tipped his head toward Aidan. "Does he mind if you and I walk over together?"

"Do you mind if I walk with you two?" Aidan countered. "I've got sixth period free."

I stood, then immediately reached for Aidan as my vision began to tunnel. *Oh no . . .*

"What's wrong with her?" I heard Tyler ask, just before Aidan's arms came around me, holding me tight as the vision took over my consciousness.

"That's it," Cece cried, tears coursing down her cheeks. "I'm out, Violet." She was tossing things into a suitcase as I sat there helplessly.

"What do you mean, out?" I asked. My hair was shorter, just barely brushing my shoulders.

"Expelled," Cece answered. "God, my parents are going to kill me!"

"It's my fault," I said. "All because I sent you snooping for clues."

I blinked hard, my vision swimming back to normal, the hum in my ears receding. I hadn't seen enough; I hadn't had time to search for any sort of clues. Cece expelled? It didn't make any sense. She was a good student, a model student. What could she possibly do to get expelled—and what part would I play in it?

"How bad?" Aidan murmured, his lips against my hair.

I let out a sigh of relief. "I've seen much worse." No one had been physically harmed, at least.

"What just happened?" Tyler asked, his voice laced with concern. "Did you have a seizure or something?"

If only it were that simple.

I stepped away from Aidan. "A vision, Tyler. My gift, remember?"

I quickly replayed the vision in my mind. I'd seen my hair short like that once before, but the memory was just out of reach.

"You okay to go to fencing?" Tyler asked, taking a step toward me. "Or should I tell Coach you're sick or something?"

"Nah, I'm fine." At least, I *would* be fine. "I'm coming, just give me a sec."

Aidan was openly glaring at Tyler now. "Why don't you give her some space," he said.

Can you please stop that? I snapped silently.

Aidan's gaze shot toward mine. *Stop what?*

I shook my head. *This whole weird possessive thing you're doing. Tyler's not . . . he's just being nice.*

Aidan's eyebrows arched knowingly. *That's what you think.*

". . . going to be late if we don't get moving," Tyler was saying, glancing down at his watch.

I just nodded.

"I'll let you two get going, then," Aidan said, his voice maddeningly polite.

With that, he turned and walked away from us. I stood there silently, watching his back as he slipped down the aisle and disappeared through the door without a backward glance.

Tyler's smirk was unmistakable as he stood there beside me watching Aidan's exit.

"After you," he said at last with a sweeping gesture toward the door. Without a word, I set off, Tyler falling into step beside me.

It was only later, as we made our way across the courtyard en route to the gym, that the memory I'd been trying to grasp earlier drifted effortlessly into my consciousness.

I'd had a vision last year—a vision of myself lying in an unfamiliar, antique-looking bed. Aidan had been there in the bed with me, gazing down at me with bloodlust in his eyes. I had looked slightly different—my hair had been shorter, barely brushing my shoulders.

Exactly like it was in the vision I'd just had.

8 ~ This Kiss

Got any plans for later?" Tyler asked, sprawled beside me on the piste. Around us, the rest of the team were packing up their gear, heading out to make the most of what was left of the afternoon. I was too tired to do anything but lie there, staring up at the ceiling.

"What, you mean tonight?" I swiped the back of one hand across my sweaty forehead. The air was hot and damp, like a sauna. Not for the first time, I wished the long row of floor-to-ceiling windows lining the far wall opened, allowing in fresh air. The studio was stuffy, and it smelled like stale sweat and dust—not particularly a pleasant combination, but a familiar one.

"Yeah, I mean tonight." He raised one arm, sniffing his own armpit. "God, I stink."

"Yes, you do," I agreed enthusiastically.

He reached for the end of my ponytail and gave it a tug. "For the record, princess, you smell pretty ripe yourself."

I sat up, eyeing him sharply. "Hey, watch it. And yes, I do have plans tonight."

"Ah, with the boyfriend, I suppose. Speaking of Mr. Moody, Jack Delafield asked me to work on a project with the two of them in the chem lab. I guess Jack's a friend of yours?"

"Yeah, Jack's dating my friend Kate. He's a good guy." But I was surprised that he'd asked for Tyler's help in the lab, even if they did share the same psychic gift.

"Kate's the cute blonde?" he asked. "Looks like Tinkerbell?"

I rolled my eyes. "She does *not* look like Tinkerbell."

He shrugged. "Does to me." He reached into his bag and pulled out a towel, wiping his face with it before stuffing it back inside. "Anyway, Jack says he's doing some sort of medical research—something about his brother. Weird, isn't it?"

"That he has a brother? Yeah," I agreed. Because pretty much everyone else at Winterhaven was an only child. "Are you going to help out?"

"Yeah, I thought I would. There aren't a lot of us here. Micros, I mean. We had more at Summerhaven."

My curiosity was piqued. "What was Summerhaven like?"

"Way more casual than here. None of this 'Mr. Bennett and Miss McKenna' crap. I guess you could say it's less traditional. Summerhaven isn't nearly as old as Winterhaven."

"No?"

He shook his head. "Wasn't founded till the 1950s or something like that. And the campus is totally different—smaller, for starters. The buildings are all wood and beams, kind of built to blend right into the landscape."

"Do you miss it?"

"Yeah, I guess. Mostly I miss the ocean. I like to surf."

"Are you any good?"

His mouth curved into a grin. "Hell yeah. I could have competed, if I'd wanted to." His smile disappeared at once. "But my dad . . . well, he was a fencer. Just missed making the Olympic team. It was pretty important to him that I follow in his footsteps."

"What happened to your dad? I don't mean to pry," I added quickly. "Feel free to tell me to shut up, if you want."

He took a deep breath, then let it out slowly. "Nah, it's okay. He had a dinner meeting with clients and was driving home after dark. A drunk driver crossed the center line and hit him head-on. They say he died instantly—blunt force trauma. Course, the stupid fucking drunk walked away without a scratch. On April Fool's Day—can you believe that?"

My throat felt tight, my windpipe constricted. "I hope he's in jail—the guy who hit him, I mean," I said, my voice tense.

"Hasn't been sentenced yet, but everyone thinks he's going to walk. First-time offender and all that, just out of college. He shows up in court looking like some kind of altar boy."

I let out my breath in a rush. "That totally sucks."

His eyes looked hard, his jaw clenched. "Man, if I could just get my hands on him . . ." He trailed off, shaking his head. "I think that's why my mom wanted to come east, to get me as far away as possible, just in case."

I took a deep breath, gathering my courage. "I lost my dad too," I said at last. "Three years ago. He was . . . murdered. Executed, actually."

"Oh God, Violet. I'm sorry. I had no idea."

"It's okay—I don't talk about it much. But I wanted you to know . . . well, that I understand what you're going through. And it *does* get easier. At least a little bit."

"Do they know who did it?"

I nodded. "It was in Afghanistan. Terrorists. He was a journalist, and they"—I swallowed hard—"they kidnapped him. There was a videotape, but I had already seen the whole thing. My visions," I clarified. "I saw . . . *everything.*"

"Fu-uck" was all he said, drawing it out to two syllables.

"That about sums it up," I said, refusing to let the images enter my mind. "Anyway, I just wanted you to know, that's all. If you ever need to talk . . ."

He reached for my hand and gave it a squeeze. "Thanks, Violet. I appreciate that."

I just nodded, pulling my hand from his grasp.

"I guess we should get going, huh? You've got those big plans and all. With the boyfriend."

"Are you going to keep calling him that?" I asked with a sigh. "'The boyfriend'?"

He smiled, the corners of his eyes crinkling. "Yeah, I thought I might."

I stood, brushing off the seat of my shorts. "You are *so* annoying."

"Just part of my charm," he said with a wink, and then wrinkled his nose. "You really need to hit the shower. Trust me, the boyfriend will thank you."

I swung my bag at him, connecting with his arm.

"Hey, it's not my fault you stink." He took a step back as I swung for him again and missed. "Okay, so you and Tinkerbell are spoken for. What about the rest of your little gang? Help me out here."

"Cece!" I said a little too excitedly, an idea forming in my head.

He raked a hand through his damp hair, leaving it sticking up in all directions. "Which one is Cece?"

"My roommate." I reached for my bag and hoisted it onto my shoulder with a smile. "How do you feel about double dates?"

I blinked hard, waiting for my eyes to adjust to the dark. "That went well, right?" I asked, lowering myself to the blankets on the floor of the chapel's loft.

I could hear Aidan digging out the candles he kept in a box in the far corner. He struck a match, and the small space filled with soft, flickering light. "If you say so," he said.

I scooted over as Aidan made his way back to the blanket and sat down beside me, draping one arm around me. I leaned into him, resting my head on his shoulder. "Well, it *was* going well till Todd walked in."

"Is that what happened, then? I admit, I wasn't quite following the subtext."

"Todd sat down right behind us, even though there were plenty of empty tables." .

"Marking his territory, I suppose," he said with a shrug.

"Yeah, but they broke up, remember?"

Aidan nodded. "Oh, that's right. Well, your little friend didn't seem to notice, if his incessant chatter was any indication."

"Oh my God—'my little friend'? You're as bad as he is. He calls you 'the boyfriend.'"

"At least he knows where things stand. Remind me to congratulate him," he said with a smirk.

"C'mon, give the guy a break. He just lost his dad, you know. Back in April."

His brows drew together at once. "No, I didn't know. Does he know about your father?"

"Yeah, we were talking about it today, after practice. It was . . . I don't know." I shook my head, searching for the right words. "Easier this time, I guess. Talking about it, I mean. Mostly I just felt angry. Really, really angry."

He pulled me closer. "I think that's normal, Vi. Especially in a situation like this, where there's no justice."

"I swear, just knowing that they're still over there, thinking they've won . . ." I shook my head. "It makes me sick."

Aidan reached for my chin, tipping my face up toward his. "You know, if it would make you feel better, I could take care of it. They deserve to die, and I would take great pleasure—"

"No, Aidan. Oh my God, the very idea of you anywhere near them . . ." I swallowed hard. "Just no, okay?"

"Violet, I'm a vampire. What do you think they're going to do to me? I could end them all in a matter of minutes, with no risk to myself whatsoever."

I squeezed my eyes shut, trying to block out the mental image of Aidan taking on my father's murderers. A shudder snaked up my spine. "You would want their blood inside you, Aidan? Tainting you? They're evil—pure and utter evil. Just . . . no."

"Of course," he said softly. "I didn't mean to upset you."

"I know. It's okay. I appreciate the sentiment, trust me. They *do* deserve to die. I just don't want their blood on your hands, that's all."

"Understood. Anyway, back to Tyler. He seems like a pretty okay guy," he conceded.

"He is, and I think he could use some friends. Jack seems to like him."

"Yeah, he said as much. He thinks Tyler can help him with his work in the lab. Which is good, because I'm pretty preoccupied with my own lately. And speaking of which, guess who stopped by today—to check on the progress of my work, she claimed?"

"Who?"

"Nicole," he said, and then corrected himself. "Mrs. Girard. Our esteemed headmistress. I'm pretty sure she's never set foot inside the science wing before."

"Hmm, that's kind of weird."

"I thought so too. I don't want to get too complacent about her—she's definitely not to be underestimated."

I nodded. "Right, the chairwoman of your vampire court. They're all females, right?"

"Actually, there are two males on the Tribunal, Luc and Goran," he said. "Impeccable pedigrees, those two, turned by the Impaler himself."

"You mean . . . Vlad the Impaler?" I said incredulously. "He's real?"

"Definitely." There was a trace of amusement in his voice. "He's like a rock star in our world. Probably the most revered male vampire ever."

"Wow. That's . . . I don't know, surreal. Where is he now?"

"Oh, I don't know. Around. He's pretty much a recluse these days."

I couldn't believe how blasé he sounded. I mean, Vlad the Impaler? He was only the most famous vampire *ever*. Well, except for Dracula, but I'd read somewhere that Stoker had actually based Dracula on Vlad, so I guess they were really one and the same. "Okay, so who else is on this Tribunal?" I asked.

"Let's see, there's Nicole, Luc, and Goran." He ticked them off on his fingers. "Adele—she's pretty scary—and Melina. That's it, besides the Eldest."

"The Eldest?"

"Yeah, the eldest living vampire, Isa. Nicole's the chairwoman, but that's more like an administrative position. All the true power lies with the Eldest, though it's a dangerous position. Isa's been in power as long as I've been alive, but every couple of hundred years or so, there's unrest among the ancients. Imagine a king with hundreds of younger brothers, all desperate for the crown—only with no familial ties to keep them in check."

"That sounds crazy. And dangerous," I added. "So what's this Isa like?"

"Pretty much exactly what you'd expect from a thousand-and-something-year-old female vampire. The only real difference between her and the Propagators is that Isa is far more concerned with quality than she is with quantity. While the Propagators are indiscriminate, Isa sees vampirism as a gift only to be bestowed on the most deserving—the smartest, strongest, bravest. She's far more calculating, more cunning, but just as dangerous."

"Do me a favor and try *really* hard not to get sent to the Tribunal this year, okay?" I still felt ill when I thought about those three days he'd spent in their clutches last year—being *tortured*, apparently.

"You got it. Things are pretty stable right now, but you never know who's plotting what and with whom. Which is why I prefer to stay out of the politics and why Mrs. Girard poking around the lab makes me nervous. Especially after Jenna's little revelation about Blackwell."

"I think we're all a little freaked out by that. Did she tell you anything else?"

"No, and I honestly don't think she knows anything. She was as much a pawn in the whole thing as we were. Anyway, we don't have much time before curfew. I told you I had a surprise for you, remember?"

"Yeah, but I don't much like surprises."

"No? Well, I think you'll like this one." The candlelight flickered across his face as he gazed down at me, his eyes the same pale blue-gray as the sky at dawn. My pulse leapt in response.

"Wow, you sound awfully sure of yourself," I said, my mouth dry.

"I am." He reached for my shoulders and drew me closer.

Electricity skittered across my skin as his lips met mine. I leaned into him, expecting his usual tentative kiss—soft and searching, until the bloodlust took over and he was forced to pull away.

He always pulled away, not because he feared his bite would turn me into a vampire—it wouldn't. Or even because he thought he might kill me. Oh, that was a possibility, I suppose—that he would lose control and suck me dry—but I was pretty sure he wouldn't. Sure enough to risk it. It was because he feared his bite would hurt, and he had vowed never to hurt me.

Besides, it went against his own personal "code"—he didn't bite innocents, didn't drink their blood. For him, it was a punishment dealt to the deserving—criminals or would-be criminals, dangerous souls who showed no remorse.

The problem, however, with this self-imposed code was that it was directly at odds with an integral part of his vampire nature—the part that made his bite necessary for sexual satisfaction. Oh, he could have sex without biting, without drinking blood, but he wouldn't actually *enjoy* it. At least, not fully.

And as far as I could tell, he'd only done it once—the sex-while-biting thing. With Isabel, his ex from the past who looked just like me. And since Isabel had been killed as a result of her relationship with Aidan, it seemed a safe bet that, in his mind, sex plus biting equaled a dead girlfriend. Yet there was no stopping the dual, intertwined needs from increasing his bloodlust whenever we made out. Thus, the need for caution.

But *this* kiss . . . this one was anything *but* tentative and cautious.

No, this kiss was slow and languorous, mind-numbingly thorough, and without any reservations whatsoever. My bones seemed to melt away inside me, my whole body growing heavy and warm as he lowered me to the blankets, his body held taut over mine, his lips never once leaving mine.

His fingers tangled in my hair, angling my head as he

deepened the kiss. I could feel his heart thrumming against mine as I opened my mouth against his, wanting more.

My hands traveled from his neck down to his shoulders, across his back. Beneath my fingertips, his muscles seemed to bunch and shift, his heartbeat quickening in response. Feeling slightly reckless now, I reached under his shirt, sliding my palms up the smooth planes of his chest.

When I heard him groan, his body tensing beneath my touch, I knew I'd gone too far. I felt him pull away and braced myself for the sight of his transformation—the red-rimmed eyes, the elongated fangs. I waited a beat, gathering the courage I needed to open my eyes.

In the silence, his thumb brushed across my cheek, drawing lazy circles against my flushed skin. Finally, he spoke. "God, Violet. I love you so very much."

"I love you, too," I replied breathlessly, willing my eyes to open and meet his.

"Look at me, then," he whispered, nudging my face with his nose. "Go on."

And so I did. The eyes that gazed back at me were a pale blue-gray and thickly lashed, no redness marring their perfection. His lips parted with a smile, revealing straight, white teeth that looked entirely unremarkable.

There was not a single hint of bloodlust in his features.

9 ~ To the Manor Born

How did you do that?" I asked, sitting up so abruptly that I nearly knocked Aidan over.

He reached up to brush back a lock of hair that had fallen across my cheek. "Amazing, isn't it?"

I nodded. "Yes, but how? I mean, what's changed?"

"Something that Dr. Byrne suggested, a slight alteration to the formula for the cure. The serum that I inject," he clarified, "not the elixir."

"You mean—you mean it worked?" I stammered, unable to believe it. "You're cured?"

He shook his head. "Unfortunately, no. But there have actually been some significant changes at the cellular level. Not enough, but I can tell we're moving in the right direction now."

"Are you sure?"

He leaned back against the blankets, his arms folded behind his head. "I injected myself with the serum two days ago, and I can already feel the changes. I slept like the dead last night, and even though the elixir should be starting to wear off by now, it isn't. I should be feeling the urge to feed, but I'm not. And you saw what happened just now. I knew I was taking a chance, but I was hoping that I was right. It looks like I *was* right." He was grinning now, happier than I'd ever seen him.

"Wow," I breathed. "So . . . what next?"

"More work, I suppose. We need to figure out exactly which systems we've altered and which remain unaffected, and then we can go from there. Here"—he patted the blanket beside him—"lie down."

I complied, fitting myself against his body, my head on his chest. "How much time before curfew?" I murmured. Because this new development—this opened up new options. *Exciting* options.

"Not enough time." His cool fingers found my neck, tracing a path down to my collarbone. "Your skin is so warm."

"It just feels that way to you," I said, but truthfully, it felt like my skin was on fire. Aidan always seemed to have that effect on me. Our connection was that visceral—it always had been, right from the beginning.

Insta-love, some would call it, but it wasn't, not really. It had taken time for the initial attraction to deepen, to shift and grow. I did the mental math—two months, a little more. Long enough to know that Aidan was gentle and kind, generous to a fault. He'd experienced great loss in his life, just like me.

"Tell me more about your family," I prompted. "Your parents and sisters."

"Okay," he said, reaching down to cup my hip with one hand. "My father . . . let's see. Looking back, I realize that I didn't know him very well. He had very little interaction with his children—at least, not while we were still in the nursery."

"You really had a nursery?" I pictured the one from *Peter Pan*—Wendy and her brothers together in one big room, their beds in rows, the children tended by the giant dog Nana.

"We really did. Anyway, my father was a quiet man. Studious. He took his duties seriously, though he didn't care for London. He much preferred our country estate in Dorset. I'm fairly certain that was a bone of contention between him and my mother. She loved town."

I closed my eyes, succumbing to the hypnotic tone of his voice. "And by 'town' you mean London?" I asked sleepily, trying to picture London at the turn of the century. The twentieth century, that is.

"Exactly. My mother preferred the hustle and bustle of London. She liked to go to parties, to attend court. It was novel to her—she had Irish roots, grew up a commoner. Being a viscount's wife was everything she'd dreamed of, and luckily for her, society adored her. And why not? She was beautiful and charming, always smiling."

"And your sisters?" I asked, suddenly aware of the fact that I didn't even know their names.

"Georgiana and Elizabeth," he said, his voice swelling with affection. "Both as beautiful as our mother, with her dark hair and eyes. Georgie was just thirteen months my junior, more like my twin. We did everything together—fought, played, tormented the nursemaids and governesses. Lizzie came six years later, the little plaything that Georgie had always wished for. She turned out be a troublemaker, our little Lizzie, always getting into scrapes."

The pride in his voice was unmistakable. "Go on," I said, wanting to know more about these long-lost girls who shared his blood.

"Georgie hadn't even had her coming-out when I was turned. I'll always regret not getting to dance with her at her ball. I watched, though," he said, his voice quiet now. "I stood outside in the shadows, watching her through a window. She'd never looked more lovely.

"At one point, I saw her glance at the window where I stood, as if she somehow knew I was there. Her thoughts were full of me, missing me." His voice was thick now. "And yet I could not show myself. She died in childbirth five years later, giving her husband the son he'd always wanted."

"And Lizzie?" I asked, my eyes suddenly damp. I only hoped her story was a happier one.

"Little Lizzie continued to get into as much trouble as possible, including a situation with a married man that didn't end well. Let's just say I had to take care of that unpleasant business myself."

My eyes flew open. "You mean you . . . what? Killed him?"

"Trust me when I say that he full well deserved what he got. After what he did to my sister . . ." He trailed off, shaking his head. "I take great comfort in knowing that I perhaps saved other women from suffering the same cruel fate as Lizzie did. Anyway, Lizzie finally married years later, after the scandal died down. I think she had a happy life. She outlived my mother by just a few years, the last of my family to go. Only then did I present myself as my father's rightful heir, claiming to be my own grandson. I had fabricated papers to prove it, and I was able to use them, along with a bit of mind manipulation, to see that the estate in Dorset passed to me. I kept it up for a while, eventually donating it to the National Trust. It still stands—Brompton Park, a historic site."

I tried to picture it, some grand English estate like Mr. Darcy's in *Pride and Prejudice.* "Will you take me there someday?"

"If you'd like." He pressed his lips to my temple.

"Definitely. Maybe next summer, after graduation. I'm sure Patsy wouldn't care. She probably wouldn't even notice I was gone," I added.

"We'll see," he said. "Next summer is a long way away, isn't it, love?"

I knew he didn't like to think of the future, didn't like to hope.

I would have to have hope enough for both of us.

I stared at my laptop screen, waiting impatiently for the search engine to load. *Brompton Park,* I typed into the box. Then I added *viscount* and *Dorset* just for good measure.

And there it was, at the top of the search results. A UK National Trust listing for a Brompton Park in Dorset, England, the former seat of Viscount Brompton. My palms suddenly damp, I clicked the link.

The page loaded, filling my screen with images of Aidan's ancestral home.

I let out my breath in a rush. *Wow.* Aidan had grown up *there?*

"Hey, what's that?" Cece asked, looking over my shoulder at the screen. "Research for your history class or something?"

I tapped the screen with my finger. "No, it's—well, it *was*—Aidan's house. His family's estate back in England."

"Oh my God, you've got to be kidding!" Cece sat down beside me. "Whoa, can you say 'posh'? Does he still own it?"

I shook my head, clicking on the gallery link. "No, he gave it to the government. It's like a tourist attraction now or something."

Cece's chin resting on my shoulder, I clicked through the photographs, one after another. A marble-tiled foyer. A curving staircase. An enormous dining room table set with an elaborate china and crystal setting. A bedroom with a short-looking four-poster bed draped with velvet curtains. More bedrooms, each as decadent-looking as the one before. Another room that could only be the nursery, looking much like the one I'd imagined from *Peter Pan.* And then I began to click through several paintings, mostly portraits.

One portrait made my breath catch in my throat—two dark-haired girls sat on an ornate purple velvet couch, a golden-haired boy standing stiffly beside them. The face looking back at me was achingly familiar, despite the old-fashioned clothing and formal pose.

There was no doubt in my mind that it was Aidan, maybe twelve or thirteen years old, with his sisters. He was gazing at the artist with a bored expression, his posture radiating a careless arrogance. It was him, and yet it wasn't.

"That's—that's *him*," Cece stuttered. "Whoa! Keep going; maybe there's more."

I reached for the mouse again and continued to click through the remaining photos, but the rest showed only the estate's gardens—a fountain, a hedgerow maze, manicured flower beds.

With a sigh, I clicked back to the main page.

"Oh my God, look at that." Cece leaned closer to the screen. "You can actually rent the place. Twenty-eight hundred pounds a week—what's that come to? Four thousand dollars, maybe?"

I nodded. "Something like that. Can you imagine?"

Cece stood, unfolding her long, trim legs. "Hey, I've got an idea! We should go in together, all of us, and rent it out for a graduation trip next summer."

"Tyler too?" I asked, raising my brows.

"I guess. Last night seemed promising, right?"

"I don't know—you tell me," I prodded. "I mean, I think he's a little obnoxious sometimes, but he was pretty funny last night. He *did* make you snort coffee up your nose, you were laughing so hard."

She eyed me dubiously. "You say that like it's a good thing."

"Well, you two seemed to be getting along."

"Yeah, it was fun," she agreed. "But . . . we'll see. Anyway, back to Aidan's house. Excuse me, his *mansion*. How cool would that be, to rent it out? Do you think he would go for it, or would that be too weird for him?"

"I don't know." I glanced back at the screen, shaking my head in amazement. "But I *would* like to see it."

"Well, get to work on him, girlfriend! Use your persuasive feminine powers, if you know what I mean."

I had to laugh at that. Yeah, that was the only weapon I had to use against him. Well, that and my stake.

And then something clicked in my mind. The bed!

Hastily I clicked on the back button, going through the gallery of photos in reverse order, until I found what I was looking for.

"That's it," I breathed, my eyes widening as I stared at the image on the screen.

It was a bed—an antique mahogany bed with four spindly posts and a blue damask duvet trimmed in gold cording spread across it. I'd seen it before, in one of my visions.

That vision—the one of Aidan and me in a bed. Together.

"That's what?" Cece asked, glancing at the screen. "A bed?

Yeah, that's a bed, all right. Looks pretty comfy, too, I'd say. Look at all those throw pillows."

But I couldn't answer her—I couldn't say a single word. I was too busy trying to remember what I'd seen, to recall the details. Mostly, I came up blank.

That was the vision I'd work on retrieving next with Dr. Byrne, I decided. Because I needed to know, once and for all, if I'd seen myself there in that bed.

Or if I'd somehow seen Isabel instead.

10 ~ Inked

I closed my eyes, concentrating on the now familiar sound of the clock. No more than thirty seconds passed before I fell into the vision, moving around inside the images in my head, searching for clues.

As far as visions went, this one wasn't particularly interesting or illuminating. Kate was sitting on Cece's bed crying; sobbing, really. Cece and Sophie were there with me, comforting her. I'd deduced that she and Jack had broken up. Which was awful, yes, as far as Kate was concerned. Still, I'd seen far worse.

I'd already decided I wasn't going to tell her about the vision—I just couldn't. But, I don't know . . . maybe I could learn something useful, something that I could use to redirect whatever was going to happen or maybe soften the blow somehow.

I hadn't had that many visions since the beginning of school, so there wasn't much to choose from when it came to my sessions with Dr. Byrne. I'd managed to master the vision recall on our third session, and now I was an old pro. I'd gone through the vision with the bed—it was definitely the one in Brompton Park, I was sure of it now—and pretty much every other vision that wasn't too painful to relive, just for the sake of practice.

An entire month had passed since the beginning of school, mostly in a blur of textbooks and pop quizzes. Cece had been elected student body president by a landslide. Temperatures had dropped, leaves had changed colors, and jackets had come out of closets.

And every single Saturday I'd met with Dr. Byrne. In all that time I hadn't been able to recall the vision with Whitney and Aidan. Not once, and not for a lack of trying. Which meant it had been a dream after all, I'd concluded.

Thank God.

Mostly I'd revisited "Crying Kate" and "Expelled Cece," studying the visions from every possible angle. "Expelled Cece" wasn't happening till wintertime—there was a significant amount of snow on the ground outside our window, I'd discovered. There was plenty of time to worry about that one.

But "Crying Kate" was coming soon—this fall, for sure. Before the Halloween Fair dance, which meant it was imminent, unless I could find a way around it. Unfortunately, I had very little to go on. Still inside the vision, I shook my head. There was nothing new to see.

I opened my eyes, allowing myself to return to the present, to Dr. Byrne's cramped office.

"How'd that go?" he asked, his chin propped in the palm of one hand, his elbow resting on the desk.

"Eh," I answered with a shrug. "Can I ask you something?"

"Of course. Anything."

I took a deep breath before speaking, carefully considering my words. "What would you do if you saw something— something about a friend—that would only hurt them to know in advance. Something that . . . well, that your friend probably couldn't do anything to prevent, anyway. Because it was . . . well, about someone else's feelings. Something that can't be controlled. Would you warn them anyway?"

"You mean like a shift in someone's affection, something like that?"

"Yes, Dr. Byrne," I said, amazed at his perception. "Something *exactly* like that."

"You know, every time you call me Dr. Byrne, I want to look over my shoulder for my dad. I know it's expected in the classroom, but maybe here during our sessions you could just call me Matthew. You called your old coach by her first name, didn't you?"

"Sandra? Sure, but she isn't a teacher."

"Actually, she is. She teaches aerobics. A PE elective."

"Really? I didn't know that." It made sense, considering she was always wearing perky little track suits. "So, Matthew, huh? You don't look like a Matthew." It just seemed too . . . I don't know, traditional, maybe? Too biblical.

A slow smile spread across his face. "What *do* I look like?"

"I don't know." I studied him, considering the question. Dark hair, dark eyes. Chiseled cheekbones with a scruffy day-old beard. "A Zach, maybe? Or a Sam. You could probably get away with Matt, though."

"My grandma calls me Matty," he said with a wince. "And don't even *think* about it."

I held up my hands in surrender. "Hey, don't worry. I don't think I could say it without laughing."

He raised one eyebrow. "For what it's worth, you don't look much like a Violet, either."

I nodded. "Yeah, I know. My middle name is Ashton—my mom's maiden name. I always liked it better."

He studied me back, his head tipped thoughtfully, his index finger resting on his cheek. "Ashton? Yeah, I can see that. Anyway, to answer your question, I probably wouldn't tell him— my friend, I mean—if I'd had a vision like you described. Have you had a lot of luck preventing things? Once you see them?"

"Not before I came to Winterhaven. But here . . . well, I'm comfortable warning people here about stuff I see. And I actually managed to prevent my gran's housekeeper from slipping and breaking her hip last year. Of course, I *didn't* see my gran having a stroke a few months later."

"It's annoying how we don't see everything, isn't it? What's the point of saving someone from one calamity only to have someone else fall victim to another that we didn't foresee?"

I let out my breath in a huff. "Exactly. Seriously, I just don't get the point of it. This gift, I mean."

"Well, what's the point of any of them, really? Except to give us a slight advantage over more normal folks. Some think we're representative of an evolved species. Maybe we are, I don't know." He shrugged. "I guess it's come in handy now and then. I'd rather be Spider-Man, though."

"Spider-Man? He wears tights, you know."

With an easy laugh, he picked up a newspaper from his desk and tossed it toward me. "Unfortunate fashion choices aside, at least I could be useful in fighting crime. Did you see this?"

I picked up the paper and scanned the headline. VAMPIRE STALKER STRIKES AGAIN, it proclaimed in bold, black type. "Vampire Stalker? What do they mean, strikes *again*?"

He looked at me like I'd grown two heads. "Haven't you been following the news?"

I dropped the paper to my lap. "Who has time to follow the news with the workload around here? What's going on?"

"Three victims so far, all in Manhattan, all female. Puncture wounds to the neck, heavy blood loss. Thus the moniker."

"It's stupid," I said. "The name. Sounds like someone who stalks vampires."

"Yeah, but you know how the media is. They love dramatic-sounding nicknames. You know, like the Zodiac Killer."

I nodded in agreement. He had a point.

"Anyway, here's the really weird part. The police have questioned all three victims, and none of them remember anything about the attack. It's like it's been totally wiped from their memory. The police think it's some crazy, delusional guy who thinks he's a vampire. Of course, we know it could be something else entirely."

"You mean like an actual vampire," I said, stating the obvious.

He nodded. "It *is* possible."

"Well, from what I understand, this would be . . . well,

unacceptable. Leaving the wounds visible like that . . ." I trailed off, shaking my head. "That's not the way they do it. It's not allowed."

"I'm glad to hear they have rules, at least."

My stomach lurched uncomfortably. "We shouldn't be talking about this. Anyway, I'm no expert." I handed back the newspaper.

He took it and laid it on the corner of his desk. "Clearly, you know enough. Anyway, just promise me you're being careful."

I looked up sharply, preparing myself for yet another lecture about the dangers of dating a vampire.

"I don't mean like that," he said, obviously misinterpreting my expression. "Though as a teacher and dorm master, of course I *do* mean like that, too." He was actually blushing. "But I meant maybe you should stay away from Manhattan for the time being. At least until Spider-Man manages to solve the crime."

"Or Batman," I offered.

"Sorry, I'm purely a Marvel man. Anyway, what should we work on next, now that you've got the whole 'recall' thing down pat? Or have I fully served my purpose now?"

The truth was, I wanted to keep working with him. I'd come to enjoy our sessions together, the time spent with someone who shared my gift—even if he *was* a teacher. *A very young, very good-looking teacher,* I thought, remembering Aidan's words.

"There must be *some* other skills you can teach me," I said, feeling my own blush creep up my neck.

"Sure," he said with a shrug. "I've got a few more tricks up my sleeve. We won't be able to meet next Saturday, though. You've got the SATs."

"Ugh, don't remind me."

"You'll do fine, Violet. Your practice test scores were great."

Surprisingly enough, they were. "Will you be proctoring it?"

"No, they like to have an empath proctor the actual test. Makes sense, really. Helps with the nerves. You'll probably have Señora Díaz." One of the Spanish teachers—I didn't know her, but I'd heard good things about her.

"Well, I guess I should go," I said, rising.

"Yeah, I guess so." He stood, rolling his sleeves up as he did so, once again exposing the bottom edge of his tattoo.

"You've got a tattoo," I said before I thought better of it. "Kind of edgy for a science teacher at a stuffy boarding school." Again, my cheeks flamed. What had loosened my tongue like that? I mean, I guess I considered him kind of a friend at this point—an ally. But still . . .

"Hey, Winterhaven is anything but stuffy," he countered, pushing up his sleeve farther, revealing the entire image inked onto his bicep. "But yeah, it really enhances my 'professorial' image, don't you think?"

I took a step toward him, examining it. I'd been right—it was some sort of dagger. Almost like a medieval-looking cross, with a daggerlike blade. Layered atop it was an elaborately scripted letter M. *For Matthew.*

He was watching me closely, as if gauging my reaction. "That's pretty cool," I said at last. "I like it."

"I'm glad you approve," he said with a laugh, releasing his sleeve.

"I was kind of thinking of getting one myself. When I'm eighteen, I mean." I stopped, totally taken aback. I had no idea where that idea had come from. It had literally just popped into my head as I said it.

Suddenly the need was there—a pressing, burning desire. I could see the image as clearly as if I were having one of my visions. A small tattoo on the inside of my right wrist. A stake—my smooth, shiny hawthorne stake—with a butterfly resting on it. I had no idea where the image had come from or what it meant. But I knew that I wanted it, that I *would* have it. Eventually.

"Well, then, here's the best advice I've heard where tattoos are concerned: Figure out what design you want, and then wait a year. If after a year you still want that same image, then get it. And yeah, eighteen is the magic number."

Eighteen. The year I would officially "come of age" as a *Sâbbat*, but he couldn't know that. Five months from now, I realized, goose bumps rising on my skin. What would happen then? I had no idea, and I was more than a little afraid to find out.

11 ~ Shattered

Ow was practice?" Aidan asked as I lowered myself to the grass beside him.

I blew out a long breath. "Fine, but I'm exhausted. The SATs yesterday just about killed me." It had been a *long* day. I lay back against the cool grass, glad I was wearing a hoodie. It was finally starting to feel like fall.

The branches of a tree arched over us, its brilliant red leaves ruffling in the breeze. The crisp air smelled vaguely of smoke and leaf mold. Fall smells.

"I still can't believe I actually sat the test," Aidan said.

"I'm glad you did." I sat up and reached for his hand, eyeing him appreciatively as I did so. He was wearing a black leather jacket with a black T-shirt beneath it. His long, jeans-clad legs were stretched out in front of him. As always, the sight of him made my breath catch in my throat. "Hey, have you gotten all your college apps done?"

"I still don't see the point, but yeah, they're done."

I rolled my eyes. "The point is, you're going to be cured by then."

"You don't know that."

"Look how close you are, Aidan. I swear, you seem almost normal now. These past couple of weeks . . ." I trailed off, shaking my head.

There had been a definite shift in his personality—he was a little more possessive than before, less sure of himself, maybe. And despite his claim that he'd been sleeping soundly at night for the first time in more than a century, he somehow seemed fatigued. Less infallible. More . . . *human*. I was worried about him, even while I was relieved. It was a confusing combination of feelings.

"Have you even had to, you know"—I glanced around to make sure no one was within earshot, then dropped my voice to a whisper, just to be sure—"feed lately?"

"Not once," he said, shaking his head. "I've had no real urge to feed."

I gave his hand a squeeze. It felt different, I realized. Maybe a degree warmer than usual. "Well, you're getting closer then."

"The closer we get, the more out of reach it seems. I swear, sometimes I think I should just give up."

"No way. You are *not* giving up. Not now." He was going to find his cure, and we were going to go to college next year— together. We'd decided on several schools, an even half dozen: NYU, Columbia, Princeton, and Emory, plus St. Andrews in Scotland and the American University of Paris.

Personally, I thought the list seemed overly ambitious, but my guidance counselor insisted that given my grades and academic record, it was perfectly reasonable. I hoped she was right.

With a sigh Aidan turned my hand over and began tracing the lines on my palm with his index finger. "Do you know what I despise the most about myself?" He didn't wait for my reply. "The fact that I have no talents no true passions. Like you with your fencing, or Max with his music. During my mortal life I was way too spoiled, too lazy to bother. But since I was turned"—he shook his head—"I've had nothing *but* time. How easily I could have mastered something—a dozen somethings. I should have composed a symphony by now, painted a masterpiece, won an Olympic medal. I didn't have a single extracurricular activity to list on my applications. Not one."

I hated the despair in his voice. "I think you're being way too hard on yourself, Aidan. Look at how much you've accomplished with your research. That's got to count for something."

"It's not the same. I swear, if I were an adult I'd be one of those men who are completely obsessed with work. You know, the ones who only go home to shower and change their clothes. Speaking of which, I've got to head back to the lab in a little while. Dr. Byrne is meeting me and Jack to try out something new."

"What about Tyler?" I asked.

"What about him?"

"Do you think he could help you guys? I mean, he's been working with Jack, hasn't he?"

He shook his head. "Too many people know my secret as it is—I can't afford the risk. Dr. Byrne tiptoes around the word, but it's clear he knows exactly what we're dealing with."

"Matthew would never tell," I said with a shrug. "He wants to help, that's all."

Aidan's sharp gaze met mine. "Matthew?"

Uh-oh. "Dr. Byrne, I mean."

"He's 'Matthew' now? Just how close are you two?" His eyes were a stormy gray now.

"It's his—I mean—that's what he asked me to call him during our coaching sessions," I stammered. "Just—never mind."

"If I ever *do* get the urge to feed again, I know who to go after first," he said through gritted teeth.

"That's not funny, Aidan. You know he's no threat to you. He's been helping you out, remember?"

He released my hand. "Maybe he needs a reminder that you're a student and he's a fucking teacher."

"Are you done?" I asked coldly, shocked by his outburst. "Because I think I've had just about enough for today." I climbed to my feet, reaching for my bag.

He caught my wrist. "I'm sorry, Vi. I'm just . . . I don't know . . . frustrated."

"With Dr. Byrne? Because trust me, he hasn't—"

"With everything. Myself. My work. Nothing feels right." He was still sitting there on the grass, gazing up at me with what almost looked like fear in his eyes.

With a sigh, I went to him, kneeling beside him. "This is right," I said, gesturing between us. "*We're* right."

He leaned forward, pressing his lips against my forehead. "Yes, we are. When I'm not being a bloody bastard, that is."

"You, a bastard? Okay, maybe a little bit." I held up my thumb and forefinger, indicating about an inch.

"Come here." He tangled his fingers in my hair, wrapping one lock around his hand as he drew my head toward his. He paused, his lips just inches from mine, his breath warm against my cheek. "Your hair's gotten longer," he whispered. "I like it."

It was well past my shoulders now, last year's little flip totally grown out. The hot Georgia sun had streaked the brown with reddish gold over the summer. I liked it; it felt somehow glamorous.

And yet I'd been thinking about getting it cut to match the shorter style I'd seen in my vision. That would be tempting fate, I realized. *Dangerous.*

A frisson of excitement shot through me, making my breath come faster.

"I'll leave it long," I murmured, my lips curving into a smile. "For now."

"Now what am I supposed to do?" Kate sobbed. "Can you believe his shitty timing? The Halloween Fair's in two weeks."

Sophie handed her a tissue, just as I'd seen her do over and over in my vision.

"I don't have a date yet. We can go together," Cece offered, which just made Kate cry harder. Around the room, objects began to shake. A brush flew off Cece's dresser and landed on the floor beside the bed. Magazine pages fluttered as if some unseen hands were flipping through them.

"I wish there was something I could do," Sophie said, her brow furrowed. "We need Marissa."

"She's probably off sucking face with Max," Kate moaned, sending the stack of magazines flying to the floor.

Kate was probably right—Marissa and Max had been spending a lot of time together lately.

I reached up to rub Kate's back. "Want me to get you some water?"

She shook her head.

"Did he even give you a reason why?" Cece asked, even though we'd already been through this before. "I just don't get it."

Kate looked up, her eyes red and damp. "He says I'm too much of a distraction lately. A *distraction*—can you believe he called me that?"

"Douchewaffle," Sophie said.

"Asswipe," I added, though we'd pretty much called him every name in the book by now—maybe even a few that *weren't* in the book.

Kate hiccupped, then wiped her nose. "He's probably hooking up with someone else and just too chickenshit to admit it."

I shook my head. "When he's not in class, he's either at football practice or in the lab with Aidan or Tyler." I'd been watching him closely to see if he was acting differently, hanging out with anyone new—anything that would lead to this breakup. Despite my efforts, I had come up totally blank. "When would he possibly have time to hook up with anyone else?"

Sophie pulled out her cell and checked the time. "I don't know, but it's time for dinner. Want me to skip it and stay here with you, Kate? We can go back to our room—"

"No way." Kate stood, her bag lifting from the floor and flying through the air, right into her hands. "I'm not hiding out like some pathetic little castoff. He's going to have to face me. Just let me go wash up."

While we waited on Kate, I went over to shut off my laptop. As soon as I touched the mouse, the screen flickered to life, back to the news site I'd been reading when the Kate drama began to unfold. Ever since I'd seen that newspaper in Dr. Byrne's office, I'd become obsessed with the so-called Vampire Stalker, checking the news each day for more information. It was almost like a fire had been lit in my belly. There might be a vampire out there hurting innocent people, and I had the power to stop him. I wanted to stop him. Correction: I *needed* to.

I'd told Aidan about the Stalker, but not about my preoccupation with him—and I don't know why I assumed it was a him, but I did. I was well aware that a female vampire could attack a female victim just as easily as a male vampire could. Still, it was a feeling, an instinct.

Aidan was worried. It could only be a Propagator, he theorized. No vampire living under Tribunal law would dare to be so brazen. After all, the most basic tenet of their code was "do not expose our kind." Leaving victims with visible puncture wounds and marked blood loss was either ridiculously careless or stupidly defiant.

Aidan had disappeared several times since learning of the attacks—at Mrs. Girard's request, I think—going to Manhattan to see if he came across any vampires who'd gone rogue. Each time, he'd returned to Winterhaven as mystified as ever.

Apparently there was a pretty well-established community of vamps living in New York City—a coven, of sorts—and they knew nothing; they had seen nothing out of the ordinary. There were no newly turned vampires, no strangers walking among them. They were inclined to believe that it was a mortal committing the acts, an impostor.

The greater the mystery grew, the more restless I became. There was this deep, seething need growing inside me, and it scared me. My *Sâbbat* tendencies? Maybe, but I didn't want

Aidan to know that they were stirring, if that was what was happening.

I shut the screen as a freshly scrubbed Kate walked back in, looking fiercely determined.

Why did Jack have to go and screw everything up? I knew with certainty that our group would never be the same again.

12 ~ Blast from the Past

I scrunched down lower in the seat, pressing my knees against the cracked green vinyl in front of me. Between the bus's noxious fumes and the blurred view outside the dusty window, I was starting to get queasy.

Beside me, Aidan looked entirely unaffected. "Jack hasn't said anything to you about Kate?" I asked him. "Seriously?"

Aidan shook his head. "I told you, we don't talk about that kind of stuff."

So Jack breaks up with his longtime girlfriend, totally out of the blue, and doesn't even mention it to his friends?

"Hey, you feeling okay?" Aidan asked, his forehead creased with worry. "You're starting to look a little green."

"I just wish we'd hurry up and get there." I let out a sigh. "I swear, I just don't understand your half of the species. What *do* you guys talk about? If personal things are totally off limits, I mean."

"Hey," Tyler said, his head popping up from the seat in front of me, "no raggin' on dudes. We've got you outnumbered."

"And surrounded," came Josh's voice beside him. "Man, how much farther?" he groaned. "Dr. Andrulis! Are we there yet?"

"Almost," Dr. Andrulis yelled back from the seat behind the driver.

Tyler was still peering over the seat at me, a scowl on his face. "You look awful. You're not gonna blow chunks, are you?"

"Go away," I said feebly. "Aidan, make him go away."

"Aw, c'mon, don't sic the boyfriend on me."

Aidan made a low noise in the back of his throat. "Vi, tell your little friend to turn around. He's starting to get on my nerves."

"Hey, man, you're a mind reader, right?" Tyler drawled. "Why don't you read mine right now."

Several seconds passed in silence—I guessed Aidan was doing exactly that. His eyes narrowed. "Right back at you, man."

"Here we go again," I muttered, even though I knew it was

really just for show. They liked each other well enough. At least, I was pretty sure they did.

The bus lurched to a stop. I glanced out the window across the aisle and saw the looming facade of the Metropolitan Museum of Art. Finally.

Dr. Andrulis stood in the aisle, his gloved hands gripping the seat backs on either side of him. "Okay, folks, listen up. I want you in groups of four—check in with me on your way off the bus and let me know who you're with. Take the list I've given you, and make sure you've got something to write with. We've got four hours, plenty of time. There are twenty-five paintings on the list; make sure you find them all. Jot down the basic information and then spend some time examining each one.

"You're going to have to pick one from the list for your research project, so make a note of the ones that interest you. Back on the bus by two p.m., no excuses. Okay, people, I think that's it."

"You with us?" Tyler asked.

Aidan nodded. "Sure, why not? C'mon, Vi." He reached for my hand and helped me up.

I stood, swaying slightly on my feet. "God, I hate buses. Why couldn't we have taken the train?"

Minutes later, we were gathered in the museum's massive

lobby, waiting for Dr. Andrulis to return with our little metal admission tags. Joshua had grabbed a map and was already cross-referencing the list we'd been given.

"Hey, do y'all mind if we take a quick trip through the Egyptian stuff first?" I asked. "I know it's not part of the assignment, but it's my favorite exhibit."

Joshua looked up from his mapping quest. "Sure. We've got plenty of time."

"I'm cool with it," Tyler said with a shrug. "As long as the boyfriend doesn't mind."

I whacked him on the arm with my notebook. "Shut up, dork."

"You're just pissy because I kicked your pretty little ass at practice yesterday."

"Only because my shoulder's bothering me," I shot back. My old rotator cuff injury had been acting up lately, probably because I'd been training so hard for our first big tournament.

With a smirk, Tyler wagged his head. "Always got an excuse."

"Whatever," I murmured, reaching up to rub the shoulder in question. Sophie had checked it out this morning and said there was some serious inflammation in the joint. Time to break out the meds.

Dr. Andrulis returned with our tags, and we clipped them to our shirts. "Have fun, kiddos," he said with a wave.

I wondered if those ever-present gloves of his were going to come off today. I could just imagine him reaching out to touch works of art whenever the guards had their backs turned. I knew his gift could be a major pain—if he wasn't wearing gloves, that is. But how cool would it be to get inside an artist's mind, to actually see and feel and hear what they were experiencing while creating a masterpiece?

It was definitely better than *my* gift.

"Hey, are we going to stand here all day?" Tyler asked. "Where's this Egyptian stuff you want to see, Violet?"

"Follow me," I said, leading the way.

Fifteen minutes later we stood in front of the Temple of Dendur, easily the most spectacular sight the museum offered. On the far side of a rectangular pool of water, the tan-colored sandstone structure stood framed behind a towering doorway, illuminated by rays of sunlight that streamed in through a slanted wall of glass on our right.

I heard Tyler's low whistle of appreciation.

"Amazing, isn't it?" I said with a smile, leading the way around the pool, toward the temple.

"Pretty incredible," he agreed. "We can actually go inside?"

I nodded. "Yep. A little bit, at least."

Joshua tapped the list he carried clipped to a notebook. "C'mon, let's take a peek, and then we've got to get going. We've got a lot of ground to cover."

Strangely, the little temple was mostly empty of visitors when we approached it. Joshua and Tyler headed toward the columned entrance on the left side of the porch; Aidan and I went right, examining the carvings etched into stone so long ago.

"I think it's some sort of tribute to Isis," I said.

"Something like that," Aidan agreed. "Hey, look at this." He took a step farther in, pointing to a line of figures at hip level. "What does that look like to you?"

I squinted, trying to make out the details. "It looks like a woman holding something—a stick maybe." I followed the line of figures. The next showed the woman raising the stick—which I now noticed had a sharpened end—over her head, aimed toward the male figure beside her. Toward his heart, actually. "Oh my God, you don't think that's—"

"You guys ready to go?" Joshua interrupted behind us.

Aidan nodded. "We'll be right there."

Mercifully, Joshua and Tyler moved away, toward the reclining sphinxlike figure at the temple's side.

"Were there vampires back then?" I whispered, still staring at the strangely familiar image.

"Of course. Remember I told you about the Eldest, Isa?

She's Egyptian, born during the reign of Amenhotep IV. Or so she claims."

"Then it's possible there were also *Sâbbats*," I mused.

Aidan shook his head. "They wouldn't have been called that, not that far back in time. It's an eastern European term, probably from the Middle Ages."

"So they were called something else," I said with a shrug. My gaze lingered on the carving of the woman. I felt a kinship with her, a link to the past. I knew exactly how she felt, stake raised, poised to strike.

The hatred, the terror—all intertwined, sharpening your focus, making the rest of the world fall away as every cell in your body honed in on the target.

The vampire's heart.

Aidan reached for my hand. "Hey, you okay?"

"I'm just . . . remembering."

He drew me closer, his face just inches from mine. "What you did that day was incredibly courageous," he said, his voice low, his gaze intense. "You, my love, are strong and brave and fierce. I have no idea what I did to deserve you, but I'm eternally grateful that you came into my life, *Sâbbat* or not."

"Are you two done whispering sweet nothings over there?" Tyler called out, loud enough for half the exhibition hall to hear. "C'mon, let's go."

He was lucky I didn't have my stake with me. If I had, I might have been tempted to use it on him. At the very least, I could have whacked him upside the head with it.

An hour and a half later, we sat around a rectangular table in the noisy museum café, finishing up lunch.

"Okay, pretty much everything else we need to find should be here in this gallery." Joshua pointed to a lavender section of the map labeled 19TH- AND EARLY 20TH-CENTURY EUROPEAN PAINTINGS AND SCULPTURE. "Second floor."

Aidan nodded. "I know where it is—all my favorites are there." The paintings from *his* time, I realized. Of course they would be his favorites.

"Let's go, then." Tyler stood, picking up the cellophane wrapper from his sandwich and tossing it into a trash can.

I threw away what was left of my salad and fell into step beside Aidan.

We'd already found what we needed to see in the American Wing, so we hurried back through and up a flight of stairs, then past a bunch of European paintings we'd already explored as well.

"A Van Gogh, a Degas, a couple of Monets," Joshua was saying, ticking off the remaining paintings on our list. "Shouldn't be too hard to find."

I checked my watch—we still had an hour and a half, so

we were good. My feet, however, were not. I glanced down at the cute silver flats I'd worn and wished that I'd opted for my running shoes instead.

"We're almost there," Aidan said, hurrying his step. "It's just past this temporary exhibition area."

Which seemed endless, I realized.

Behind us, Joshua had stopped and was staring up at a framed photograph on the wall. "Look at this," he called out. "It's an early photograph—1895, it says." He took several steps to the right, where a framed painting depicted the exact same scene. "Pretty cool, huh?"

I took the map and checked the listing for temporary exhibitions on the second floor. "Photography and late impressionism," I read out loud.

Fascinated, I moved from one pair to the next. I'd never seen photographs this old. It was like peeking back in time, back to Aidan's time.

He stood silently beside me as I gazed up at a photograph of two women in voluminous skirts with bustles, their blouses buttoned up to their throats. Sisters, I mused, noting their resemblance, and then moved on to look at the accompanying painting.

"Ho-ly shit!" came Tyler's voice from somewhere around the corner. "Violet, you've got to come see this!"

"What?" I asked, hurrying toward his voice. "It can't possibly be *that* exciting."

"Oh yeah, it is."

I turned the corner and found him staring up at one of the larger photographs on the wall. It was a nude, I realized. Even from halfway across the gallery space I could see the bare breasts.

"Oh, give me a break," I said, rolling my eyes. "What are you, twelve years old? You didn't get this excited in the sculpture garden—"

I stopped short, sucking in my breath. The picture . . . oh my God!

"She looks just like you!" Tyler said, putting words to my thoughts.

Not again.

I stepped closer, examining the photograph as my heart thudded against my ribs. It looked like a dance studio, with a wooden barre on one wall opposite a long row of mirrors.

In the middle of the open, airy space stood a woman— and okay, she wasn't totally nude, thank God. She was wearing some sort of tulle tutu-looking thing that came to her knees. Her back was to the camera, but her face and entire body were visible in the mirrors, bare boobs and all.

"And here, look at this." He was pointing to the bottom

right corner of the frame, where a tall guy with golden blond hair stood leaning against the wall, his face in profile. Though he was mostly hidden in shadows, everything about him was eerily familiar.

My gaze flew to the cardboard description tacked to the wall between the photograph and the accompanying painting, and I flinched. OPERA DANCER IN LONDON, 1892, it said, and beneath that the artist's name—Guillaume Fournier.

I quickly did the mental math. Aidan was born in 1875. That would have made him, what? Seventeen in 1892. It was all falling into place. An opera dancer in London, one who looked just like me, her blond-haired lover looking on while she was photographed. He was seventeen when he met Isabel, still seventeen when he was turned. This must have been just before—

"What the hell?" Joshua said, stepping up beside me.

"Yeah, Vi, put some clothes on," Tyler teased.

I saw Joshua's gaze move lower, toward the boy in the corner. His eyes narrowed perceptibly. "Is that . . . ?" Because he *knew*, I realized. Tyler was totally in the dark, but Joshua would know that it was entirely possible.

I swallowed hard, looking at the painting now. It was pretty much exactly the same as the photograph, except the boy in the corner was gone. Allowed to watch protectively while she was photographed, but not vital to the actual work of art.

My stomach lurched uncomfortably, the salad I'd just eaten threatening to make a reappearance. I had to do something, I realized—*say* something before Tyler realized that this was freaking me out way more than it should.

I swallowed hard. "Yeah, okay. She looks like me; I get it. Can we move on?"

Tyler turned to face me, his eyes wide. "She looks *just* like you."

"Nah," Joshua said, shaking his head. "I mean, there's a resemblance, I guess, but that's all. See, her mouth is different and . . . well . . . no offense, Violet, but this chick's tits are bigger."

I wanted to kiss him. Clearly he knew something was up, and he was covering for me.

"Hey, no offense taken," I said with a shrug.

"Where'd you guys go?" Aidan called out.

"In here!" Tyler yelled back. "You gotta come see this."

No.

But it was too late. Aidan was there, right behind me. I turned in time to see his stunned expression before he shuttered it, replacing it with a look of nonchalance.

"That's it?" he asked, his voice deceptively smooth. "You're all worked up over a bit of nudity? I think you need to get out more, Bennett."

Tyler raked a hand through his hair. "Dude, you are *not*

going to pretend you don't see it, too. C'mon, she looks just like her."

Aidan just shrugged.

Joshua started flipping through the list again, looking bored. "It's not even full frontal," he muttered. "We've still got another six paintings to find—we should get moving."

Tyler stood there, openmouthed. I knew he'd seen it—that shock of recognition on Aidan's face before he'd wiped it clean. For a moment there, Aidan had looked as if he'd seen a ghost.

Because he *had* seen a ghost.

It's you, isn't it? I asked him in my head. *There in the corner of the photograph. Watching her.*

His eyes met mine, and he nodded. *I'd completely forgotten about it. I had no idea it would ever be shown in public, much less somewhere like this.*

I knew it was entirely unreasonable that I should be jealous, but sometimes your head and your heart don't exactly agree. Oh, man . . . I felt sick. I took a deep breath, then exhaled slowly, willing my racing heart to slow.

"Josh is right," I said coolly. "We're wasting time." Without a backward glance, I turned and walked away.

"You're not mad at me, are you?" Aidan said, sliding into the scabbed seat beside me. We were the last ones to board the bus, taking the very last row of seats, away from everyone else. "C'mon, Vi, you can't be mad."

I let out my breath in a rush. "I'm not mad."

"Are you sure? Because you're acting like you are. Ever since we saw that picture—"

"How do you think I feel?" I snapped, shaking my head in frustration. "For once, put yourself in my shoes. Imagine that picture was me instead, and the guy looking on was my ex-boyfriend. You know, watching me cavort around *naked*. How would you feel?"

"You never mentioned an ex-boyfriend."

"You never asked," I shot back.

"And besides, she wasn't naked. Not from the waist down, at least."

Was he really that obtuse? "You're being a dick."

"Am I?" He reached up to brush my cheek with the back of one hand. "I'm just trying to understand—"

"Understand what? Why I don't like to imagine you with *her*?"

"My God, Vi, it was over a hundred years ago. I was a different person then."

"You looked the same, except for the clothes," I said stubbornly. "I *saw* you."

He tipped his head back against the seat, looking tired.

Defeated. "What can I do, Violet? How can I possibly make it up to you? I can't erase my past. My mortal past," he corrected. "None of it was even worth remembering."

"Do you remember that day?" I asked. "The day that photograph was taken?"

"I do now."

"Tell me about it," I pressed, overcome with a reckless desire to feed my morbid curiosity.

"No," he said resolutely. "I don't want to talk about it."

"You're kidding, right?"

He shook his head. "Sorry, but no."

And then, I swear I didn't do anything—not consciously, at least—but images began to flood my mind. I shut my eyes and pressed my fingers against my temples as the images shifted into focus.

Isabel was standing in the studio, the one from the photograph, holding a scrap of fabric across her naked breasts. She was walking toward me. No, toward Aidan, I realized. I was seeing the scene through his eyes.

A high-pitched buzz softened into recognizable sounds—the muffled notes of a piano; the sound of something striking the floor in perfect rhythm; voices. All muffled. From another room, another studio, perhaps.

"You liked watching as Guillaume photographed me," Isabel

said, smiling flirtatiously. "It excited you, didn't it?"

Somehow I expected her to sound like me, but she didn't. Her accent was pronounced, her voice more breathy than mine.

"Perhaps it did," a male voice answered. Aidan, though he sounded different—far more British, more refined. Older, somehow.

Isabel took several steps toward him, moving gracefully across the wooden floor. "Show me, then," she said, releasing the scrap of fabric she'd been clutching to her chest.

"Enough!" I cried out. "Stop it."

"I didn't do anything, Violet," Aidan said, his features stony.

"You did. You breached my mind."

I shook my head. "How? I wasn't trying, I swear."

"I guess you're getting stronger. The closer you get to your birthday, the stronger your *Sâbbat* tendencies will become."

"You don't know that," I argued, even though it made perfect sense. Still, I didn't want to think about—didn't want to consider the possibilities. "Anyway, my birthday is still five months away."

"And each day that passes brings you one day closer."

"Well, aren't you Mr. Philosophical today," I said sourly, then dropped my head into my hands. "I'm sorry, Aidan," I said, my throat tight. "I don't know what's wrong with me."

He reached for my hand and brought it to his lips. Prickles of electricity ran up my arm, making me shiver. "Today was a strain. That picture . . ." He trailed off, a muscle in his jaw flexing. "You have no idea how sorry I am. Sorry that it exists. Sorry that you saw it. Sorry that I lived such a shallow, callous mortal life."

"Don't," I said, shaking my head. He had every right to his past, relationships and all. Just because I hadn't ever been seriously involved with anyone before him didn't mean I should expect the same from him—especially considering just how long his past was. "You have no reason to apologize, Aidan. Seriously."

He shook his head. "I have so many regrets, Vi. But you"— he brought my hand to his heart—"you're the one thing in my life that I *don't* regret. This heart beats only for you."

"You're going to make me cry," I said, my voice thick.

Aidan laughed. "Don't cry, love. Tyler knows something's up—even now, he keeps turning around to watch us."

"That's Tyler's problem." I leaned toward Aidan, pressing my lips against his jaw, just where it curved down toward his throat.

Together, we slid down in the seat, away from prying eyes. I heard him sigh, felt the muscles in his jaw relax. "Was that for Tyler's benefit or mine?" he asked, his voice a hoarse whisper.

"Take your pick," I answered coyly. But speaking silently

inside my head, I told a different story. *For you*, I said. *Always for you.*

He grasped the back of my neck and drew my face toward his, kissing one damp eyelid, then the other. *Until the day I die*, came his voice inside my head.

I took it as a good sign that he'd said "until I die" rather than "until I'm destroyed."

"You two, there in the back," bellowed Dr. Andrulis from the front of the bus. "I want to be able to see your faces."

My cheeks flaming with embarrassment, I scooted back in the seat, sitting up straight now. Aidan did the same. As the bus lurched forward, I laid my head on his shoulder, trying to ignore the snickers from several seats away.

Tyler, no doubt.

13 ~ Timeless

Okay, what do you think?" I spread my arms wide and turned in a slow circle. I'd spent all summer dragging Whitney from one vintage shop to the next, putting together the perfect costume for the Halloween Fair dance. More than anything, I hoped Aidan appreciated the effort.

Cece let out her breath in a rush. "Oh. My. Freaking. God! You look amazing!"

I laughed nervously, glancing in the mirror above my dresser. Okay, I looked good, but not *that* good. Cece, on the other hand . . .

"You know you look gorgeous, right?" I asked her.

She smoothed her hands down the front of her gown. She was supposed to be some sort of Greek goddess—I wasn't quite sure which one, but it didn't matter, really.

The draped white fabric hugged her body, setting off the rich hue of her skin to perfection. One shoulder was left bare, dusted with sparkly gold powder that matched the metallic shadow on her eyelids.

Somehow she'd managed to pile her hair high on her head and wrap it with gold wire. Strappy gladiator sandals completed the look.

"I can't wait to see Tyler's face," I said, reaching up to adjust my enormous hat. "How am I going to fit through the doorway in this thing?"

Cece laughed. "Don't worry, I'll help you. Anyway, I don't think Tyler's all that interested in me."

"Well, he *did* ask you. It's not like he had to. He could have hung with us regardless, right?"

She shrugged. "I guess. What do you think—pink lip gloss or this berry-colored one?" She held up two plastic tubes.

"Hmm, I vote for pink. You don't want to take the focus away from your eyes."

"Pink it is." Leaning across the dresser so she could see her reflection in the mirror, she carefully applied the gloss, then put the tube into the little purse she was carrying. "Okay, you ready?"

I took one last glance at myself in the mirror and smiled. Yeah, I was ready.

"Let's go meet the guys," Cece said with a grin.

When we stepped into the East Hall lounge two minutes later, they were there waiting, standing by one of the long brown couches. Aidan had his back to us, his hands shoved into his pockets as he gazed out the window. Beside him, Tyler watched our approach with wide eyes.

"You call that a costume?" Cece called out to him. "Cheater."

He had applied black construction paper circles to his regular clothes—rumpled khakis and a white button-down shirt.

"It's a costume," he protested. "I'm polka-dot Tyler."

Cece shook her head, laughing. "That is *so* lame."

"Hey, I thought it was creative. You look amazing, by the way." He eyed her appreciatively, a glint in his clear green eyes.

"Thanks," she murmured, actually fluttering her lashes at him.

I gave her my "I told you so" look as Tyler turned to appraise my costume. "And you . . ." He trailed off, nudging Aidan in the ribs. "I definitely think the boyfriend will approve." With that, he took Cece's hand and led her away.

Taking a deep breath, I smoothed down my dress. The lady at the vintage shop had called it an Edwardian tea gown—a reproduction, of course, but a good one made from delicate black lace over a beige shift. The fluttery hem fell against my calves, tickling them.

I'd paired it with several strands of fake pearls and low-heeled black kidskin shoes. The wide, sweeping hat on my head, trimmed with silk flowers and ostrich plumes, completed the ensemble.

"Okay, you can turn around," I said. "They're gone."

Almost as if in slow motion, he turned to face me. "I was trying to savor the element of surp—"

The word died on his lips, his eyes growing wide.

"Circa 1905," I said quietly. "Or thereabouts. What do you think?"

I was suddenly assaulted with images that weren't from my own eyes. Instead, I saw myself standing there, rooted to the spot. Words were tumbling through my head at a dizzying rate, so jumbled I could barely make any sense of them.

But a few . . . a few stood out. *Stunning. Gorgeous. Beautiful beyond compare.*

I'd never felt such powerful emotions—they overwhelmed me, took my breath away. Blindly I reached for the couch. My knees buckled, and I would have fallen if not for Aidan's arm, which had somehow found its way around me, steadying me.

"Are you okay?" he asked.

I swallowed hard. "I just . . . I need to catch my breath. What happened?"

"You breached my mind again," he whispered. "Just now."

I shook my head, hoping to clear it. "Not on purpose."

"Is everything all right, dear?"

I looked up to find Mrs. Girard standing there, watching us with a puzzled expression.

"I'm fine," I managed to reply, unable to meet her pale, washed-out brown eyes. *Vampire eyes.* "I just got dizzy there for a second."

Mrs. Girard nodded. "Perhaps you should go see Nurse Campbell, then. I can call her now and arrange—"

"No, I'm fine," I interrupted. "Really." The last thing I wanted was to get sent to the infirmary. After all, I'd missed most of the dance last year. This year, I planned to enjoy every second of it.

"You'll keep an eye on her, Mr. Gray?" she said to Aidan.

"Of course," he answered with a curt nod.

"Very well, then. You two make quite the elegant pair, don't you?" With a wave, she hurried on her way.

Only then did I get a good look at Aidan's costume. A black tuxedo with tails, a white vest and bow tie, finished with a top hat. Likely vintage, I realized. Probably from his own closet.

"Trevors got it ready for me," he explained. "Cleaned up nicely, considering its age. Circa 1905. Or thereabouts."

All the breath left my lungs in a rush. "How did you know?"

A smile danced on his lips. "I asked Cece, but she wasn't very forthcoming. However, your friend Whitney was far more accommodating."

"She didn't," I breathed.

"She did."

I had to laugh. It sounded exactly like something Whitney would do.

"I had to promise to send her a picture, however. Tonight. She was *very* specific."

"Then let's go find a photographer," I said.

"Indeed." He offered his arm. "I suppose I don't need to tell you how beautiful you look," he said, smiling down at me as we went out into the crisp, cool night and set off across the quadrangle toward the gym. "You must have heard—"

"Every word," I interrupted, my skin flushing hotly at the memory. "Every thought."

Beneath the light of a nearby lamppost, I could see the color rise in his cheeks. *A vampire who blushes.* His adorable factor ratcheted up a few notches.

"Oh, I almost forgot." He paused and produced a small

plastic container. "Here," he said, opening it and reaching inside. "These are for you. I thought they might look nice pinned to your dress."

In his hand lay a small circlet of perfect white blossoms. I breathed in their fragrance, sweet and citrusy. "They're beautiful," I said.

His face lit with a smile. "Back before I was turned, you had to be careful with flowers. Flowers had meaning; you risked giving a girl the wrong idea if you didn't choose with care." He cleared his throat, looking slightly embarrassed all of a sudden. "Anyway, the orange blossom means 'eternal love.' I've never given them to anyone before now."

"Thank you," I said, reaching out to run one trembling finger over the velvety petals. It was more than a simple corsage—the blossoms were somehow attached to what looked like a delicate silver brooch with tiny faceted crystals glinting in the moonlight. This was a piece of jewelry disguised as a corsage, I realized. "Can you pin it on me?"

He pinned the delicate blooms just above my heart. "There," he said, taking a step back to examine it. "That's perfect." He held out a hand, and I took it. "Ready?"

I nodded, my heart near to bursting. "Ready."

By the time we entered the gym, the dance was in full

swing. The music was loud, the bass thumping. The decorating committee had gone with a headless horseman theme—fitting, considering Washington Irving was said to have founded the school—and the gym was completely transformed.

The walls had been covered in black crepe paper with cut-out silhouettes of the horseman with his jack-o'-lantern head, all lit from behind. Twinkle lights were strung across the rafters, giving the entire space an eerie, ghostly glow.

It took us a full fifteen minutes to elbow our way through the crowd and find our friends—the ones who weren't already out on the dance floor, that is. I'd managed to spot Cece and Tyler in the thick of it, looking like they were having fun. I thought I'd caught a glimpse of the top of Joshua's head, too.

Everyone else was in a clump beside the refreshment table—Sophie, Kate, and Marissa. Jack was nowhere to be found, of course. The traitor.

"Hey, where's Max?" I yelled into Marissa's ear as Aidan and I joined them.

"With the band, setting up," she yelled back, gesturing toward the stage on the far side of the room. "They're playing the next set."

"Cool."

Marissa nodded. "Wait till you hear them—they're awesome." Her dark eyes shone with obvious pride beneath the false eyelashes and dramatic makeup. Punk-rock chic, she'd called it, and it looked perfect on her. She really *did* look like a rock star's girlfriend.

"You want something?" Aidan called out, tipping his head toward the drinks.

"Try the punch," Kate suggested a little too enthusiastically. Which made me wonder if someone had somehow managed to spike it.

I shook my head. "Just a Coke."

I took the icy can he handed me and went to stand beside Sophie. "Who's Joshua dancing with?"

"I think her name is Bronwyn. She's a shifter. Seems nice." Sophie leaned closer. "Be warned—Kate is in a mood tonight."

"Is Jack here?" I whispered, moving one of Sophie's fairy wings out of my rib cage.

"Yeah. Alone, thank God. You look great, by the way. So does His Lordship." She glanced over at Aidan, who stood with his hands in his pockets, watching me. "I can't even look at him without getting woozy. He is seriously rocking that tux."

"Tell me about it. Oh, wait—do you have your phone?" The cell phone restriction had been lifted for the dance, mostly because everyone's doubled as a camera these days. "I need someone to snap a picture of us so I can send it to Whitney."

"She spilled the beans about your costume, huh? He tried to work over Cece, but she wasn't going for it." Sophie reached into the little drawstring bag she wore on her wrist and pulled out her phone. "But yeah, of course I brought it. Wait, is he going to show up? In the picture, I mean?"

"Why wouldn't he? Oh, you mean because . . ." I trailed off, realization dawning on me. Only one way to find out. "Hey, Aidan," I called out, miming taking a picture. "Myth or fact?"

"Myth," he yelled back with a lopsided grin.

Of course. Otherwise, he wouldn't have promised Whitney a picture. I hurried over to his side, allowing him to wrap one arm around my waist.

"Say cheese," Sophie commanded.

We ignored her, waiting for the flash.

"What do you think?" She held up the phone, screen out, so we could see. "Good?"

It was the first picture we'd ever had taken together, I realized, my eyes scanning it hungrily. If only I weren't wearing the hat.

Still, it was good. Aidan looked beautiful—young and perfect and handsome. The dark smudges that usually marred the skin beneath his eyes were gone. I'd never seen him look so healthy, so vibrant.

162

So alive.

Whatever was in that serum was obviously doing *something* right.

"Perfect," I said, reaching for the phone. "Just let me text it to Whitney."

"You want to dance?" Aidan asked as soon as I handed the phone back to Sophie.

I nodded, reaching up to steady the flying disc on my head. "Let's lose the hats first, okay?"

"I'll hold them," Kate offered sourly. "It's not like I'm doing anything else."

"Thanks." I carefully dislodged my hat and handed it to Kate, smoothing down my hair as best I could without a mirror.

As if on cue, the music switched to a slow song. "Hey, perfect timing," Aidan said, tipping off his top hat with practiced ease.

"Go on." Kate snatched it from him with a scowl. "I swear, watching the two of you together is making me want to puke."

"Ugh, I can't take it anymore," Marissa said, shaking her head. "She's killing me. I'm going to go watch Max set up." She flounced off, tossing her hair over one shoulder.

Sophie turned toward me with a sigh. "It's okay. Go on, have fun."

I allowed Aidan to lead me away, toward the dance floor. I glanced back apologetically at Sophie, alone now with a surly Kate. Silently I promised to return and drag them both out to dance with us as soon as the slow song ended.

We'd find Cece and Tyler, maybe even Joshua and his date too. This was our senior year, our last Halloween Fair. We were supposed to be having fun—*all* of us, together.

Of course, the moment Aidan took me into his arms, gazing down at me with those gray-blue eyes of his, every coherent thought flew right out of my head. I'd accidentally breached his mind again, but there was only a single word there in his thoughts, a word echoed in my own thoughts: *love*.

I smiled up at him, realizing that for the first time in a very long while, I was completely and genuinely happy. Things were good. No, they were great.

All I needed was for Aidan to find his cure, and then things would be perfect. That wasn't too much to ask, was it?

14 ~ Oh, No, You Didn't

On my way to the dining hall on Monday, I paused by the fountain, leaning against the cool stones. The noon sun was high in the cloudless sky, cutting through the chill in the air.

Aidan? I called out in my mind, reaching out to him telepathically.

Nothing.

He'd been a no-show in calculus, which was pretty unusual these days, at least without advance warning. I knew he'd been working in the lab the night before—he, Jack, and Dr. Byrne usually worked together on Sunday nights after dinner. I'd actually tried to talk to him telepathically before I'd gone to bed and had gotten no response. At the time I'd just figured that he'd been caught up in his work, too preoccupied to notice.

But now . . . now I was worried.

"Hey, you going to lunch?" came a voice behind me, and I turned to see Tyler headed my way.

"I guess," I said. It just wasn't like Aidan to disappear, not anymore. Something was wrong, my instincts told me.

Tyler peered down at me curiously. "You look like you just lost your best friend. What's up?"

"Just worried about Aidan, that's all. Have you seen him today?"

He shook his head. "Nah, but it's not like I've been looking for him. Why?"

I shrugged. "He wasn't in calc this morning."

"Maybe he's sick. Did you try the infirmary?"

I knew he wouldn't be in the infirmary—vampires didn't get sick. "I'm sure he's fine," I said, sounding way more sure of it than I felt.

"Don't worry, he's a big boy." Tyler swept a hand through his hair, pushing it off his forehead, a now familiar gesture. "Hey, can you give me your friend Kate's cell number?"

"Why do you need it?" Silently, I called out to Aidan again in my mind.

Tyler glanced back over one shoulder toward the building that housed the dorms and dining hall. "I was supposed to meet up with her later today, but I need to cancel."

"Why would you be meeting up with her?" I asked distractedly. *Still no reply from Aidan.* "Anyway, just tell her at lunch."

He shook his head. "Nah, can't do that. Too public."

I just stared at him, completely confused now. "What are you talking about?"

His mouth curved into a grin. "I'm pretty sure I'm not supposed to tell you."

"Not supposed to tell me what?" *Oh God, no.* At the end of the dance on Saturday night, Cece hadn't been able to find Tyler anywhere. Kate had been missing in action too, but we'd figured she'd called it an early night and gone to bed.

"Please tell me you didn't. I swear, I will *kill* you—"

"Just do me a favor and don't tell Cece, okay? She's a nice girl and I don't want to hurt her."

"Don't tell her *what*, Tyler?" I took two steps toward him, closing the gap between us. "What exactly did you do?"

At least he had the decency to look embarrassed. "You want the play-by-play?"

"God, no. I think I'm going to be sick."

"You're not jealous, are you?"

"Jealous? Why would I be jealous? I'm pissed off. How could you do this to her? To *either* of them?"

"It's not like me and Cece were going out or anything. I just took her to the dance. You know, as buddies."

"And then left the dance with one of her best friends? What are you, a complete moron? Please tell me you were just—that you didn't—"

"I thought you didn't want the play-by-play." He folded his arms across his chest, looking way too pleased with himself.

"Oh my God, you *did* hook up with her. What the hell was Kate thinking?"

"Well, from the sound of it, I'd say she—"

"Just shut up." I shook my head, hoping to clear it of the unpleasant images flooding my brain. "I thought you were my friend, that I could trust you—"

"This doesn't have anything to do with *you*, now, does it? Though I'm kinda flattered—"

"I said to shut up." Instinctively, I raised one hand toward him.

"Don't," he said, grabbing my wrist. There was a glint in his eyes that I'd never seen before—almost menacing. "You can take it out on me later, at practice."

"Let go of me," I spit out.

I glanced around nervously, almost expecting Aidan to appear out of thin air in a murderous rage. But then I remem-

bered that he'd changed; that he seemed more human than vampire these days.

For a moment, Tyler continued to manacle my wrist, his gaze challenging mine. And then his gaze slid lower, to my mouth.

When his head dipped toward mine, I took a step away from him, wrenching my wrist from his grasp.

"What the hell is wrong with you?"

"Just testing out the 'jealous' theory," he answered with a shrug. "Sorry about that." His usual cocky grin was back, making me wonder if I'd imagined the brief flash of malice I'd seen in his eyes.

This was *Tyler*, I reminded myself. A friend.

A friend who'd screwed over my roommate. With Kate, of all people. Vulnerable, hurting Kate.

"You are in *so* much trouble," I said, pointing a finger at his chest.

He brushed aside my hand, then took a step toward me. "Are you going to tell her?"

"I have no idea what I'm going to do. You suck, you know that?"

He shook his head. "I'm sorry, Violet. She was there, offering it up. What can I say? I'm a guy."

I wasn't buying that. "That's the lamest excuse in the book. Seriously, can you say 'cliché'?"

"She was available; you're not. Let me know when that changes."

Feeling drained, I let out my breath in a rush. "Just go away, Tyler. I've got to find Aidan."

"Course you do. Tell him I said hey."

"Hey is for horses," I said completely nonsensically, repeating something that Gran liked to say.

"See, now? That's why I like you, Violet." With a low chuckle, he walked away.

"I hate you," I muttered under my breath, somehow feeling as if he'd come out on top, the jerk.

I wasn't lying when I said I had no idea what I was going to do about Cece. On the one hand, telling her would just hurt her, and would surely put an enormous wedge between her and Kate, and rightfully so. Hurting or not, it had been a shitty thing for Kate to do. She knew how Cece felt about Tyler. That should have made him off-limits.

On the other hand, how could I *not* tell her? Eventually it would come out—the truth almost always did—and Cece would never forgive me for keeping it from her. She was my bestie, after all. Besties didn't lie to each other. Or, for that matter, withhold important information. Hadn't I always said that was just as bad?

With a heavy sigh, I headed toward the dining hall. One

thing was for sure—Kate and I were going to have a little heart-to-heart.

Just as soon as I found Aidan and made sure he was okay.

He was in the infirmary after all. Which didn't make any sense. But as soon as I found my friends in the dining hall—Kate *and* Cece included—and set down my lunch tray, Suzanne Smith walked by, pausing at our table.

"Hey, I just saw Aidan in the infirmary," she said with a grimace. "He looked awful."

Which meant my lunch sat abandoned while I hurried over to the infirmary as fast as I could.

As soon as I stepped inside, the medicinal smells assaulted me—antiseptic and something sharper. I glanced around, seeing no one in the reception area.

"Hello?" I called out.

Nurse Campbell bustled in from the back. "Oh hello, dearie," she said in her cheerful Irish brogue. "I suppose you're looking for Mr. Gray."

"Is he okay?"

She hurried to my side, speaking quietly. "I've never seen anything like it, not with his kind. I suppose he'll recover— they always do. Still . . ." She trailed off, shaking her head. "Odd. Very odd, indeed."

"Does Mrs. Girard know he's here?" I asked.

She nodded. "Of course. She just left. Unfortunately Dr. Anderson was here when I admitted him, and not Dr. Peters."

I could only assume that meant that Dr. Peters knew what Aidan was, but not Dr. Anderson. Interesting.

"He's given him a thorough examination," she continued, her mouth pinched with worry. "Severe exhaustion, he said, and ordered a full blood panel. I can't exactly comply with that one. We'll have to substitute someone else's blood sample to send off to the lab."

"You can draw some blood from me," I offered. "Can I see him first?"

"Of course, dearie. Might do him some good. Come right this way." She led me past the two curtained treatment cubicles, back to a long corridor with several closed doors on either side.

She opened the second one on the right, and I followed inside. Aidan lay on a narrow cot in the windowless room, a sheet pulled up to his waist.

He turned his head toward us, his eyes sunken and shadowed, his face a dull, sallow color. "I was just about to call you," he said, smiling weakly.

My breath hitched in my chest, panic rising at the sight of him. Suzanne was right—he looked awful. I hurried to his side and reached for his hand. "What happened to you?"

"I'll just give you a moment," Nurse Campbell said, shutting the door softly behind her. I listened as the sound of her footsteps faded down the hallway.

He sighed, a deep, rattling sound coming from his chest. "I injected a new serum last night. Afterward, I felt perfectly normal. I remember walking back to my room, the underground one, just to be safe. But then Mrs. Girard found me down by the river, just before dawn. Here," he said, shifting over several inches, making room for me on the edge of the cot.

I sat, reaching up to feel his forehead. It felt strangely warm—for him, at least—and slightly clammy. "How did you get there? What were you doing?"

"I have no idea—no recollection of anything after walking to my room. I've had bad reactions before, but nothing like this. I'm slightly . . . alarmed."

I was too. "Well, what were you doing when Mrs. Girard found you?"

He shrugged. "Passed out cold. My clothes were ruined— apparently I had a run-in with Jenna at some point in the night."

My alarm rose a pitch. "What? How?"

"Last night was a full moon. I was supposed to have met her after curfew. Unfortunately, she doesn't remember much of what happens when she's in wolf form. But I had quite a few deep gashes when Mrs. Girard found me this morning."

My gaze quickly skimmed his supine form.

"They've all healed by now. Which means the serum didn't cure me, of course. But I already knew that."

"But it did something." I leaned down to kiss his forehead. "You look terrible."

"I *feel* terrible. Weak. I think I might go home tonight, let Trevors look after me for a day or two. Apparently Luc is in town, checking into this whole Stalker situation. I'd like to talk to him."

I nodded. "Okay. It's probably the safest place for you right now. With . . . you know, others. Like you," I clarified.

"I think I'm actually going to have to travel by traditional means. Once the sun goes down, I'll have Mrs. Girard call a car service."

"Is there anything I can do?" I felt so helpless, so powerless.

"Don't you have a tournament to prepare for?"

I did, on Friday. In Manhattan, at a private school on the Upper East Side. I nodded.

"I should be back by then. I'll be fine. I don't want you to be distracted."

I rolled my eyes in frustration. "How can I not be distracted? Look at you." I dropped my voice to a whisper. "Vampires aren't supposed to get sick. They're immortal, remember?"

"Only until destroyed."

Was that it, then? Was he somehow trying to destroy himself? Messing around with the serum, injecting it indiscriminately, no matter the consequences?

He reached for my hand. "Next time I'll—"

"Oh, no, you don't," I said, cutting him off. "No next time. There's got to be another way to test it out."

His grip on my hand increased. "I've told you before, there's no other way. No vampire rats to test it on first. This is a risk I'm prepared to take."

Tears burned behind my eyelids. "What about me? What if I'm not comfortable with the risk?"

He closed his eyes, his breathing suddenly sounding labored. When he opened his eyes again, his gaze was pleading. "Don't do this, Vi. Don't make me choose. Not when you know that you're the reward, either way."

My heart felt like someone had it in a vise, twisting it cruelly. "Next time might destroy you, Aidan."

His eyelids fluttered closed again. "It very well might. Then again, it might cure me."

Please be careful, I said in my head, hoping he could hear me now.

I'm always careful, he answered.

"I've been trying to talk to you telepathically all day," I said, aloud this time. "Since last night, actually. You never answered."

"You're very faint, even now. I think whatever happened temporarily knocked out that ability. It's coming back, though."

"What would I do if I lost my Aidan channel?" I teased, but in truth the very idea terrified me. I liked it too much—the specialness, the intimacy of it.

A smile danced on his lips. "The same thing you'll do when I'm cured. Talk to me the regular way."

"We'll lose that?" I hadn't really considered it before.

"I assume we will. It's not something I could do before I was turned. I suppose you'll still be able to talk to *other* vampires, though."

Because I'd still be a *Sâbbat*, even if he wasn't a vampire.

"You need to rest," I said at last, reaching down to plump the pillow behind his head.

He nodded sleepily. "Stay with me?"

"Can you scoot over a little more?" He did, and I wriggled down, fitting myself beside him, my head resting on his shoulder. "Sleep like the dead, vampire boy. I'm not going anywhere."

15 ~ Strange Bedfellows

Hey, good job," Tyler said, elbowing me in my side. "Yeah, you too." I'd won the girls' match, and he'd won the boys'. This had become a pattern, actually. I had a feeling we'd both be going into the All-Ivy tournament at the end of the semester as top seeds.

I reached up to pull the ponytail holder from my damp, sweaty hair. From the bleachers, Cece and Sophie waved at me, then gave me a thumbs-up. With a smile, I held up five fingers. *Five more minutes.* And then we'd have an entire weekend to ourselves, just the three of us. Well, and Patsy, too. Luckily, Kate had some sort of glee club meeting, which had saved me the trouble of *not* inviting her.

Tyler leaned in toward me. "Hey, the redhead is pretty cute," he whispered.

"You did *not* just say that."

He shrugged. "What is it with you and all the hot friends?"

"I swear, Tyler, if you even *think* about it, I'll—"

"Aw, I was just messing with you. Anyway, where's the boyfriend? I figured he'd be here tonight."

"Yeah, me too," I murmured, my gaze sweeping across the emptying bleachers.

Aidan? I called out telepathically.

Nothing.

I assumed he was still at his apartment just off Fifth Avenue—he'd never made it back to school that week. We'd texted a little, but I'd been busy practicing for the tournament, and he was still recovering from whatever had happened to him on Sunday night.

Trevors was taking good care of him, he insisted, and he preferred his own bed. He promised he was fine, just taking some extra time to make sure.

Of course, he'd also promised that he'd come to my tournament. Worry shot through me, quickening my pulse.

"So what are you guys doing tonight?" Tyler asked, drawing me from my thoughts.

"I don't know. Just hanging out, I guess. Why? Aren't you taking the bus back to Winterhaven?"

"Nah, I got a weekend pass. My mom was supposed to come and take me back to Connecticut for the weekend, but she canceled on me. So sure, I'd love to tag along."

"What do you mean, tag along? You can't come stay at Patsy's with us."

His brow furrowed. "Why not?"

"Why not?" I rolled my eyes. "Well, let's see. For one, Cece's barely tolerating you, and who can blame her? Two, after that little crack you just made, I'm not letting you within ten feet of Sophie. And three, where were you planning on sleeping?"

"Your mom's got a couch, doesn't she?"

"Stepmom," I corrected.

"And hey, without the boyfriend you ladies are without an escort, aren't you?"

I shook my head. "We can take care of ourselves just fine."

"C'mon, Violet, don't make me beg. I don't want to waste my pass and go back to school. Please?"

I just stared at him, amazed as always by his boldness.

"Pretty please? I'll take all of y'all out to dinner," he offered. "My treat. Anywhere you want to go."

I turned to watch Cece and Sophie make their way down

the bleachers toward us. "It's up to Cece," I said, shaking my head. "And if she says no, that's it, end of story. No more pressure."

"Yes, ma'am." He reached into his bag for a baseball cap, pulling it low on his brow.

I noted the red, white, and blue *T* on the cap. "A Rangers fan?"

"You got a problem with that? Let me guess—Braves fan, right?"

"Of course," I answered with a shrug. "Season tickets my whole life, on the first base line. Well, till my dad died, at least."

He nodded, his eyes softening a measure. "My dad and I went to Arlington every year for the Rangers' opening day."

I felt that familiar tug of kinship with him, as much as I hated to admit it. "How far is that from Austin?"

"Not far. 'Bout three hours in the car. We'd make a week-end of it. It was . . ." He shook his head, a faraway look in his eyes. "Nice. Good times, you know?"

I nodded, my mind flooded with images of my dad sitting beside me in the folding seats, the air redolent of hot dogs, popcorn, and beer. I could almost hear the crack of the bat, the blaring notes of the organ pumping up the crowd. My dad always insisted on wearing the same ratty blue hat he'd bought at the old stadium back when he was twelve, claiming that it brought the team good luck—his own personal version of a rally cap.

"Yeah, I know what you mean," I said at last, an uncomfortable lump in my throat. "Let me go talk to Cece and Sophie."

Tyler just nodded.

Ten minutes later we were all piled in a cab, headed toward Patsy's apartment. Patsy was at some fancy work event, not expected home till after midnight—which was why she hadn't been able to come to the tournament. I'd texted her to warn her about the strange guy she'd find sleeping on her sofa, but she hadn't seemed to care. This was one of those times when I actually appreciated her parental indifference.

"Ouch, those *were* my ribs," Cece cried, glaring at Tyler, who was squeezed in beside her.

"Sorry," he muttered, and I wondered how I'd ever let him talk me into this.

Cece had said she didn't mind, but the two of them hadn't stopped squabbling since we'd gotten into the cab. It was going to be a *long* weekend if this kept up.

"Right here is good," I called out to the driver. "This corner." We could walk the last couple of blocks. Anything to get the two of them off of each other.

We paid and clambered out onto the sidewalk. The night

air was crisp and cool, and I reached down to zip up my fleece jacket. A line spilled out of the yogurt shop on our right; the sound of laughter carried on the breeze along with the scent of waffle cones.

For perhaps the twentieth time that night, I reached out telepathically to Aidan.

Still nothing. If he was home, he wasn't more than twenty blocks away. Our telepathy should have been good and strong.

"I've got to take a piss," Tyler said, heading toward a darkened alley between two buildings just up the block.

"What is he doing?" Sophie asked.

I let out my breath in a rush. "Tyler! You can't just—"

"Hey! Violet!" a familiar voice called out.

I turned to find Dr. Byrne standing on the sidewalk behind us, his hands thrust into his jeans pockets. "What are you guys doing here?" he asked, his forehead creased.

"Weekend pass," I answered, glancing over my shoulder, looking for Tyler. He was still in the alley—relieving himself, I supposed. *Idiot.*

Dr. Byrne's gaze swept across our group. "All of you?"

I turned back to face him and nodded. And then I remembered—tomorrow was Saturday, our usual coaching day. I hadn't even thought to cancel. I reached a hand to my temple. "Oh my God, I'm so sorry. I totally forgot about our session tomorrow. So . . . yeah, obviously I'm not going to make it."

His lips curved into a smile, the tension in his face lessening a fraction. "Yeah, I kind of figured that."

A flush heated my neck. "Hey, what are you doing here, anyway?"

He looked slightly taken aback at the question. "I was visiting a friend. About to return to school, actually." He shook his head. "I just wish you guys had an adult with you."

"We're fine, Dr. B.," Sophie said. "Anyway, it's still early."

He glanced down at his watch. "I guess, but with this Stalker guy on the loose, it makes me a little uncomfortable."

"Oh hey, Dr. Byrne," Tyler said, rejoining us on the sidewalk.

"And look, we've got Tyler, too," Sophie offered.

Dr. Byrne leveled a steady gaze at Tyler, who was pulling up his fly. "I'm not sure that makes me feel any better," he murmured.

"Has the Stalker struck again?" I'd been so busy preparing for the tournament that I'd gotten lax in checking the news.

"Yeah, this past weekend. Here, why don't you let me walk you guys wherever you're headed."

I shook my head. "We're just going to my stepmom's apartment a couple blocks away. We're fine. Seriously," I added.

He didn't look convinced. "You sure?"

"I think we're perfectly safe as long as we stick together," Cece said. "It sounds like the Stalker attacks girls who are off alone somewhere. At least, that's what my mom said."

Dr. Byrne nodded. "True. So far, at least. Just . . . pay attention, okay?"

Cece held up two fingers. "Scout's honor."

"Okay, I'll see you back at school on Sunday. Take care." With a wave, he turned and walked off, glancing back over one shoulder before disappearing into the crowd by the yogurt shop.

He seemed genuinely concerned, I realized. A knot of anxiety curled in my belly—not because of the Stalker; logically, we weren't likely to be targeted. But—I wasn't sure—things just seemed somehow off, especially with the total radio silence where Aidan was concerned.

I needed to talk to him, to make sure he was okay. If he wasn't going to answer telepathically, then I was going to have to find him.

But first things first. I needed to get everyone settled in at Patsy's. Then I'd start with Trevors, I decided.

My stomach growled noisily, interrupting my thoughts and reminding me that we hadn't yet eaten. "Hey, didn't you promise us dinner?" I asked Tyler.

"You feel like Chinese?" he replied, tipping his head toward the takeout across the street.

Cece nodded. "That'll do. I'm starved!"

"You and me both," Sophie said with a sigh. "C'mon. Tyler's treat, remember?"

"You can't go by yourself," Cece whispered, shaking her head. "No way."

I glanced back at Tyler, who was sprawled on the couch with the remote in one hand, flipping through the TV channels at lightning speed.

"Nice flat-screen," he called out.

I let out a sigh. "Yeah, whatever." He'd planted himself in front of it the moment we'd walked in, and so far no one had succeeded in prying the remote from his greedy fingers.

I leaned in toward Cece. "What am I supposed to do? *He* can't go."

Cece rolled her eyes. "Obviously."

"So what do you suggest, then?" I asked.

"Hey, what are you two plotting over there?"

"Shut up, Tyler," Cece bit out. "Or I swear I'll make Violet kick you to the curb."

"Who peed in your cornflakes?" he shot back.

"Oh, let's see." Cece tapped her chin thoughtfully. "Wait— it was *you*, wasn't it?"

Before Tyler had a chance to reply, I grabbed her hand and

tugged her into the kitchen. "Seriously, Cee, I can send him back to school. Just say the word—"

"Nah," she said, cutting me off. "S'okay. I mean, yeah, he's hot, but he gets on my nerves. I just like to give him a hard time, that's all."

I nodded, feeling a weight lift from my shoulders. "He totally deserves it," I said, reaching into the sleek stainless-steel refrigerator and pulling out two bottles of water. "Want one?"

"Yeah, thanks." She took the proffered bottle and leaned against the countertop as she twisted off the cap. "Anyway, don't worry, I'm not letting Tyler off the hook that easily. I mean, whatever." She waved one hand in dismissal. "We've known each other a couple of months, big deal. But Kate? I just don't get it."

I let out a sigh. "I don't either."

"Turns out I wasn't all that into Tyler, after all, but Kate didn't know that. What if I really liked him?"

"I don't know what she was thinking," I said with a shrug. "I realize the whole thing with Jack really messed her up, but still. There's just no excuse, you know?"

"Well, I hope she enjoys her weekend. *Alone.* And speaking of alone . . ." She trailed off, watching me as I took a long drink of water. "C'mon, you gotta take me with you. Over to Aidan's,

I mean. Sophie can stay here with he-who-can't-be-trusted-to-keep-it-in-his-pants."

"Yeah, and you're going to leave him alone with Sophie? You just said he can't be trusted."

"Don't worry, Sophie can handle him. She's like the impenetrable fortress."

I choked on my water, literally snorting it through my nose.

"Wait, ewww." Cece screwed up her face. "I didn't mean it like that. God, I just meant . . . you know, that she's way too sensible to let him get to her, that's all."

I glanced back toward the living room. Tyler was sitting up now, his elbows on his knees and his chin resting in his palms as he stared at the screen. He must have finally found something worth watching for more than a few seconds.

An uncomfortable thought flitted across my mind. "You don't think that he and Kate actually . . . I mean, they were just messing around, right?"

Cece's eyes widened. "You're kidding, right? This is Kate we're talking about."

"Yeah, but, you know . . . she and Jack had been going out a long time. This is different."

"Yeah, but Jack was just a one-time hookup at first." She plucked a shiny red apple from the big wooden bowl on the countertop. "Hey, can I have one?"

"Of course. Help yourself to whatever you can find."

"Anyway," she continued, rubbing the apple on the hem of her shirt. "It was a couple of months before they actually started . . . you know, actually going out."

Huh. I hadn't known that. "So, back to Tyler—"

"Hey, what'd I miss?" Sophie padded in wearing a tank top and pajama bottoms, her hair damp and smelling like coconut shampoo. "What did he do this time?"

"For once, nothing. There's water in the fridge, if you want a bottle."

"Nah, I'm good. What's up?"

Cece hooked a thumb in my direction. "Crazy girl here actually thinks we're going to let her trot off to Aidan's by herself tonight."

Sophie's green eyes widened a fraction. "What? Now?"

"Just for a little bit. I swear I won't stay long. I just want to check on him, that's all, before Patsy gets home."

Sophie appeared unmoved. "Yeah, I don't think so. Not alone, at least. You heard Dr. Byrne."

"Matthew, you mean," Cece cooed, waggling her fingers at me.

I rolled my eyes. "Fine, one of you come with me, then. Do you want to draw straws?"

Sophie shook her head. "It's okay, I'll stay. As much as I'd love a peek at His Lordship's mansion, we can't leave Cece here alone with Tyler. She's likely to claw his eyes out or something. Not that he doesn't deserve it," she added.

"You sure?" I asked, my gaze straying to her thin little tank top.

Clearly, Sophie was following my train of thought. "Hey, I didn't know we were going to have bedtime company of the male persuasion. Besides, I am *not* my roommate."

"No, it's just"—I shook my head—"something stupid he said, that's all."

"I don't even want to know." Sophie folded her arms across her chest. "You got a sweatshirt I can borrow?"

"Follow me," I said, leading her and Cece to my bedroom.

"Hey, if there's gonna be a pillow fight, I'm in," Tyler called out. "Or maybe some girl-on-girl wrestling—"

I slammed my bedroom door, effectively shutting him up.

16 ~ Tea for Three

T his is it," I said, stepping up to the shiny black lacquered door.

Cece let out a low whistle. "Nice."

"You ain't seen nothing yet," I quipped. My hands were shaking, I realized.

Aidan? I tried one last time.

Still nothing.

"Okay, here goes." I reached for the bell, pressing it firmly and then stepping back to wait beside Cece.

In seconds, I heard footsteps on the opposite side of the door. I sucked in my breath expectantly, my heart pounding against my ribs.

The door swung open, and Trevors stood there peering down at me. His face was drawn, his brow furrowed. "Miss McKenna?"

"It's—yes—Violet," I stammered, wondering where this sudden case of nerves had come from. It was only Trevors, I reminded myself.

"Of course. Violet. Please, come in." His voice was kindly as he stepped aside, gesturing toward the expansive marble-tiled foyer behind him.

As soon as I stepped across the threshold, Cece beside me, a shiver raced down my spine. Something was happening—I couldn't explain it, but it felt as if my senses had become heightened. Colors were more vivid. The heated air from the radiator brushed against my skin, making it flush hotly. And the weirdest part? It was almost as if . . . as if my entire body was *vibrating*.

"Are you okay?" Cece whispered.

I couldn't answer, couldn't say a single word in reply. Instead, I was hyperfocused on my right hand, my fingers flexing at my side.

My stake. I wanted my stake. It was in my bag; if I could just get it, just wrap my fingers around the satiny shaft—

"Hey, snap out of it!" Cece reached for my forearm, giving me a little shake. "What the hell's wrong with you?" she whispered harshly.

I shook my head. "I . . . I don't know." But I *did* know. It was almost like a voice in my head, an alarm.

Vampire, it was screaming.

Calm her, came another voice in my head. *Let her know that you aren't a threat.*

Trevors?

He was watching me intently, seemingly unaware that I had just breached his mind—and I was pretty sure that I had.

"I am *so* sorry," I said at last, shaking my head, forcing myself to take a deep, calming breath. "I think I need to sit down."

"Of course," he said, leading us into the living room. "You're always welcome here, even in Master Gray's absence."

The word "absence" reverberated in my head. Aidan was absent. He wasn't here.

Cece cleared her throat, nudging me in the ribs.

"Oh, Trevors, this is my friend Cece Bradford. She's my roommate at Winterhaven. Cece, this is Trevors, Aidan's . . . um, his . . ." I trailed off, unsure.

"Employee," Trevors supplied. "Household manager, I suppose you could say."

But I heard another word in my head, spoken silently with great pride: *butler.* He preferred the term "butler," I realized, but somehow deemed it old-fashioned. Out of date.

Shaking my head, I forced myself to break whatever tenuous connection there was between Trevors's mind and mine.

With a sigh, I took a seat on the sofa. Cece sat beside me. Aidan's absence seemed like a big, gaping hole. I'd never been here without him. "Aidan's not here?" I asked, running my fingers along the familiar velvet cushions beneath me.

Trevors shook his head. "No, he's with Luc Mihailov. They left just yesterday. I'm not convinced that he's well enough to travel, but . . ." He paused. "If you'll excuse me for a moment, Miss McKenna, I'll make some tea. You're looking rather pale, if I might be so bold."

"Sure, of course," I mumbled.

Cece nodded enthusiastically. "Tea sounds nice."

"Very good, Miss . . . Bradford, wasn't it? Just let me put the kettle on, and then we can chat."

As soon as Trevors disappeared, Cece put a hand to my forehead. "Okay, what's going on? You don't feel hot or anything."

I shrugged, noting that the uncomfortable sensations had lessened the moment Trevors left the room. "I think some *Sâbbat* stuff is going on. My instincts are starting to kick in or something." It was the only explanation that made any sense.

Cece's dark eyes looked troubled. "Do you think he's a threat? Trevors, I mean?"

"I don't think so. I mean, Aidan said I was one hundred

percent safe with him—some sort of 'life debt' he owes him, or something like that."

Still, butterflies fluttered in my stomach. I'd brought Cece here, to a house where we were alone with a vampire who wasn't Aidan. What in the world had I been thinking? If something happened to her, if I couldn't protect her . . .

I let the thought trail off, refusing to examine it further. This was Trevors we were talking about, not some random vampire. Aidan trusted him, and so should I. Hadn't Aidan left me alone with him, late at night, when he'd gone off to feed? Whatever this life debt was, it meant that Trevors would protect me in the same manner that Aidan would, and I was sure that the protection extended to my friends, too.

Aidan and his kind were *not* dangerous—at least, not to people like me and Cece.

But where had Aidan gone off to with Luc? And more to the point, why hadn't he told me? None of it made any sense.

I physically felt Trevors's presence the moment he stepped back into the room carrying a large silver tray. He set it on the sideboard, removing two dainty teacups from the cabinet below. "Cream and sugar?" he asked, seemingly oblivious to my reaction.

I attempted to silence the warning bells going off in my head, to subdue the weird sensations. "Both, please. Lots of sugar," I added.

"Same," Cece chimed in.

"Careful, it's hot." He handed a cup to Cece, then to me.

I wrapped my hands around the delicate china, hoping the warmth would quell their trembling. This was crazy. I didn't get this way around Mrs. Girard, I realized. Maybe her constant presence created some sort of immunity? I had no idea, and no one to ask.

Trevors sat opposite us, regarding me thoughtfully. "I assume we can speak freely in Miss Bradford's presence? I believe Master Gray said that your roommate is aware of the situation."

I nodded. "We can talk. Cece knows everything."

"Very well." He leaned forward in his seat, one forearm resting on his thigh. It was a posture that suggested urgency, and my anxiety level ratcheted up a notch in response. "I'm worried about him," he continued. "He's not been himself these past few weeks. And now . . . well, I'm sure I needn't tell you how atypical his current condition is. For our kind," he clarified. "Vampires don't just fall ill."

"It's that serum he's injecting," I said. "I don't know what it's doing to him, but it seems to be getting worse."

"And yet he feels as if he's experiencing positive effects from it, as well," Trevors said with a nod. "I just don't know what to think."

I took a sip of my steaming tea, watching Trevors over the rim of the cup. "But what does Luc have to do with any of this?" I asked. "He's on the Tribunal, right?"

Trevors raised one brow. "He is, indeed. But he's also a friend of Master Gray's. Or perhaps I should say they are friendly. To a degree, at least."

"So I shouldn't be worried?"

"Not about Luc," he answered cryptically.

Cece leaned forward, placing her now-empty cup on the coffee table in front of us. "Well, where did they go?" she asked.

Trevors shrugged. "I'm not certain. Paris, perhaps?"

I let out my breath in a rush. "Paris?"

"Paris is the seat of the Tribunal these days."

"He's going to the Tribunal?" I groaned. "Why would he do that?"

Trevors sighed heavily. "I wish I had answers for you, Miss McKenna. Truly, I do."

"You really care about him, don't you?" I said softly. "More than just a household manager would."

He smiled wanly in reply. "Of course I do. I assume he's told you of my debt to him?"

I shook my head. "Not the specifics."

"Would you care to hear the story?"

Would I ever. There was so much about him I didn't know;

each little tidbit was a piece of the puzzle falling into place. "Of course I would."

Beside me, Cece nodded enthusiastically.

"Very well." He leaned back against the chair's cushions, a more relaxed position than before. "I'd known Master Gray in my mortal life, you see. I was head butler at Asbury House, Lord Tewksbury's London home in Grosvenor Square. Viscount Brompton's town house was right across the square; young Aidan was a childhood playmate of Tewksbury's eldest son. Trust me, the two got into a fair amount of mischief."

I couldn't help but smile, imagining it. "I'm not surprised."

"Anyway"—he waved one hand—"years later, long after Aidan had disappeared, presumed dead, I had the misfortune of crossing paths with a female vampire who had, in her mortal life, suffered at the hands of my employer, Lord Tewksbury.

"Lucinda was the most dangerous sort—a vampire bent on vengeance. I became an unwilling pawn in her plot. She turned me, intending to use me to destroy Tewksbury and everyone he loved.

"When I proved uncooperative, she decided that I simply needed to be persuaded. First she threatened my daughter, a grown woman who was living in London and working as a seamstress. Lucinda killed her immediately—a show of strength. She wasn't playing around, and she wanted me to know it. My wife had long since passed, a victim of influenza, and the only family I had left was my granddaughter. Camilla was beautiful and smart, off at school, hoping to become a teacher someday. Lucinda gave me an ultimatum—I could join her in her plot, or Camilla would suffer the same fate as her mother.

"By that time," he continued, "I'd become acquainted with London's vampire community. I was pleasantly surprised to find Aidan, alive and well. So to speak, of course," he added. "I turned to him for help; I had no one else. Aidan was very . . . how shall I put it? Very *angry* in those days. And he was far stronger than me, given that he was turned as a young man."

Cece's eyes were wide. "I can't believe someone would . . . well, you know, do *this* to you, at your age."

"There are plenty of vampires who were turned at my age, Miss Bradford, though most were willing, attempting to evade death. Who knows"—he shrugged—"years later, had I been facing the same certain fate, I might have chosen this path. One never knows . . ." He trailed off, a faraway look in his eyes.

"So Aidan helped you?" I prompted.

Trevors nodded. "He saved Camilla and destroyed Lucinda. As punishment, he was sentenced to twenty years of confinement by the Tribunal. When he was released, I pledged my life to him. I will serve him in whatever way necessary, as long as I walk this earth. It's an excellent arrangement, actually. He needs someone to manage his household, and I enjoy doing so. It's a comfortable life for me, and I strive to make his equally so."

"That's . . . amazing," Cece said.

I let out my breath in a rush. "Twenty years? They imprisoned him for twenty years for saving a child's life?"

"For destroying a vampire," Trevors corrected.

I shook my head in disbelief. "A murderous vampire! Who was killing people for no reason. I mean, isn't *that* against your rules?"

"Lucinda's punishment would have been far more severe than his, had she succeeded with her plot. Besides, twenty years isn't so very long to a vampire. In the face of immortality, it's just a blip in time, really."

"I guess so," I said, unconvinced.

In twenty years, I'd be thirty-seven. Would this brief time spent with me seem so inconsequential to Aidan, just a minute blip on his radar?

No. Because Aidan would be long cured by then—mortal again, and close to my own age. He *had* to be.

"He could have just saved Camilla," I said. "If he hadn't destroyed Lucinda, he wouldn't have been punished. He could have turned her over to the Tribunal instead."

Trevors regarded me with one raised brow. "He could have,

yes. As I said, Aidan was very angry then. He didn't know who had turned him, and any female vampire in London was suspect, as far as he was concerned. He would have destroyed them all and willingly paid the price, given the opportunity. I knew that when I sought his help."

"You only wanted to save your granddaughter," Cece offered. "Anyone would have done the same."

He acknowledged her kindness with a nod. "My only regret is that I wasn't able to save my daughter, too."

"What happened to Camilla?" I asked, hoping the sacrifice had been worth the price.

His mouth curved into a smile, the corners of his eyes crinkling with obvious delight. "I'm pleased to say that she went on to live a very long, very happy life. She became a teacher, married, and had five children. Some of her descendants live here in New York today, though most of the family remains in Britain. I keep close tabs on them all, each and every one of them," he added, his voice filled with pride.

"That is so cool," Cece said. "Being able to see all those generations, I mean."

"Indeed, though I'm also forced to witness them age and eventually die. It's all part and parcel of this curse."

I leaned forward in my seat, curious. "Say Aidan *does* perfect the cure. Will you take it?"

"Would you think me a foolish old man if I said I wasn't certain? I've had nothing but time to ponder the question, and yet I cannot say what my answer will be when that day comes. And it *will* come, Miss McKenna. For Aidan's sake, we must have faith. In all these years, I've never seen him so determined."

I just nodded, unable to reply. My emotions were too raw, too unsettled. I wanted to believe that I was the reason for Aidan's newfound determination.

And yet . . . the responsibility weighed heavily on my mind. Was his single-minded, desperate pursuit of the cure causing him to act carelessly? Had he grown too hasty, hoping to beat the clock because of me?

He would deny it, of course. He was obstinate—and brilliant, I reminded myself.

Beside me, Cece cleared her throat. "We should probably get going," she said, glancing at her watch.

Looking down at my own, I grimaced. "Patsy's going to be home soon." I stood, setting my empty cup on the table. "Thanks, Trevors. For the tea *and* the talk. I really appreciate it."

He nodded. "Of course, Miss McKenna."

"If I leave you my cell number, will you call me if you hear from him? In case, you know . . . I don't hear from him first?" I hoped it wouldn't come to that, but I was starting to realize that there was still an awful lot about Aidan I didn't know.

I understood why he kept some of his history from me—he wanted me to know him as he was now, as the boy he would be when he was cured. I got that. Really, I did. But to fully understand him, I had to understand his past. It was a part of him, no matter how strenuously he denied it. Shielding me from it served no purpose, as far as I could tell.

Trevors rose, leading us out toward the foyer. "I'm sure he'll contact you as soon as he's able," he assured me. "But yes, of course." He gestured toward a pad of paper and pen on the console opposite the front door.

"Thanks," I said, scribbling my name and number.

Trevors turned toward Cece and extended one hand. "It was very good to make your acquaintance, Miss Bradford. I hope we'll meet again soon."

Cece beamed at him as she shook his hand. "I hope so too."

It was only when he reached out to take my hand that I remembered he was supposed to be the enemy—at least, the *Sâbbat* part of me thought he was, if the way my body recoiled was any indication. My urges had calmed while we had sat talking, but now they were back in full force.

"Sorry," I mumbled, forcing myself to suppress the shudder that snaked down my spine as I gripped his cold hand in mine.

"It's entirely understandable," he answered with a smile. "I appreciate your restraint."

Restraint. I supposed that was the right word. Because at present, every cell in my body was screaming in alarm. My fingers were itching for my stake, desperate to use it.

Instead, I was shaking the vampire's hand and leaving him my number.

Trevors's gaze met mine, questioning. "It's fascinating, really. I've never before met one of your kind. *Sâbbat.*"

"Yeah, me either," I answered with a shrug. I didn't know how, but someday—somewhere—I would find those other girls like me.

And when I did . . . well, I had no idea what I'd do once I found them. I only knew that I somehow must.

For now, that would have to be enough.

17 ~ Under Where?

Aidan reached for my hand, bringing it up to his lips. "I'm sorry, Vi. I just didn't want—"

"Me to worry. Yeah, I know. It's still no excuse." I snatched my hand away as I slid into a seat at our usual lunch table. "You should have at least called and told me you were going away."

He ducked his head, looking somewhat sheepish as he slid into the seat beside me. "But then I would've had to tell you where I was going. You would have worried yourself sick, when you had the tournament—"

"That you were supposed to come to. Did you think I wouldn't notice?"

"Okay, okay." He held up his hands in surrender. "So I'm an idiot. A complete moron."

"Keep going," I prodded, waving one hand in a circular motion.

"A . . . jerk? Help me out here, I'm running out of appropriate insults." His jaw was set, but his eyes were smiling.

"Hey," a voice called out, and I looked up to find Tyler standing across the table from us as the lunch crowd shuffled in around him. "I think I might have left a pair of boxers over at Patsy's this weekend. Let me know if she finds 'em, okay? I liked that pair. Worn and comfy, you know?"

I winced, feeling Aidan tense beside me. "What?" was all he said. Rather restrained, actually. I had to give him credit.

Tyler was grinning now. "Yeah, when you were a no-show on Friday, Violet asked me over for the weekend. Didn't she tell you?"

I let out a sigh. "Cece and Sophie were there too. Oops, you left that part out, didn't you, Ty?"

"Hmm, I guess I did. Sorry 'bout that." He nodded in Aidan's direction. "Guess I should be grateful that you're just a mind reader and not something more dangerous, huh?"

There was something in his tone that made my heart skip a beat. Had he somehow figured it out? Or was I just paranoid?

Don't react, Aidan said inside my head. *Just ignore it.*

"I should go get some food," I muttered, rising on shaky legs.

When I returned to the table five minutes later, everyone was there. Well, everyone except Joshua, who still sat with the other shifters at meals, and Jack, who had always eaten with the football team anyway.

Max had joined our little group. He and Marissa sat at the end of the table, in shouting distance to Max's bandmates, who now occupied the next table over.

Kate and Cece were there, sitting as far away from each other as the rectangular-shaped table allowed, with poor Sophie stuck somewhere in the middle, playing the role of neutral party.

"So, what'd you guys do this weekend?" Kate was asking Sophie as I slipped back into my seat beside Aidan.

Sophie shrugged. "You know, just hung out. It mostly rained."

Which was true. We'd stayed in, watching movies for the most part. I assumed that she didn't know that Tyler had ended up spending the weekend with us. I had no idea how well that would go over. Didn't want to find out, really.

"It was pretty quiet here," Kate said. "Luckily these two let me hang with them." She hooked her thumb toward Marissa and Max, who were deep in conversation—about the merits of Linkin Park's newest album, it would seem.

Since when did Marissa like Linkin Park?

I turned toward Aidan, who was sitting quietly beside me. "You're not hungry?"

"Not really." He shook his head. "I think I might head over to the lab."

Weird, because the new serum had increased his appetite for actual food, along with other more humanlike traits. Maybe it was starting to wear off or something.

"Sure, whatever," I said, trying to sound nonchalant. *You've still got a heck of a lot of explaining to do,* I added silently.

He smiled. "We'll talk after sixth period, okay?"

As soon as Aidan vacated his seat, Tyler was there, holding a tray cluttered with food. "You leaving?" he called out to Aidan's back. "I'll take that as a yes," he said when Aidan continued on without looking back. With a clatter, he set his tray down and slipped into the seat beside me.

He was seemingly oblivious to the tension that crackled around him now. Cece was visibly ruffling; Kate lowered her gaze, her cheeks flushing pink.

"Uh, Marissa," I muttered, looking at her entreatingly. "Could you maybe help us out here?"

Mercifully, she did.

Aidan and I were walking over to the chapel after sixth period when I stumbled, my vision tunneling as everything went dark.

Patsy was standing on a golf course. Everything was green, which meant it wasn't late fall in New York. But then I noticed the palm trees swaying in the breeze behind her. She was somewhere tropical. It could be any season, I reasoned. She stepped up to a tee, bending down to place her pink ball atop it. As she straightened, her body jerked. I heard her gasp as she swatted at her right arm.

"Hey, you okay?" an unfamiliar man called out. He had an accent—Australian, maybe? I'd never seen him before. He was tall, with short brown hair and blue eyes. Good-looking, I guess, in an unremarkable way.

"I need my EpiPen," Patsy replied, hurrying over to the golf cart. There was a tone of urgency in her voice. She was deathly allergic to bees—she never went anywhere without an EpiPen. I saw her digging around in her bag, saw her movements become more and more frantic. "Damn it, where is it? Oh God, no. I switched bags last night. . . ." Her eyes grew wide with panic. Her lips had already begun to swell; red rings circled her eyes. "Call 911," she choked out, reaching for one of the cart's roof supports to steady herself.

And then it was over. I was sitting on the curb, cradled in Aidan's arms. "Hey, you okay?" he crooned.

I shook my head. "This one was bad. Patsy. A bee sting," was all I managed.

"She's allergic?"

"Yep, goes into anaphylactic shock. Carries an EpiPen. She was on a golf course somewhere, on a trip, I think. But she didn't have it with her." I closed my eyes, taking a deep, calming breath. "The EpiPen, I mean."

Aidan kissed my temple. "It's okay. You can work with this."

I swallowed hard. "I guess. She's never going to listen—never going to believe me."

"Just make sure she's got an EpiPen," he offered.

"It's not like I can follow her around twenty-four seven. What am I supposed to do? She doesn't always tell me when she's going away. God, she could be in Hawaii or somewhere like that right now, for all I know." My head was spinning.

What if . . . what if the bee sting *killed* her? What if I'd just witnessed her death, just like I'd seen my dad's? Panic made my heart race, my palms dampen.

"Look, Vi, you just saw her this weekend," Aidan reasoned. "She probably would have mentioned a trip, don't you think?"

"Yeah, I guess," I conceded. "I'm going to have to work on replaying this one. I have to see what's going to happen. To make sure . . . you know, that she's going to be okay. With no EpiPen, if she doesn't get to a hospital right away, it'll be too late."

Aidan nodded, apparently understanding the gravity of the situation. "Do you want me to call Dr. Byrne now?"

"No, you're right—she wasn't going anywhere anytime soon. It can wait till Saturday. I hope," I added. "Here, help me up."

He stood, reaching for my arm and pulling me to my feet. "Want me to walk you back to the dorms?"

"No, I'm good. What, did you think you were going to get off that easy?"

"You're cold." He took my hands, rubbing them between his own. "Let's get to chapel, and then I'll talk."

"You bet you will," I shot back.

Minutes later, we settled ourselves into a pew near the altar. Aidan had lit the sconces along the walls—telekinetically, of course—and a warm, soft light filled the chapel.

"You want my scarf?" He unwound it from his neck and held it out to me.

I took it, not because I was cold but because I loved that striped scarf. It held his scent, and I loved to snuggle into it.

"Thanks," I said, draping it around my neck. "Okay, now tell me why you went to the Tribunal."

"I didn't have much choice. Luc insisted, as did Mrs. Girard. I guess you could say I was ordered there. They just wanted to see me, to check on my condition. It's not something they've seen before."

"And?"

"And that's it. I wasn't in any trouble or anything like that.

It was just a . . . well, an informational visit. With Luc as my escort."

I didn't like the sound of that but decided to keep my opinion to myself. "How did you get to Paris?" I asked instead.

"We flew."

My eyes grew wide with surprise. *Flew?*

He reached for one end of the scarf and wound it around my neck. "Yeah, commercial airliner. Nighttime flight," he added, seeing my confusion. "How did you think we traveled across the ocean?"

"I have *no* idea." An image of Aidan flying like a bat flooded my consciousness. I had to admit, it was kind of funny.

"Well, we can move faster than the human eye can see, but we can't walk on water," he said with a shake of his head.

"Yeah, whatever. Okay, so you flew. Commercial. And they just talked to you, that's all?"

"They examined me, asked about the serum. That's about it. They're supportive of my work, you know. They're not opposed to a cure, to offering a choice to those who may not have had one when they were turned."

"I'm glad to hear they're sensible." *Yeah, right.*

"Well, I'm not sure I'd call them sensible," he said, obviously missing my sarcasm. "I have a feeling that Isa would be happy to cure vampires she deems unworthy *without* their consent. Anyway, the trip wasn't a total waste of time. Luc found this." He dug into his bag and produced a book—a very old book, by the look of it.

"What is it?" I asked, running my fingers across the ragged, split leather cover. There were words etched in gold—in a strange-looking alphabet that I didn't recognize.

"It's Serbian," he said, lifting the cover and flipping to a spot near the back where a folded piece of paper was tucked inside. "But Luc translated this section for me."

He unfolded the page, which was filled with a precise, slanted script. The word *Sâbbat* immediately jumped out at me.

"He found something about *Sâbbats?*" My heart was pounding now, my hands shaking as I reached for the page.

Aidan nodded. "He did, indeed. *Sâbbats*, and their male counterparts, the *Megvédio*, or Protectorate."

"The what?"

He tapped the page. "Read it."

There exists an ancient legend of the *Sâbbat*, a name that is rarely spoken aloud, for it is feared that doing so establishes a connection between the minds of the two—vampire and slayer. The *Sâbbat* is a hunter of vampires, a slayer—a female, born on a Saturday. Only three exist at any given time, a child of the order born to replace the deceased. It is a blood legacy, passed from mother to firstborn daughter, lying dormant for generations until triggered by necessity.

As she approaches her eighteenth year, the *Sâbbat* discovers her purpose, becoming possessed of a hatred for the vampire and a burning desire to hunt and destroy. She is brave, fierce, and dauntless. Her weapon is a stake made from the wood of the hawthorn tree, trimmed in size and sharpened to a deadly point. She takes the mark of the *Sâbbat* on the wrist of her dominant hand.

At the time of self-discovery, her male counterpart, the *Megvéd*, reveals himself to her and offers his protection. He is strong, fearless, and cunning. He possesses no powers equal to the *Sâbbat*'s—he offers only assistance and companionship. Unlike the rare *Sâbbat*, the *Megvédio* are more plentiful in number, aware of their status at a young age. Their status, too, is a blood legacy, conferred from second-born son to second-born son. Like the *Sâbbat*, the *Megvéd* bears an identifying mark.

Only the rare *Megvéd* finds his *Sâbbat*, on account of her scarcity at any given time. Thus, it is considered a great honor. Their bond is strong, psychologically and psychically. He becomes her mate in every sense, their mission singular—to rid the earth of vampires.

It has been suggested that the *Sâbbat* is often born with a face that will attract a certain vampire— the face of a lover, or that of a beloved family member, a sister or mother. In this way, the vampire shall be drawn in for the kill.

In such an instance, the vampire in question will be exceptionally dangerous, infamous, or influential, thus posing a greater threat to humankind. Therefore, one might assume that any given *Sâbbat* might be born with the specific purpose of destroying a particular vampire, though of course her proclivities would assure that she would destroy a great number of other vampires as well.

I had to pause there, to let that sink in. I mean, the whole protector thing was bad enough, but if I was reading this right, then it was saying that I was not just meant to kill vampires but to kill Aidan specifically. Any other vampires I managed to off in the process would be considered collateral damage. But my true target? The guy I loved.

And my protector, whoever he was . . . I supposed his mission was to make sure I did it. *Nice.* I reached a hand to my temple, feeling dizzy all of a sudden.

"You okay?" Aidan asked.

"Yeah, I'm fine," I lied, feeling sick to my stomach. My hands shaking, I looked back down at the page and continued to read.

> It is also believed that the fate of the *Megvéd* is irrevocably tied to that of his *Sâbbat.* If she fails in her quest, and her blood runs through a vampire's veins, the *Megvéd*'s life is extinguished.
>
> Beyond these facts, very little is known of the *Sâbbat* and her *Megvéd.* There are no known written records detailing either her methods or her history, and the legend remains shrouded in much secrecy and speculation.

That was it. I glanced up at Aidan, not quite sure whether I should laugh or cry. "Luc's sure that's what it says?" I tapped the book's cover, trying not to sneeze as dust wafted up toward my nose. "I mean, you're sure he didn't mess up the translation or anything?"

He shook his head. "Luc is fluent in all Slavic languages, even long-dead ones. That's what it says."

"Well, don't I get a protector then?" I asked, my voice laced with sarcasm. "Where's my *Megvéd*, or however the heck you say it?"

He folded his arms across his chest. "Ah, but you're not eighteen yet."

"It said 'as soon as she makes her self-discovery.' Been there, done that. I've already killed three vamps, remember?"

"Oh, I remember all right. You're brave, fierce, and daunt-less, just as it says." The admiration in his voice nearly stole away my breath.

"Anyway," I said, "didn't you the notice the wording? It said 'as she approaches her eighteenth year.' That's pretty vague. So maybe sixteen, seventeen was close enough."

"Maybe," he conceded.

"And what's the deal with that whole 'mate' thing? That's just creepy. This isn't the Dark Ages. I get to choose my own mate, thank you very much."

His lips curved into a smile. "You don't have to convince *me*."

"And all that stuff about bearing a 'mark.'" I shook my head. "I don't have any birthmarks or anything."

"Well, actually you've got a little mark here"—Aidan pat-ted a spot on the back of his own neck, near his hairline—"nothing much, really. Just a few tiny red spots or something."

"On the back of my neck? You've noticed that?" I asked in amazement.

"Yeah, I spend a fair amount of time hovering around your neck, obsessing over it." He cleared his throat. "Just a peril of the condition, I suppose."

Something stirred inside me. *His teeth. My neck.* I swallowed hard, tamping down the sudden, pressing need. It was my turn to clear my throat uncomfortably. "That's just what's left of a stork bite I had when I was a baby." My hand rose to the spot in question, my fingers probing but feeling nothing. "Wait, you don't think that's what they meant?"

"I have no idea. Probably not, though. I think those are pretty common, aren't they?"

"Yeah, I think so." I slumped against the pew's wooden back. "Wow, we're like the blind leading the blind here. For every answer we uncover, we find a half a dozen more questions. You think Mrs. Girard knows anything about this? She said something before about meeting others like me."

"She says she's encountered several *Sâbbats* over the years, but she's always gotten the hell away from them as fast as she could, without stopping to question them. All I can do is take her word for it. She's never mentioned the *Megvédio* before. You could go talk to her, I guess."

"I guess," I said, unconvinced. Truthfully, I didn't really trust her any more than I'd trusted Blackwell.

"I thought you'd be happy to see the 'same face' theory explained. I guess that eliminates the whole reincarnation thing."

"Thank God," I breathed. It was bad enough that I looked like Isabel. The idea that maybe I *was* her, reincarnated? I didn't even want to think about it.

Aidan reached up to rub his jaw. "It still doesn't make a lot of sense, though. I just don't see how I fit the criteria—dangerous, infamous, or influential. I'm none of those."

I shrugged. "I hope that when my protector dude shows up, he brings me a manual. *Sâbbat for Dummies*, or something like that."

"So long as you don't pledge him your troth in gratitude."

"My what? Never mind. Why do you keep looking at your watch?" He'd glanced down at it three times in the past five minutes or so.

"I'm supposed to meet Jack and Dr. Byrne at the lab. Was supposed to," he corrected. "Five minutes ago."

"Go, then. It's okay—I told Sophie I'd study with her this afternoon, anyway." I reached for the book, tucking the translated page back inside. "Can I keep this?"

"Of course. It's yours."

"You're not going to inject more serum into yourself, are you? Just when you're finally well again?" I studied his face. His color had returned to normal, the dark smudges beneath his eyes a bit less prominent than before.

He reached for my hand, lacing his fingers through mine. "Not today. Today we're just working on some stuff. But hopefully by the weekend—"

"Just go." I snatched my hand away. Instantly, I regretted it—he looked as if I'd just punched him in the gut. "I'm sorry. It just scares me, is all."

"I'm frightened too," he said softly. "Mostly afraid that I won't perfect the cure till it's too late, till you've moved on. Grown up. Forgotten me."

"I promise that's not—"

"Don't make promises you can't keep, Vi." His voice was sharp now. "Seriously, I don't expect you to wait around forever. As I said, there are two ways this thing can end: I find my cure and find it fast, or you destroy me and end this, once and for all."

I shook my head. "There are other options, Aidan. Anyway, do you honestly think I could destroy you?"

"Who knows what you might be capable of, given time. We still don't know enough about any of this stuff." He picked up the book and flipped through the pages. "Maybe your *Megvéd* will have your answers for you. Maybe he can—"

"Ugh, just go," I interrupted, refusing to listen to more. "Seriously, I don't want to talk about this now." I stood, taking back the book before making my way to the chapel's aisle. "I'm going to go call Patsy and have a little chat about the importance of always carrying an EpiPen. Especially on the golf course."

"Sounds like a good idea," he said, joining me in the aisle. "Maybe I'll walk you back after practice tonight?"

I nodded. "Sure. I'll wait for you."

He leaned forward, pressing his lips gently to mine. "Oh, and when you talk to Patsy, don't forget to ask her about Tyler's underwear. They're his favorite pair, remember?"

I rolled my eyes. "How could I forget? Worn and comfy."

He slung his bag over one shoulder, grinning now. "Apparently."

With a laugh, I unzipped my bag, stuffing the ancient book inside. When I looked back up again, Aidan was gone.

"I hate it when you do that!" I called out, my voice echoing in the empty space.

18 ~ Four out of Five Dentists Surveyed . . .

You want to try one more time?" Dr. Byrne—
Matthew—asked, and I nodded.

This was our last session before Thanksgiving
break. I needed to get it right this time. My head was pounding
from the effort—a throbbing ache just above my eyebrows.

I'd managed to replay the same part of the vision I'd seen
before, right up to where Patsy grabbed the golf cart for sup-
port, but nothing further. Which terrified me. What if I was
blocked from seeing it because subconsciously I knew I was
going to see something awful?

He laid a comforting hand on my shoulder. "Hey, it's
okay, Violet. I'll talk you through it."

"I know. Just . . . let me catch my breath for a second." I was actually sweating, despite the fact that he kept his office on the chilly side.

"Sure, take your time." He lowered himself into the chair beside mine. For a moment, we simply sat there in companionable silence. Finally he turned toward me. "You know, it doesn't always work. Trying to go forward, I mean. It's not exactly the same as a replay. I've only been able to do it a couple of times, and I've had a lot more practice than you."

I sighed, realizing it was probably hopeless. There was so much I still didn't understand about my visions, so much I couldn't control. "Hey, that reminds me—have you ever had a vision where you were kind of sucked under, having a hard time getting back out of it? Almost like there was a band around your chest or something, making it hard to breathe?" It had only happened one time—last spring, just before Julius's attack. It had totally freaked me out, and no one had been able to explain it.

"Just once, and it scared the hell out of me. I'd seen something where . . . well, let's just say that one of the possible outcomes meant lights-out for me. Anyway, I assume it had something to do with the fact that, in that particular vision, I was the one in danger, and the danger was imminent."

"So . . . why the reaction? Any theories?"

He shrugged. "Not really. How about you?"

I shook my head. "Nope. Anyway, I guess you managed to stop whatever you had seen from happening."

"Sure did. I assume you did too—you know, since you're sitting here in my office now."

"Yeah, but mine was a little different." Because I hadn't seen anything that had threatened me, specifically. Unless . . . unless Julius had been lying, telling Blackwell what he wanted to hear but never intending to turn me over to him after I'd destroyed Aidan.

Maybe Blackwell knew Julius was lying; maybe that's why he sent Jenna into the fray to save the day. Of course, that still didn't explain why he would sacrifice himself—

"You ready to try again?" Matthew asked.

I nodded. "I'm ready."

For fifteen minutes, he talked me through it. It was the same as always—the ticking clock and his voice, almost hypnotizing. Each time, I'd fall back into the vision, and each time it stopped at exactly the same place.

"You want to call it a day?" he offered, glancing down at his watch.

I reached up to rub my temples. "Anxious to get rid of me, Dr. Byrne?"

"Hey, it's Matthew, remember? And not at all. We can do

this all day, if you want. You sure you're okay?" He stood over me now, his brows drawn.

"I'm fine—just a little headachy. Anyway, I want to try one more thing, if you don't mind." The holidays were coming up, which meant winter. Which meant I needed to be one hundred percent sure that what I'd seen on my first day back—Aidan going after Whitney—had been a dream, and not a vision.

I'd give it one last try, and then I'd put it to rest. Because this one was different. I'd been able to recall all the others, each and every vision I'd had since school started—all but this one. One last attempt, and then I'd be sure.

"You want to tell me about it?" he asked. "Some details, maybe? I could guide you—"

"No, I'm good."

"Seriously, Violet. You know it works better when you tell me what we're dealing with."

"I know, but . . . not this time, okay?"

His eyes seemed to darken a hue. "Why do I get the feeling that this has something to do with Aidan? If you're sensing some sort of danger, seeing something that—"

"I told you, I'm not in any danger with him. Seriously, you spend almost as much time with him as I do. Probably more. Have you ever felt in any way threatened by him?"

He regarded me coolly. "No. But like I said before, it's not the same."

"It *is* the same," I said stubbornly.

He leaned toward me, his voice a harsh whisper now. "For Christ's sake, Violet, he's a vampire. How can you even . . ." He trailed off, shaking his head. "Just . . . never mind."

What had he meant to say? Trust him? Touch him? Kiss him?

"He trusts *you*," I said at last. "He thinks you're some kind of genius. Did you see what happened to him the last time he injected the serum that *you've* been working on with him? I swear, it almost killed him. Who knows what kind of damage it's done, and he's *still* messing around with it, injecting it into himself like he's some sort of lab rat."

He leaned back against his desk, looking stunned. "What are you saying, Violet? You think I'm trying to hurt him?" He pushed forward off the desk, raking a hand through his hair as he paced before me. "God, Violet, I'm trying to *help* him."

I let out my breath in a rush. "I know you are. I'm sorry. Please, just"—I shook my head—"just let me try this my way, okay? I could try it on my own, back in my room, but I have better luck with you talking me through it."

"You like to do things the hard way, don't you?" he said with a tight smile. He slumped back into the chair behind his desk. "You remind me of my brother, James."

"Seriously, Matthew, I didn't mean to sound ungrateful." I rose, stepping up to his desk. "I meant it when I said he thinks you're a genius. I don't understand half of what he says about the work you're doing together, but I know he feels like he's finally getting close. Thanks to you," I added.

He shook his head. "Unfortunately, there's no protocol to follow. No way to test it out, except on him. I wish there was another way, I really do."

"Yeah, me too." My gaze fell upon the framed photographs arranged on the wall behind him. In one, he was standing on the deck of a sailboat with his arm around a guy who looked just like him, only older, maybe a bit heavier. And then it hit me . . .

"Wait, you have a brother?"

He nodded. "I was always a bit different from everyone else at Winterhaven. I've gotten used to it."

"You know Jack Delafield has a brother too, right?"

He nodded. "Ah, but Jack and I are not the same."

"Wow, that's pretty cryptic. Care to explain?"

He folded his hands behind his head as he leaned back in his chair, looking more relaxed now. "I just meant the circumstances are different, that's all. Jack's the older sibling; I'm the younger. Aidan's got a theory about that, one I tend to agree with, so that's significant."

I nodded, remembering Aidan's explanation. "That whole thing about the Rh factor, right?"

"Right. Anyway, you want to try this last recall or not? On your terms," he added.

"Yes." I slipped back into my chair with a sigh. "Thank you."

I knew I had to push everything else from my mind, to focus my sixth sense as best I could. I could do it, I told myself. I'd done it dozens of times. This shouldn't be any different— not if it had been a vision.

When I left his office a half hour later, I was pretty sure that it wasn't.

"Violet? *M'ija?*"

I sat up, clumsily pulling the earbuds from my ears. "Did you call me, Lupe?" I yelled.

"You've got company!" Lupe shouted back, and I hurried out into the hall. Leaning over the banister, I saw Whitney standing in the foyer below.

Lupe kissed her on both cheeks, then stepped back, studying her with a scowl of disapproval. She made a clucking sound with her mouth. "*Mi Dios,* haven't they been feeding you?"

"Yeah, but I miss your chicken fried steak," Whitney replied with a laugh—avoiding the question, I realized. "No one makes milk gravy like you do."

Which was true, but still.

"We've got plenty of leftovers in the fridge, if you're hungry," Lupe offered.

Last night's Thanksgiving dinner had been a true feast: smoked turkey and Virginia ham with all the fixings—cornbread dressing, collard greens, dumplings, pole beans—and even my favorite Jell-O mold. I patted my stomach appreciatively, glad Patsy had agreed to fly down to Atlanta with me. It felt great to sit around the long dining table, a family again, even if what we considered family was a bit of a hodgepodge these days.

After all, Patsy wasn't really related to Gran. Gran was my real mother's mom. As for Lupe, her only son had never married and never had kids. He lived in California, and since neither Lupe nor her son liked to fly, she pretty much spent all her holidays with us.

And now Melanie, the home health aide, had joined our motley crew. Apparently she had family somewhere near Dahlonega but had opted to spend Thanksgiving with us instead. Clearly, Gran and Lupe had grown to care for her and were thrilled to have her. Even Patsy seemed to really like her. Actually, the two of them were off now getting mani-pedis at Patsy's favorite salon. They'd tried to convince me to come with them, but I had opted to stay home and wait for Whitney.

"Thanks, but I'm still full from last night," Whitney was telling Lupe now. "Trust me, my grandma sent us back home today with two dozen Tupperwares full of leftovers. I think we're going to be eating turkey for the rest of our natural lives."

"Well, go on, then." Lupe shooed her toward the wide, curving stairs. "But you girls let me know if you get hungry, *si?*"

"Will do," Whitney agreed, then hurried up the stairs, taking them two at a time.

"Look at you!" I said, wrapping her in a hug as soon as she crossed the threshold. "You look great!" *Thin.* She looked way too thin, but I wasn't going to say it, I wasn't going to start in on her right away, no matter how badly I wanted to. It would only put her on the defensive. No, I had to ease into it.

We both plopped down onto my bed, a beautifully carved four-poster that had been my mother's when she was a kid.

Whitney reached for a pillow, clutching it to her chest. *Hiding herself.* "I can't believe you're flying back tomorrow!" she said with a scowl. "We've only got one day to hang out. This sucks."

"I know, right? I wish your grandparents had come to you this year, instead of you going there." They lived in Alabama, a four-hour drive away. "What time did you leave this morning?"

Whitney rolled her eyes. "At the butt-crack of dawn. You know how my dad is."

Oh, I knew. It didn't matter where you were going—Stone Mountain, Olympic Park, even the mall—he'd swear that everyone else on the road was going to the same place. If he was driving us to Six Flags and the traffic was heavy on I-20, everyone else was surely headed to Six Flags too—the park was going to be packed, he'd complain. And then we'd get there, and the parking lot would be half empty.

Still, at least Whitney's dad had been around to take us to places like Six Flags. My dad was never home, always off on assignment in some dangerous, faraway place. And Patsy? She was way too busy to be bothered. Not that she would have set foot into an amusement park anyway.

"So, how's school?" I asked Whitney, forcing aside the mental image of Patsy riding a roller coaster, as amusing as it might be.

"Pretty much the same as always. Competitive. Sometimes I wish I'd stayed at Windsor Day, though I guess it would have been weird there without you."

I playfully punched her arm, wincing at the sharp feel of bone that my knuckles encountered. "Hey, I was at Windsor for two whole years without you, remember?" I leaned over to my nightstand and plucked off a pack of gum. "You want some?" I offered as I took a piece for myself and popped it into my mouth.

She wrinkled her nose. "Is it sugarless?"

"Of course. Four out five dentists surveyed recommend Trident to patients who chew gum," I intoned.

"Oh my God, you remember that?" she asked with a laugh. It was a game we played when we were kids, trying to stump each other with slogans from television commercials. "But no thanks, maybe later."

Wow, Whitney was refusing gum? That wasn't like her. I turned the pack over, checking the nutritional information. With a shrug, I tossed it back on my nightstand, watching as Whitney pulled the hair band from around her wrist and combed her long blond hair back with her fingers before securing it in a ponytail.

I was always envious of her ability to get her hair into a perfectly neat ponytail without a brush or mirror, something I couldn't accomplish no matter how hard I tried.

But then, everything about Whitney had always been so natural and effortless—just like our friendship, even now.

We were so much alike, after all. At least, I always imagined that we would have been, had I not been forced to go through life hiding a vital piece of myself from the rest of the world, her included.

"Guess who I ran into last week?" she asked, drawing me from my thoughts.

"Who?"

"Talia Simpson—remember her?"

I did—she had been one of our best friends in lower school. But she'd moved outside the Perimeter the summer after fifth grade and switched schools, and I hadn't seen her since.

"Wow," I said. "Talia Simpson. I'm not even sure I'd recognize her."

"Oh, her cousins live down the street from my Aunt Jo, so I see her every once in a while. Anyway, I ran into her at the mall. She asked about you, so I told her that you'd moved to New York. I showed her the picture of you and Aidan."

"Oh, yeah?"

She raised one blond brow. "Let's just say she was suitably impressed. She asked for your e-mail address. I hope it's okay that I gave it to her."

"Sure. Hey, don't you have some auditions coming up?" She was applying to several conservatory programs, planning on majoring in dance.

"Yeah, but my parents are still giving me a hard time about it. They want me to go prelaw, UGA or Tech. They just don't get it."

"That totally sucks." I couldn't even imagine that kind of parental interference. I was on the opposite end of the spectrum—

more

me what I wanted to major in. Probably

n't quite sure yet. "They're at least letting

ther-

though, right?"

ween

" She released the pillow and reached

"Wow, your taste in music has really

you,

lling through the songs.

been

, that's all. Anyway, the fact that they're

ditions means they haven't totally ruled

said

get your acceptances, and then talk to

uch it means to you."

ances, you mean. Ooh, this is a great

away

the shuffle icon, and music began to

I look

nking,

list, I realized. I suddenly wished our

don't

distance, wished I could reach out to

d I'm

missed him.

up."

t plenty of acceptances, Whit," I said,

Aidan

mind. "Just give your parents a little

ll her

to, you know"—I took a deep breath,

know

—"put on a little weight between now

g fear

be so worried about you."

rrowed a fraction. "I can't gain weight

would

itions."

, after

KRISTI COOK

I shook my head. "I don't know. I think with a few
pounds you'd still—"

"Please don't start in on me, Violet." There were tears g
ing in her eyes. "I have to listen to this all day, every day. Be
my parents, my shrink, my dietician—it never ends."

I took her hand in mine. "You know how much I lov
right? But seriously, I'm worried about you. You've neve
this thin. What do *you* see when you look in the mirror?

A single tear slid down her cheek. For a moment, sh
nothing—she only stared off toward the window.

"C'mon, Whitney," I pressed. "Talk to me. Please?"

Finally she nodded. "I know it's nuts," she said, wipin
the tear. "I mean, I realize I'm too skinny. But still, when
at myself . . ." She trailed off, shaking her head. "I keep th
'Just another pound or two and then I'll stop.' But then
stop. I can't. You have no idea what it's like trying to prete
normal, when deep inside I know I'm completely screwe

I had to tell her, I realized. Not everything—not tha
was a vampire and I was a *Sâbbat*. But I needed to t
about the visions. I wanted her to understand that I *di*
what it was like, that I totally understood the paralyzi
of discovery.

Oh, I knew it would mean walking a thin line, that I
be risking her scorn and disbelief. I'd heard the storie

234

all. I remembered what happened to Cece's old roommate, Allison.

But this was different. This was Whitney. How could I possibly expect her to fully open up to me if I wasn't equally forthcoming with her?

Okay, make that semiforthcoming, because I'd already established the fact that I couldn't possibly tell her everything.

I mean, sure, she liked to read as much as I did. As a reader, she was clued in to think "vampire" or "werewolf" whenever she came across a character that seemed to fit the bill. But that was fiction. In real life, you just didn't think to yourself, "Hey, that guy sitting next to me in English is awfully pale. I wonder if he's a vampire."

Because real life didn't work that way. Well, except that mine did.

Still, I'd stick with the psychic stuff. That, at least, was considered within the realm of possibility. There were stores everywhere selling tarot cards and crystals, toll-free numbers to dial for psychic readings. Just watch a little late-night TV and you'd see plenty of commercials for both.

What you would *not* see are ads for products to, say, protect yourself from your friendly neighborhood vampire. Yes, I knew where the line was, and I wasn't going to cross it.

"I *do* understand," I said, giving her hand a sympathetic squeeze. I smiled at the friend I'd known since kindergarten— the friend who'd seen me through braces and crushes and even my father's death—and I told her everything.

Okay, *almost* everything.

And the crazy part? She believed me.

19 ~ Lockdown

I had just walked into sixth-period fencing class when the alarm sounded. At first, we assumed it was just a fire drill.

"Okay, folks, you know what to do," Coach Gibson said. "Leave all your bags and equipment here. Let's exit the building in a quiet and orderly fashion, shall we?"

But then a voice came over the public address system. "Attention, this is a Code Yellow. I repeat, Code Yellow. All students must remain where you are until you receive further instructions. Teachers, perform a head count immediately and call it in to the admissions office. Dorm masters, please report to your posts for a head count, as well. Thank you."

Apparently we were under lockdown.

"What's going on, Coach?" someone called out as we milled about, confused.

"No idea," he answered with a shrug. "Let's do the head count, and then I'll go downstairs and see if anyone knows what's happening. Everybody sit."

So we did. I found a spot beside Tyler on a mat. Everyone remained silent as the coach walked among us, counting. "We seem to be missing one," he said, then counted us again. "Where's Suzanne?"

"I think she's at the infirmary," someone offered. "She wasn't feeling well at lunch."

He nodded. "Okay, we're good, then. You guys sit tight; I'll be back in a bit." He pulled open the door that led to the back stairwell—the fire exit—and stepped out. As soon as the door slammed shut behind him, everyone started talking at once, the sea of voices rising in an incoherent, nervous buzz.

Fire drills were always announced in advance, and no one had ever mentioned a Code Yellow—at least, not as long as I'd been at Winterhaven. So yeah, I was a little nervous, overly aware of the fact that our teacher had just left us alone.

"I wonder what you're supposed to do if you're in the bathroom," Tyler said, raising his voice to be heard over the din. It was a good question, actually.

"I wish I had my cell phone," came a voice behind me, and I turned to see who it was—Sarah Mason, an empath like Marissa. She was usually the girls' team second seed, behind me, which meant she didn't like me very much. I could only assume that her current choice of seat had something to do with Tyler, since she was looking at him now with puppy dog eyes.

"What are we supposed to do, just sit here and do nothing?" she whined.

"I guess we could practice," Carlos offered, rising to his feet. Carlos was the captain of the boys' team, although he usually ranked in the bottom third. He was a good leader, though.

"I don't think we're supposed to be practicing," Sarah argued, and I had to admit I agreed with her. Who went on about their business during a lockdown?

"You were the one complaining about doing nothing," Carlos said with a shrug, then sat back down.

Tyler leaned toward me, his breath warm against my ear. "I've got my cell in my bag," he whispered. "C'mon."

He stood and held a hand out to me, and I took it to stand, following him as he picked his way through the crowd to the cubbies by the door, where our bags were stashed. I didn't even bother to ask why he was breaking the rules by carrying his cell around campus. Nothing Tyler did surprised me.

"Max has sixth period free," he said, crouching down to

rummage inside his bright turquoise bag. "I'll text him—maybe he knows what's going on."

I'd almost forgotten that Tyler and Max were roommates. Considering how much time Max spent with Marissa, I doubt Tyler saw much of him, but still. It shouldn't surprise me that they were friendly, despite the fact that they were polar opposites, as far as I could tell.

I stood there watching while he typed his message. *Dude, whassup? U know?*

Not fifteen seconds later, there was a ping. *A body. In woods by river.*

Tyler's eyes, widened with shock, met mine for a brief moment, and then he started typing furiously. *What u mean, a body? Dead?*

We waited a bit longer for Max's reply this time. *Think so. Lots of police and EMTs. That's all I know.*

Tyler's reply was brief. *Thx.*

"What the hell?" he said aloud. "I didn't hear any sirens."

"Me either. Do we tell them?" I tipped my head toward the rest of group.

Tyler shrugged. "Your call."

"I don't know. Kind of sounds like speculation at this point, you know?"

"Agreed." Tyler's gaze met mine. "So, what now?"

"I need to talk to Aidan," I blurted out. Not that I expected him to know anything more than Max did, but just because I needed to hear his voice.

"Here," Tyler said, handing me his cell. "But be quiet about it, or everyone's going to want a turn."

"I don't need the phone," I said, gesturing for him to put it away. "I can talk to Aidan without it."

Tyler reached for my arm, his eyes narrowing. "What do you mean?"

Uh-oh. How was I going to get out of this one without revealing too much? "What do you *think* I mean?" I hedged. "We're at Winterhaven, remember?"

"And you're a precog, remember?" he shot back.

Crap. I should have known that Tyler would want a better explanation than that. Sometimes I forgot how smart he was. "I can't explain it, Ty. Okay? It's just some weird . . . anomaly."

He looked confused. "So you're saying you're a precog *and* a telepath?"

I shook my head. "No, I'm not really telepathic. It's just . . . with him."

"You're only telepathic with *him?*" His voice rose a pitch. "What the hell does that mean?"

"Shhh," I said. I reached for his hand and dragged him into the girls' dressing room, as far away from everyone else as possible. "I told you, I can't explain it. But he and I have this weird psychic connection, and yeah, we can communicate telepathically. It's not really that big a deal."

He looked at me skeptically. "You don't think it's that big a deal? Seriously? It's not normal, not even by Winterhaven standards. You're either a telepath or you're not, Violet."

"Will you just shut up and let me talk to him?" I begged, suddenly desperate to hear Aidan's voice in my head.

He held up both hands, palms out. "Hey, go for it."

"Just . . . be quiet for a second, okay?"

Without a word, he folded his arms across his chest, leaning back against the row of lockers that lined the far wall.

"Thanks," I said, then took several deep breaths, trying to focus. Aidan had been screwing around with the serum over the break, and he'd had another bad reaction over the weekend. It wasn't nearly as bad as the last time, but bad enough that I worried our connection might be temporarily down again.

Still, I gave it a try. *Aidan?* I called out, hopeful.

There was no reply, though I did feel the telltale tickle in my head. It was faint, but it was there—our connection. I tried again. *Hey, Aidan? You there?* I was trying my best to yell telepathically, which was not an easy feat.

And then I heard it, a faint whisper in my head. *Vi?*

I turned so that my back was facing Tyler. *Where are you? What's going on?*

Nothing. I waited, willing the connection to strengthen. There was a brief buzz in my head, and then, *Violet?* again, so faint and indistinct that I wasn't certain I hadn't imagined it.

I turned back toward Tyler. "It's not working."

His gaze was unflinching. "If you say so. Want me to go get my cell for you?"

"No, it's okay. Just . . . never mind, I'll find him later. We should probably go back inside." The loud, raucous voices hadn't quieted any since we stepped out, meaning that Coach Gibson was still MIA.

"Nah, I like it better in here." He pushed away from the lockers, taking two steps toward me. "So, how was your Thanksgiving?"

"It was nice. How 'bout yours?" I regretted the words the instant they left my lips. It had been his first Thanksgiving without his dad.

"It sucked," he said. "My mom made this big production of making me carve the turkey—you know, since I'm the 'man of the house' now. First she cried, then she drank, and finally she passed out. All the makings of a memorable meal."

"I'm sorry, Ty."

"Nah, it's okay. My grandma put her to bed, and I took the

train into the city and hung out with Max and his family for the rest of break. Oh, and I ran into Kate."

I let out my breath in a rush. "Please say you didn't."

"Why do you care?" he said with a smirk. "She's a lot of fun, even if we can't speak telepathically to each other like you and the boyfriend can."

My face flushed hotly. "I wish you'd stop screwing around with my friends. Seriously, it really pisses me off."

"Why do you always assume that I'm just screwing around with them? Maybe I really like Kate."

"No, I meant it literally. Stop *screwing* my friends."

He just shrugged, which only made me more furious.

"You realize that she isn't over Jack yet, that she's totally on the rebound, right? She's probably just using you."

"Hey, I'm totally down with that." He reached down to readjust the colorful string bracelets he still wore around one wrist. "She can use me anytime she likes. Anyway, I'm touched by your concern for my feelings."

I shook my head. "You're disgusting."

In the distance, a siren wailed. The public address system crackled back to life. I cocked my head to one side, listening. "Attention, please. The Code Yellow remains in effect. I repeat, Code Yellow remains in effect until further notice. Thank you."

Tears suddenly burned behind my eyelids. "I can't believe

we're standing here arguing when there's apparently a dead body out there. What if it's a student?"

He nodded, and the tension between us dissolved at once. "I'd say chances are pretty good it *is* a student. Or a teacher, maybe. Where the hell is Coach Gibson?"

"We should go inside," I said, craning my neck to see what was going on back in the studio. It looked like almost everyone was still sitting around talking. Faces looked pale, pinched with worry.

Tyler winked. "Yeah, wouldn't want to give anyone the wrong idea."

I rolled my eyes. "That's not what I meant."

"I know, Violet." With a cheeky smile, he reached for my hand, grasping it firmly in his. "C'mon, we'll tell 'em what we know."

20 ~ The Scooby Gang

As soon as sixth period ended the following day, we assembled in the chapel, all of us. Even Jack, though he made sure to keep his distance from Kate.

"What are you guys thinking?" he asked, moving to stand beside Aidan.

"That we should stay out of the woods," Cece offered.

"That's a given," Joshua said. He slipped into the first row, stretching his feet out into the aisle. He must have grown a full foot since last year, I realized, surprised. "Seriously, Cece, don't even think about it," he continued.

Beside me, I saw her roll her eyes. "Yeah, no shit, Sherlock. Only my astral self goes out there, and I'm pretty sure the Stalker can't touch her, badass that she is."

"I just wish we knew what we were dealing with," Aidan said. "Luc feels sure it's an imposter, not an actual vampire. But how does an imposter do that type of damage?"

Jack grimaced. "I think there are ways."

"Yeah, but why here?" I asked. "It just seems like too much of a coincidence that he'd strike here, doesn't it? I mean, what are the chances?"

"We're not that far from Manhattan," Marissa reasoned, "and the train runs down along the river. It's possible that it *is* a coincidence. He might have been on his way somewhere and just happened to cross paths with the victim."

The victim. She'd been identified as a local woman—a drug addict, apparently, who'd obviously been in the wrong place at the wrong time. But unlike the Stalker's previous victims, who'd been discovered in time for life-saving transfusions, this one hadn't been so lucky. The groundskeeper had discovered her bled-out body out in the woods, apparently several days after she'd been left there.

I shuddered, horrified by the idea of something so awful happening so close by. "Luc's sure there's no one new in the area? A rogue vampire who'd do something like this? I swear, it's almost as if he's trying to send a message, thumbing his nose at Mrs. Girard or something."

"Or *her* nose," Aidan added. "We have no real reason to assume the Stalker's a he."

"All the victims have been females," Kate said with a shrug.

Sophie turned to face Kate, who was sitting behind and to the right of her. "Yeah, but it's not like they were sexually assaulted or anything."

"Yeah, I guess." Kate leaned forward, resting her elbows on the back of the pew in front of her. "I can't believe the police have nothing, though. There has to be some sort of evidence left behind. Fingerprints, footprints, something."

"Not if he's careful," Jack said. "An experienced criminal knows better than to leave any clues at the scene of a crime."

Everyone nodded in agreement.

"Well, it's not like he murdered this woman and then disappeared into thin air," Kate argued.

"He could, if he's really a vampire," Aidan said. "In fact, he could do *exactly* that."

Kate nodded. "Yeah, but even so, there's got to be a trail of some sort, and I bet we're more equipped to discover it than the police are. Hey, maybe if we ask Jenna—"

"Of course!" Jack said excitedly. "In wolf form, she should be able to sniff something out. Even in human form, her senses are heightened—better than ours, for sure." He turned toward Aidan. "She can scent a vampire, right?"

Aidan just nodded, his arms folded across his chest, which I couldn't help but notice seemed far less defined than I remembered. He looked almost . . . gaunt.

"You want to talk to her?" Jack asked Aidan. "Jenna, I mean."

"Not really," Aidan muttered, shaking his head. "But I will."

I turned toward Cece and Sophie, who were staring curiously at Kate. Beside her, Marissa was doing the same. I couldn't blame them—after all, that little exchange with Jack had been the most those two had said to each other in weeks. For a second there, it had almost seemed like old times, and everyone appeared to be holding a collective breath, waiting to see what would happen next.

Of course, after Tyler's little revelation yesterday, I should have known better. Clearly, Kate was finally moving on. I just wished it had been a healthy kind of moving on, rather than a fling with a guy who was sort of dating one of our friends.

Then again, who was I to judge? I was dating a vampire.

Cece glanced down at her watch. "I've got to head over to student council, guys. God, I hate this new schedule."

"It's definitely a pain," I agreed. "We've got a half hour of fencing practice before dinner, but it's not going to be enough, not with the big All-Ivy tournament coming up."

After yesterday's lockdown, the school administration had set a temporary new curfew. Everyone had to be inside, accounted for, by sunset. All extracurriculars—clubs, meetings, practices—had to be shortened and crammed in before darkness fell. My own schedule was a mess, and I had only fencing to deal with. I had no idea how Cece could possibly fit everything in.

We stood and shuffled into the aisle. Aidan and Jack moved away from the rest of us, their heads bent in quiet conversation.

"I'm going back to the dorms," Sophie said.

"I'll go with you," I said. "Just let me say good-bye to Aidan."

Sophie laid a hand on my shoulder. "Hey, speaking of Aidan, he looks awful. Well, by Aidan standards, at least," she amended. "Did he have another bad reaction or something?"

"Yeah, over the break. Maybe you could . . . you know, do your thing with him. See if you can sense what's going on."

"Do you think he'll let her?" Cece asked.

"I don't see why not. I don't know why I didn't think of it before."

Sophie nodded. "Only problem is, I've never touched him before. Which means I don't have a baseline to go by. But I can still give it a try—can't hurt, right?"

"I've really got to run," Cece said, looking almost apologetic. "I'll see you guys later."

"Wait for me," Marissa said, hurrying to Cece's side. "I'm supposed to meet Max at the café."

Kate set off too, not-so-coincidentally timing her exit to match Jack's, I noticed.

"Hey," Aidan called out to me and Sophie, "you two heading out?" He quickly closed the distance between us.

"Yeah, but first we've got a proposition for you," I said.

He smiled, his eyes twinkling mischievously. "Hmm, now that sounds intriguing."

I looked entreatingly to Sophie.

"Here's the thing—would you mind if I took your hand for a second?" she asked him. "I just want to see if I can . . . you know, sense your condition."

His eyes narrowed a fraction, but he was still smiling as he looked back and forth between the two of us. "She put you up to this, didn't she?" he asked, tipping his head in my direction. "Because of the reaction."

"Maybe," Sophie answered with a laugh. "But honestly, I *am* curious."

"It's okay, I don't mind." He held out one hand to her. "Do you want one hand or two?"

"Two usually works best," she said. "I get a better read that way."

He complied, extending both hands in her direction.

For a moment, Sophie seemed to hesitate. She bit her lower lip, a shadow flitting across her face. Finally, she extended her own hands, grasping his firmly as she closed her eyes and took a deep breath.

Not ten seconds passed before she snatched her hands back, her eyes flying open. "Oh my God. Wow." She suddenly looked a little pale, slightly shaken.

"What's wrong?" I asked her, a knot in the pit of my stomach.

She swallowed hard. "It's just . . . I don't know, my readings were all over the place. Some were totally flatlined, like he's . . . you know, dead. But his heart's still pumping, and there's this systemic infection in the blood cells." She shook her head. "I've never seen anything like it."

"You sure you're okay?" I'd never seen her react like this after applying her gift.

She nodded, covering her mouth with one hand. When she let it fall, her fingers were visibly trembling. "It's just that when I was touching him, my mind was flooded with fear. Just . . . pure, undiluted fear." She turned toward Aidan, as if she'd just remembered that he was still standing there. Her cheeks were splotched red now. "God, I'm sorry, Aidan."

"Hey, no need to apologize," Aidan said softly. "Considering the circumstances, it's not surprising. You know, just nature's way of telling you to get away, and fast."

Sophie nodded, looking as if she wanted to do just that.

"Hey, Sophie," Joshua called out. "Can I ask you a huge favor?"

"Sure," she said, moving toward him, still looking a little dazed.

"Can you take a look at my wrist?" he asked. "I think I might have sprained it playing basketball."

I watched the pair move off toward the back of the chapel, talking quietly. She would feel better after a more "normal" diagnosis. Somehow, Joshua always seemed to know how to step in and rescue a situation.

Grateful, I turned back toward Aidan. "You still don't look good," I fretted.

"I'm fine," he said absently, taking a seat in the front row. He held out a hand to me and I took it, sitting down beside him. "So, apparently Jack's work in the lab with your little friend is going well."

"With Tyler, you mean?" I shook my head in annoyance. "Would it really be so hard for you guys to call each other by name?"

Aidan ignored that jab. "Jack says he's highly skilled at compressing molecules. I think I'm going to ask him if he'll help me out this week. That is, unless you have any objections."

I shrugged. "Why would I care?"

"I just thought I'd ask. You know, in case there's some drama going on with him that I'm not aware of."

"Oh, there's always some sort of drama going on where Tyler's concerned." I briefly wondered if Jack knew that his lab partner was busy hooking up with his ex. "But no, no objections from me. He's *all* yours."

"Thanks. I think," he quipped.

"Hey, Violet?" Sophie called out, and I turned toward her. "Joshua's sprain is really a hairline fracture. I'm going to walk him over to the infirmary, okay?"

"Sure, I'll catch you later. Feel better, Josh."

"I hope I didn't throw off her sensors or anything," Aidan said, smiling ruefully. Suddenly his expression turned serious. "I'm supposed to give you a message from Mrs. Girard. She wants to see you."

My heart gave a little leap against my ribs. "What? When?"

He looked at his watch. "Right about now, actually."

"Great. Do you know why?"

"No idea, Vi. Just . . . be careful, okay?"

"I hate it when you say things like that," I said, shaking my head. After all, I was *always* careful. I didn't need reminders.

"Do you have your stake with you?" He gestured toward my bag, and I couldn't help but widen my eyes.

"You want me to take my stake with me to meet with the headmistress? Seriously?"

He nodded. "I think you should probably have it with you wherever you go, yes."

I carried my stake with me in my bag whenever I left campus, but back on school grounds I usually left it in my closet, away from prying eyes. "Fine. I'll stop by my room and get it on the way."

"Thank you. Want me to take you?"

"Sure, why not," I conceded. "Whatever Mrs. Girard wants to see me about, it can't be good. You know that, right?"

"There's only one way to find out." He stood, pulling me to my feet.

"You sure you can do this?" I leaned into him, tucking my head beneath his chin. "In the shape you're in right now?"

I felt his lips in my hair. "Two days ago, I couldn't. Luckily, this particular ability seems to rebound rather quickly. Anyway, hold on tight."

So I did.

A hiss and pop, and we were there in my dorm room, standing near the foot of my neatly made bed.

"Huh. So this is your room." He released me, taking a step away from the bed. I watched as he turned in a slow circle, examining the small space. "Pretty nice," he said at last. "It *feels* like you."

"You've been in here before," I reminded him. Once, last year.

"Yeah, but just over by the window. I didn't get a chance to look around."

I glanced around the room, trying to see it with fresh eyes. Much of the wall space was covered with artwork—mostly music posters, interspersed with a couple of prints from our favorite movies. Everything else—the lamps, bedding, plastic bins, and fabric-covered corkboard—was done in our favorite colors, pink for Cece and lavender for me. We'd gone with a shabby-chic look, I supposed. There were sheer, fluttery curtains trimmed in grosgrain framing the room's single window, and distressed floral slipcovers on the love seat. Gran would have called it a "hot mess," but I thought it was perfect.

"The messy side is Cece's, by the way," I said, noting her unmade bed and the unruly stack of magazines on her nightstand. Luckily, she hadn't left any undies lying around the floor. At least, not today.

A smile danced on his lips as he reached for my shoulders and pulled me up against his chest. "Somehow that doesn't surprise me."

"I hope the door's locked," I murmured. "We're engaging in some serious rule-breaking here. "

Behind me, I heard the lock click. "We're good," Aidan said, taking a step back. "But yeah, I guess I should let you get over to Mrs. Girard's office before she comes looking for you."

I nodded, exhausted. It was like it all finally hit me at once—the new *Sâbbat* stuff, the lockdown, the curfew. Not to mention the murder, right here on school grounds. That's what freaked me out the most, I realized—the fact that it had happened here, in what was supposed to be a safe haven. I sank to my bed, feeling queasy all of a sudden.

"You okay?" he asked, sitting beside me and wrapping one arm around my shoulders. "I know it's been a pretty unsettling couple of days."

I let out my breath in a rush. "It's just . . . that poor woman. I mean, I realize she was just some junkie, but still." I shook my head. "She didn't deserve to die like that."

"Don't worry, Vi. We'll figure it out. All of us, working together."

I laughed uneasily. "Yeah, our little Scooby Gang."

"Our what?"

"Didn't you ever watch . . . never mind." Of course he didn't. "You're right—I should probably get going."

He nodded, and we both stood. "Want me to take you?" he offered.

"No, I'll walk. You should go, though." I headed into the closet, standing on tiptoe as I reached up to the shelf above my shoes. "The last thing we need is Mrs. G. coming to look for me and catching you here." My fingers closed around the satiny shaft, and I hurried out, crouching down to stuff the stake into my bag. "I'll see you at dinner, okay?"

When I didn't get a response, I stood, my gaze sweeping across the room—the apparently empty room—and let out my breath in a huff.

I really *did* hate it when he did that.

Just as I'd done so many times in the past, I settled myself into the chair across from the headmaster's desk. The headmistress's, in this case.

She smiled at me, looking as chic and poised as ever, not a hair out of place. Her pale brown gaze was direct but kind. Despite Aidan's warnings, it was hard to remember to remain wary in her presence. She still seemed exactly like the kindly dorm mistress I'd first met at Winterhaven, not a powerful, centuries-old vampire.

I thought of her predecessor. Dr. Blackwell's strength had been mind control—apparently his powers had been unparalleled among their kind. I wondered what Mrs. Girard's strengths were. Whatever her powers, I just didn't feel the alarm in her presence that I knew I should. Where was the reaction that I experienced with Trevors?

"Thank you for coming, Miss McKenna. Better late than never, as they say."

"I'm so sorry—"

"No need to apologize, *chérie*," she interrupted, waving one hand in dismissal. "This isn't official school business, not precisely. I was just thinking that perhaps it's time we had a little chat. I spoke to Mr. Gray today, and he tells me that your *Sâbbat* tendencies remain mostly latent."

I nodded. "I've noticed some slight changes, but nothing significant. Nothing that's affected my relationship with Aidan, at least."

Again, she smiled. "The connection you share is particularly fascinating. I can only wonder if your feelings for him will somehow neutralize your hatred for our kind in general."

"I wish I knew. When I'm with Aidan, even with you, I don't feel anything unusual. But other vampires . . . well, I do feel the stirrings of *something*."

"Hmm, interesting." She leaned back in her chair. "Though I must admit, I wasn't aware that you'd encountered any others."

"Just Trevors. You know, Aidan's . . . his . . . butler." *Butler?* I felt stupid just saying it.

"Of course. How could I forget Trevors? I wonder, then, if you'd feel similar stirrings in the presence of another vampire? One with whom you aren't familiar."

"It's possible," I said. "The feelings were pretty intense. If I hadn't known Trevors and hadn't been sure that he was someone I could trust, well . . ." I shook my head. "I was pretty desperate to get my hands on my stake. It actually took a lot of restraint to ignore my instincts. And I *know* Trevors. I like him."

She nodded, looking pensive. "So, let's say that this so-called Vampire Stalker crossed your path. Do you think you could sense his or her presence?"

I sucked in my breath. "So you think the Stalker is really a vampire?"

"Other members of the Tribunal don't agree with me, but yes, I do. A clumsy one—one who doesn't care about discovery, it would seem. My best guess is that it's a newly turned vampire, someone young, perhaps. Anyway, winter break is almost here. I presume you'll be spending the holidays in Manhattan?"

I just nodded.

"Well, you see my concern, then? If you were to somehow cross paths with this murderous vampire, well . . . I realize you've already slain three vampires, but they were threaten-ing your friends' lives. Would you be able to act so swiftly, so decisively, without such an incentive as saving your friends?"

I shook my head. "Honestly, I don't know."

"It could be a dangerous situation, Miss McKenna. Far too risky. Conversely, what if you encounter a vampire on a busy Manhattan street, and your instincts *do* kick in? I can only assume that a *Sâbbat* newly into her powers might find herself struggling with control much in the same way a newly turned vampire does." She visibly flinched, presumably imagining me going all Buffy, right in the middle of Times Square.

I had to bite my lip to keep from smiling, just imagining it myself.

Mrs. Girard's gaze met mine. "You must see why I'd feel more comfortable if Mr. Gray accompanied you whenever you ventured out."

"You mean all the time?"

"Whenever possible. Admittedly, he's compromised his own abilities with his work toward the cure. But together, I think you'll be safe."

So basically she was just asking me to spend as much time as possible with Aidan over the holidays? Hmm, okay. I was down with that. "No problem," I said with a nod. "We'll stick together like white on rice."

"Thank you," she said with an amused smile. "And thank you for that charming colloquialism."

I studied her features, searching my instincts. She seemed genuine—but then, so had Dr. Blackwell. Still, I didn't sense any sort of manipulation. I only sensed sincerity. Worry. Aidan *meant* something to her, I realized.

Because she had created him? Was there something akin to a parental bond between a vampire and those she had turned? I had no idea.

Almost immediately, thoughts that weren't my own flooded my mind. Just words and phrases, snippets.

Edward's son. Royal blood; our crown jewel. He can't know, not yet. Not till war erupts.

Accompanying the words was one single image—Aidan's face.

21 ~ Friendship 101

A fter breaching her mind, I got out of Mrs. Girard's office as fast as I could. She hadn't appeared to notice that I'd been eavesdropping on her thoughts—she'd seemed a little distracted, actually. And as far as I could tell, she was being totally up front with me.

But there was obviously something she knew about Aidan, something that was there in the back of her mind the entire time she was talking to me. I couldn't really make heads or tails out of the jumbled thoughts, but maybe he could. I needed to talk to him.

Glancing over at the window, I watched as the bright

orange sun melted into the horizon. *Great.* I couldn't talk to him now, thanks to the stupid new curfew.

Beside me, my cell phone started to ring. Patsy, according to the ringtone. Cursing her bad timing, I connected the call. "Hey, Mom."

"Hey, hon. You got a sec?"

"Sure. Wait—did you get your EpiPens?"

I heard her sigh. "Yes, Violet. They're right here in my purse."

"Okay, good." I sat down on the bed with a satisfied smile. "Go on."

"I really need to talk to you about something."

"Okay," I said, wondering where she was going with this.

"Actually, it's about *someone*," she corrected. "I should have told you about him while we were at Gran's, but . . . I'm sorry, Violet. I guess I chickened out."

Oh no. She was going *there*. "Well, now's your chance," I said.

"You know how much I loved your dad, right?"

"Uh, yeah. I guess so."

"I'll never forget him. Never."

I just sat there silently, willing her to hurry up and get it over with.

"Anyway, I met someone. Over the summer. Paul's a really

nice guy, Violet. Smart, too. I think you'll like him. He's, um, legal counsel for the Australian embassy."

I remembered the guy I'd seen golfing with her in my vision. Tall guy, short brown hair, blue eyes. Australian accent.

"And?" I prodded.

"And he's invited me to go to Turks and Caicos with him before Christmas. I'd like to go, but I hate to leave you home alone over the break."

"It's okay, Pats—Mom, I mean. You should go. Have some fun."

"Really? You're sure?" I could hear the excitement creeping into her voice. Did she really think I'd say no? "You could go to Gran's if you really don't want to be alone," she offered. "But I'll be back on the twenty-fourth, so it's not like I'd be missing Christmas or anything like that."

"Seriously, I'll be fine."

"Thanks, Violet. You have no idea how much this means to me."

I was pretty sure I didn't *want* to know. It's not like I expected her to sit home, loyal to my dad's memory forever—not at all. She was young, and I expected her to eventually move on, find someone new, fall in love. I certainly wasn't going to hold it against her if she did just that. I just didn't want the details, that's all.

"Though I . . ." She cleared her throat. "I don't want to give the impression that just because I'm gone, you and Aidan are free to do whatever you want. Regular rules still apply, right?"

"Right," I agreed, my voice tight. She was free to go gallivanting off to the Caribbean with her new fling, but I had to be home by midnight? Of course, technically speaking, her rules had never specified that I had to be home *alone*. "You have to promise me one thing, though, or the deal's off," I said, brushing aside my annoyance in favor of more serious issues.

"Oh yeah?" she asked, a trace of amusement in her voice.

"Yeah. You have to promise me that as soon as you get off the phone, you'll put an EpiPen in your golf bag, okay? Plus, make sure you have one in each of the bags you're going to bring with you. Better to be safe than sorry, right?"

"Fine," she said with a laugh. "I promise, if it'll make you feel better. I swear, since when did you become so fixated on my bee-sting allergy?"

I shook my head in disgust. I mean, okay, I got that she didn't believe in psychic stuff. But she'd lived with me since I was little. Over the years, she'd seen enough evidence of my gift that you'd *think* she might take my warnings seriously by now.

Just take the effing EpiPens, I silently urged.

A knock sounded on the door. "Violet?"

"Hey, I've got to go," I said into the phone. "Someone's at the door."

"No problem. I'll e-mail you my itinerary as soon as we book, okay?"

"Sounds good. I'll talk to you later, then. Bye." I ended the call just as another rap sounded on the door. "It's open!" I called out.

Kate stepped inside, looking as if she'd been crying. *Uh-oh*.

"Hey, since when do you knock?" I teased, collapsing back on the bed.

She sat down across from me on Cece's bed. "Since everyone started treating me like a social outcast, that's when. Where's Cece?"

"Over at Marissa's, studying for their English final. I thought you were in their class."

"I am. Obviously I wasn't invited."

Oops. I shifted uncomfortably on the bed. "Oh. Sorry about that."

"How long is everyone going to stay mad at me? Seriously, is what I did *that* bad? It's not like Cece and Tyler were serious or anything."

"Are *you* and Tyler serious?" I asked. "I mean, I don't really understand it. One day you're devastated about Jack, and the next you're off hooking up with someone else, someone you knew that Cece was interested in. And yes, it *was* that bad. Couldn't you have at least waited until the day *after* the dance?" More than a month's worth of pent-up frustration came spilling out. I wanted to make her understand that she'd broken a basic tenet of Friendship 101.

Abruptly, Kate stood. "Never mind. I should have known that you wouldn't understand."

"Well, how 'bout you help me understand, instead of just storming off," I shot back.

"What's the point?" She swiped at her eyes with her sleeve. "You're just going to take Cece's side."

I took a deep, calming breath. "Look, I love Cece. But I love you, too. You know that. I owe you so much." How could I forget Kate standing there beside me, facing down Julius? She'd done everything to stop him and the two females; when that didn't work, she'd made sure I had my stake in my hand when I needed it. "But why Tyler? I mean, I know you were hurting—I get that. But couldn't you have found someone else to mess around with?"

"I happen to like Tyler," she said softly.

"You *like* Tyler? What do you mean, you like him? What about Jack?" Because she'd loved Jack. They were going to be together forever, she'd claimed.

Kate glanced over at the corkboard on the wall. A pushpin

fell out, the picture it anchored fluttering to the floor. She held out her hand and the picture flew into it. It showed her and Jack wearing their matching pirate costumes from last year's Halloween Fair dance. They had their arms wrapped around each other, Kate's lips pressed against Jack's cheek. Someone must have snapped it while I was off in the chemistry lab, watching Aidan smash things up.

"*Jack* broke up with *me*, remember?" she asked, ripping the picture in two and dropping the pieces to the floor with a flourish.

"He's a total moron, Kate. I'm not saying you shouldn't have moved on. But . . . Tyler? I mean, he was at that dance with Cece."

"I know, and I'm sorry, okay? I told Cece I was sorry. What more do you guys want from me?"

It was a good question. I guess I just wanted to understand. "He told me that the two of you hung out some over Thanksgiving break."

Her eyes widened. "He told you that?"

"He has a habit of telling me way more than I want to know."

Kate was watching me curiously now. "I'm starting to think that maybe you're jealous," she said, her tone accusatory.

"What, of you and Tyler?" I almost laughed aloud. "I've got Aidan, remember?"

"Yeah, you do *now*," she agreed with a nod, her hands on her hips. "But what happens if he doesn't find his cure in time?"

I just stared at her, unable to believe what she was insinuating. "So what are you saying?" I finally asked. "That I'm trying to keep Tyler to myself, just in case? For backup? Seriously, Kate, that's messed up."

She just shrugged. "Hey, you said it, not me."

Something was digging into my hand. I glanced down and saw that I was still clutching my cell phone, my grip so tight that my knuckles were turning white. Inhaling sharply, I dropped it on the bed beside me. "To answer your stupid question, if for some reason the worst *does* happen, I'm not going to hop right into another relationship. There's nothing wrong with being alone, you know."

For a moment, she said nothing. She just sat there, tears flooding her eyes.

"Hey, are you okay?" I said, standing up and taking a step toward her.

"Yes. No." She shook her head. "I don't know. It's just that I . . . I don't want to be alone." A single tear slid down her cheek.

I sat down beside her, wrapping my arms around her shoulders.

"It's just that my mom's been alone all these years," she

said, her voice muffled against my shoulder now. "She always seems so sad and lonely, as if I'm not enough for her. I don't want to be like that."

I'd met Kate's mom, a Broadway star, just once. She seemed really perky and outgoing, a lot like Kate. Of course, I knew that appearances weren't always what they seemed. "You're not alone, Kate. You've got us."

"Yeah?" She sniffled. "Then tell me why Cece and Marissa are off studying without me."

I reached over to Cece's nightstand for a tissue and handed it to her. "Didn't you blow *them* off the last time they were studying for an English test?"

"Yeah, but that was back before Halloween. I was still with Jack then," she said, dabbing her eyes.

"Okay, do you hear yourself? You can't have it both ways, Kate."

She blew her nose loudly. "Yeah, thanks a lot, Dr. Phil. So what do you suggest I do? I want things back the way they were before. With all of us, I mean."

"Well, why don't you just go over there now? I'm sure they didn't even think to ask you, since you don't usually study with them, that's all."

She bit her lower lip. "You really think I should go over there?"

I nodded. "Definitely."

She stood up. "Okay, but if they spit on me, I'm blaming you."

I had to laugh at the mental image. "They are *so* not going to spit on you."

She looked at me skeptically. "Yeah, famous last words."

I walked her to the door, hoping beyond hope that Cece and Marissa gave her a warm welcome when she showed up. Enough was enough—it was time to welcome Kate back into the fold, even if she didn't quite get why we had been so upset with her.

I paused by the door, studying her closely. "So you really like Tyler, huh?"

She shrugged. "He's cute. Besides, we have a lot of stuff in common."

It was my turn to look skeptical. "You do?"

"Well, we're both tellies. And, you know, neither of us has a dad."

I wasn't sure the last one counted, since Tyler had only recently lost his dad, whereas Kate had never known hers. Still, I decided to keep my mouth shut.

Violet? Aidan's voice, in my head. *How'd it go with Mrs. Girard?*

Give me a couple of minutes, I answered. *I'm with Kate.*

She was watching me strangely. "You're, you know"—she gestured toward my head—"talking to him, aren't you?"

"Sorry," I said, smiling apologetically. "I'm . . . we were just . . . done."

"You guys are so freaking weird." With a toss of her head, she hurried out, closing the door behind herself—telekinetically, of course.

And she called *us* weird.

22 ~ You Gotta Have Faith

I can't believe we're doing this," I said, glancing around Aidan's little room. I hadn't been there since last spring, but nothing much had changed—it was still as spartan and utilitarian as it was before, a far cry from his luxurious town house in Manhattan.

"It was either here or the East Hall lounge. I figured we needed some privacy. Anyway, technically we're still in the dorms, so you're not breaking curfew."

"True." I sat down on the narrow little daybed. "So, how's it going in the lab?"

Aidan leaned against the door, his arms folded across his chest. "Pretty good. Jack was right; Tyler's been really helpful.

I'm going to head back over there later tonight. We've got a bit more work to do on this new serum."

"How? You know, with the curfew and everything?"

"Well, Byrne's faculty, so it's not a problem for him, and obviously I can come and go as I please. We can make do without Tyler till tomorrow afternoon. Anyway, what happened with Mrs. Girard yesterday?"

I took a deep breath before responding. "Like I said, not much. She claims she's worried about me wandering around the city by myself over break. You know, in case I run into the Stalker. I guess she's afraid my instincts will kick in and I'll somehow screw things up."

He furrowed his brow. "And that was it?"

"Pretty much." I reached for the daybed's lone pillow and placed it against the wall. Scooting backward, I settled myself against it before continuing. "She was mostly suggesting that you and I stick together."

"Hmm, okay. What did your instincts tell you?" he asked.

"That she was being sincere."

"That's good, then, right?"

"Right. But . . . there was something else." I'd put off telling him about my little chat with Mrs. Girard until now, taking time to sort through the snippets. There wasn't much, but I'd written it all down, in case any of it meant anything to him. I reached into my hoodie's pocket and pulled out the folded slip of paper. "I hope I got it all," I said, flattening it out on my knee.

He sat down beside me on the bed. "Got what?"

I read off the hastily scribbled phrases. "'Royal blood. Crown jewel. Edward's son.'"

"That's . . . odd," he said.

"I know, right?" Nervously, I tapped the page with one finger. "But here's the important part—these were all thoughts she had while she was thinking of *you*."

"You're sure?" he asked, his voice laced with incredulity.

I nodded. "I'm sure. And they had to have been her thoughts, because they definitely weren't mine. And there's more." I glanced down at the last line I'd written. "'He can't know, not till war erupts,'" I read aloud. "That's all I've got."

He raked a hand through his hair. "Does she know that you were eavesdropping?"

"I don't know, Aidan," I said with a shrug. "When I accidentally breach a vampire's mind, I've sort of made it a policy *not* to ask them if they noticed."

"Okay, run it by me again. Slowly this time."

So I did.

When I finished, his features were blank, unreadable. "Okay," I said, "you better tell me what you're thinking right now, or I'm going to have to breach *your* mind."

"She can't possibly be correct" was all he said.

"She was talking about you, right?" I pressed. "I assume your father's name was Edward?"

He stood, looking pensive. "Charles. My father's name was Charles."

"Then who's Edward?" I asked, confused.

He began to pace. "The prince of Wales. Later the king of England, Edward VII. There were rumors about him and my mother, but I never imagined . . ." He trailed off, shaking his head, then slumped into the chair beside the door.

"You don't think . . ." I didn't even want to say it.

There was a faraway, dazed expression on his face. "I guess that would explain why my sisters looked nothing like me."

"Wait, you think it's true? Just like that?"

"It's certainly possible—the timing is right, and it would explain a lot. What I don't understand is the significance, as far as Mrs. Girard is concerned."

"I don't know, but she sounded . . . I don't know, really *proud* when she was thinking about it. She called you her 'greatest creation' before, and now you're her 'crown jewel.' It's like she's got big plans for you, or something." My palms started to sweat, just thinking about it.

"And all she asked of you was that we stick together over the holidays?"

"That was it." I nodded. "And like I said, she seemed genuinely concerned. Maybe it's really more for your safety than mine—I just don't know."

"She's hinted that perhaps a war is brewing. I always assumed she meant a war between the lawful and the lawless— you know, us against the Propagators. Maybe there's something bigger, something I'm not privy to. Still, I don't see what my parentage has to do with it, even if I am Edward's bastard son."

I watched him closely, trying to gauge his mood. I didn't want to prod him for details if this revelation was too upsetting. But I was curious—how could I *not* be?

"Do you think your father knew?" I asked.

He shook his head. "I don't know, but I suppose it didn't matter one way or the other. You know how the laws of primogeniture work. He was married to my mother; therefore, I'm legally his son. Was his son," he corrected.

"You still *are* his son, Aidan. I mean, I'm still my father's daughter, aren't I? Even though he's gone," I added.

"It's just been"—he shook his head—"so very long. I can barely even remember him. It was so many lifetimes ago, and our relationship ended when I was only seventeen. And now, after all this time, to learn that perhaps he wasn't my father after all. I just don't know what to think."

"He raised you. Loved you. In my book, that makes him your real father, no matter what."

He nodded, his gaze meeting mine. Pain was etched in his features, reminding me of the humanity at his core. "Does this change the way you feel about me?"

I almost laughed. "Because you're illegitimate? Are you kidding me?" Still . . . I could barely believe it was true. "You really think your mom might have had an affair with the king of England?"

"He was only the prince of Wales at the time. But yes, why not? He had a reputation for having mistresses. Of course, he never acknowledged any illegitimate children, but he must have had several. And my mother . . . well, as I said, she spent a lot of time in town without my father. And she was a particular favorite of his—Edward's, I mean."

For a moment, I digested that in silence. It was just so . . . incredible. But then, wasn't everything in my life these days? "So does that mean you're related to the current royal family?" I said at last. "The Windsors? Now that I think about it, you *do* kind of look like Wills."

He reached a hand to his temple, a pained look on his face.

"Sorry," I said. But there *was* a bit of a resemblance. They were both tall with blond hair and light eyes. And there was something else, too, something indefinable. Something almost regal, I realized with a start.

"Let's say it *is* true," he said. "That I *am* Edward's bastard son. What I find most disturbing is that Mrs. Girard is somehow invested in it. Taking pride in it, if you've correctly interpreted her feelings. It almost sounds as if she has plans to use me—and the truth of my parentage—in some way."

That was exactly the impression I'd gotten when I had been in her head.

A muscle in his jaw flexed perceptibly. "And if that's true, then—"

"Then she doesn't really want you to cure yourself," I finished for him, catching on. "She needs you as a vampire. Some sort of royal-blooded vampire. Her crown jewel."

He paused a beat before replying. "Exactly."

"Ugh, I really don't like where this is going."

"I don't either, but I'm not quite sure what I can do about it," he said, "short of leaving Winterhaven—and I have far too many reasons to want to stay."

Our eyes met, his full of several lifetimes' worth of desperation. I scooted off the bed and hurried over to him, allowing him to pull me onto his lap.

"Are you going to be okay?" I murmured.

"As long as I have you, I will be," he answered, his voice

thick with emotion. "I can't let any of this distract me, not now. I've got to press on, work night and day if need be. I'll do whatever it takes, no matter how difficult. As long as I have just a single day as a mortal with you, it will all have been worth it."

There was a sharp burn behind my ribs—my heart, maybe? It might have broken just a little bit. Because a single day would never be enough. Not ever.

"I should take you back," he said, resting his chin on the top of my head now.

"Probably," I agreed reluctantly. "And you should get back to work."

He sighed heavily. "Do you truly believe it will ever happen, Vi? Me, perfecting the cure? Becoming mortal again?"

"I really do," I said. It was just like faith. I didn't really understand this cure, couldn't do anything to affect it one way or another. It was out of my hands entirely. Still, I *had* to believe. And I did, with all my heart.

23 ~ Dogfight

A large mocha, no whip," I told the woman behind the counter at the café, then shuffled to the end of the counter to wait. I glanced down at my watch, surprised to find that I had so much time to kill before dinner.

Coach Gibson had canceled practice—he had broken a tooth or something like that and had a dentist appointment in the city. When I'd first found myself with the unexpected free time, I'd reached out telepathically to Aidan, but he'd been in the lab working, completely immersed in something that apparently involved a Bunsen burner. I'd pretty much tuned out the rest. It was all gibberish to me, his science-speak.

Cece was off at play rehearsal—or maybe it was tennis practice? I wasn't sure, but I knew she was busy. She was always busy. Tyler was at the infirmary getting tested for strep throat, even though Sophie had already diagnosed him. I had no idea where everyone else was. I figured I'd take a walk around campus and get a bit of exercise.

Five minutes later, I took my steaming-hot cup and headed outside. Despite the chill, it was a beautiful day, the sky a brilliant blue, not a cloud in sight. I took a sip of coffee and glanced up, shielding my eyes from the sun as a flock of Canada geese squawked by overhead. They were headed down toward the river. I decided to follow them.

I took the path that led toward the chapel, my pace brisk as I cupped my mocha in both hands for warmth. The crowd of students milling about thinned out as I left the quad and hurried past the movie theater, turning down another path that meandered along beneath a canopy of bare, spindly braches.

I was going to miss this place when I graduated, I realized with a pang of regret. If only I'd come as a freshman and had those two extra years to discover my gift, to make both friends and memories. I felt cheated, robbed of the true Winterhaven experience. How could a place come to mean so much to me in so short a time?

It was a shame that with all the gifts and talents represented at Winterhaven, no one possessed the power to stop time. I let out a sigh as I hurried my step, following the path as it curved around the chapel's stone facade and continued down toward the woods.

A few minutes later, the path began to slope downward. My breath was coming faster now as I pressed on, heading toward the wrought-iron bench at the end of the path, where it met the split-rail fence that marked the edge of the woods. I wasn't sure what purpose the fence served—it was pretty easy to climb between the rails, and I was sure that many students did, looking for a secluded spot. There were only so many places on campus that offered complete and total privacy, after all.

It seemed like an odd place for a bench, especially since it faced the campus rather than the woods. It was a long way to walk to sit and stare back in the direction from which you'd come. But the view was great this time of year—if you sat backwards, that is. You could see all the way down to the river, and if you craned your neck, you could just make out the Tappan Zee Bridge in the distance.

As I drew closer, I saw that the bench was occupied by a lone figure turned toward the woods, her arms thrown over the bench's back. I stopped short, not wanting to draw attention to myself. Squinting, I tried to identify her. A wave of familiarity washed over me, and I turned to leave just as she called out to me.

"Hey, Violet," Jenna said without even turning around.

"How did you . . ." I trailed off. She was a wolf; she probably smelled me.

She finally turned to face me. "You might as well come sit down. I won't bite."

So I did, still clutching my now-cold coffee in one hand. "Can you identify every single student by scent?" I asked her as I slid onto the bench beside her.

"Pretty much." She wrinkled her nose. "You have a lingering vampire scent, like he's rubbed off on you or something. It's really nasty, to tell you the truth."

"Sorry about that," I said, though I wasn't sure why I was apologizing. She was the one who'd insulted me, after all. "What are you doing out here?"

"Not that it's any of your business, but I was taking a clean set of clothes out to the shed over there." She pointed off to the right, down by the edge of the woods, where I could just make out a gray-shingled building with a tin roof. "That's where I change when I shift. Anyway, it's nice out, so I decided to sit."

She turned to face me, and once again I was struck by just how beautiful she was. She wasn't wearing any makeup, and yet she looked like she'd just stepped off the cover of a magazine. It wasn't fair.

"What about you?" she asked, sounding slightly bored. "What brings you out to my neck of the woods?"

I tamped down my feelings of inadequacy. "Fencing practice was canceled, so I'm just getting some exercise."

"And no vampires to play with? I guess you'll have to settle for a wolf, instead."

"Aidan's working in the lab," I said. "He does that, you know."

She shook her head. "Such a waste of time."

My gaze snapped toward hers. "Why do you say that?"

"How long has he been working on that cure of his? Like, a hundred years or something?" She reached up and twirled a lock of her hair around one finger. "If he hasn't figured it out by now, he isn't likely to ever get it right."

"It hasn't been that long" was all I said in reply. She was baiting me. I don't know why—maybe just to get on my nerves.

She shrugged. "If you say so."

I decided to change the subject. "So, I heard you checked the woods for the Stalker's trail and didn't find anything."

She glanced down at her fingernails, examining them closely. They were perfectly manicured, painted a deep bloodred. "Nope, the trail was cold. There were plenty of human scents, but they were all familiar, and the only vampire I scented in the woods was Aidan."

I sat up sharply, straightening my spine. "And what's that supposed to mean?"

"Don't get your panties in a twist. I meant just what I said—either the Stalker is a vampire who somehow managed to cover his scent or he's human. Or, who knows"—she shrugged—"maybe this was just some sort of copycat attack gone wrong. How should I know? I'm a lycan, not a detective."

"Well, thanks for trying."

She rolled her eyes. "Yeah, sure. Whatever."

"What's your problem, exactly?" I asked, feeling my hackles rise. "It's not like I've ever done anything to you."

Her sharp gaze pierced mine. "I don't like vampires, and I don't like people who hang out with vampires. Is that really so hard to understand?"

"One vampire saved your life, and another offered you shelter. Doesn't that mean anything to you? Or are you so self-centered that—"

"Oh, save me your little speech. I repaid my debt to Aidan, remember? He wouldn't still be here otherwise. Anyway, it's mostly biological, if you must know."

"Fascinating," I said mockingly.

She eyed me closely. "But vampires can't be trusted. You know that, right? Blackwell was a prime example. It doesn't surprise me one bit that he sold out Aidan—or tried to, at least. That's just their way."

"Is that what your pack told you? You know, the people who were going to marry you off at sixteen? The ones who tried to kill you?" I didn't even try to hide my disgust.

"You can say what you like about us, but we don't lie—not to each other, at least. It's biologically impossible."

"Because you can hear each other's thoughts?"

"Yeah, unfortunately. Anyway, I'm not going to play games and pretend I like you, when I don't." She eyed me sharply. "I know you're used to being treated like a pet, but lycans don't take pets like vampires do. We don't play around with humans, manipulating them. It's not our style."

I raised my brows. "So you're saying I'm Aidan's pet? His little human plaything?"

"Hey, if the shoe fits. He keeps you on a pretty short leash, doesn't he? Like I said, that's a vampire thing. Kind of degrading, though, if you ask me."

I shook my head, seething inside. "You don't know *anything* about my relationship with Aidan."

"You say that now, but I've seen it before. Soon enough you'll be all like, 'Ooh, make me immortal so we can be together forever!' It's so pathetic."

I almost laughed at the absurdity of that. As if that was

ever going to happen. I was a vampire slayer, not a vampire wannabe. "I can promise you that I will never, ever say that. Not in a million years."

Her mouth twitched with a smile. "Sure you won't. They *all* do, eventually."

"Whatever." I took a sip of my cold coffee, mostly just to keep myself from saying anything more. I wasn't going to give her the satisfaction of seeing me rattled.

She stood, zipping up her jacket as she did so. "Well, this has been fun, but I'm going to head back."

"Go for it," I said, wiping my mouth with the back of one hand.

She looked off toward the campus buildings looming in the distance, then back at me. I could have sworn I saw indecision flit across her features. "I'll leave you with this," she said at last. "I suggest you convince Aidan to stop injecting himself with whatever the hell it is he's working on."

I couldn't help but bristle. "Is that a threat?"

"Just a friendly suggestion," she said with a smirk.

Oh, how I wanted to wipe that smirk off her face. "Gee, thanks, Jenna. I'll take it into consideration."

"You do that," she said with a wink, then sauntered off.

I watched her retreating form until she disappeared over the rise, and then I let out my breath in a huff. How in the world had I *ever* thought she might be a friend?

I shook my head, trying to clear it of her condescending tone. If only I'd walked in some other direction, anywhere but here. I made a mental note to avoid this particular bench from now on. It was obviously way too close to her doghouse.

It was a wonder the girl had any friends at all, I mused. Then again, people were generally drawn to her type—attractive girls who exuded a cool confidence and indifference to the negative opinion of others.

I gazed off toward the river, wondering where the geese had gone. The gray water was still and wide, undisturbed. For several minutes I sat in total silence, watching in quiet fascination as the rays of golden sunlight cast rippling shadows across the water's surface.

Briefly, I considered reaching out to Aidan again, wanting to hear the sound of his voice in my head. But then I remembered Jenna's little "pet" comment, and decided against it. He kept me on a short leash? Is that really what she thought?

Shaking my head in annoyance, I stood. What did it matter what Jenna thought? My relationship with Aidan was none of her business, and I refused to let her snarky comments get under my skin. In fact, forget speaking telepathically—I'd drop by the lab and see if I could convince him to go with me to dinner.

And then I sank back to the bench with a groan. My

ears began to hum, my vision to tunnel. As I waited for the onslaught of unpleasant images, all I could think of was how glad I was that Jenna wasn't there to witness it.

I was in the lab. At least, it looked like a lab. There were microscopes along the wall and what I was pretty sure was a Bunsen burner on one of the black-topped tables. I saw a pair of hands before me, holding a dropper. They were extracting a liquid from a small vial and dropping it into a test tube. One drop. Two. Three. Then the vial was capped and put into a little wooden rack. The hands reached for a second vial. . . .

And just like that, it was over. No more than a second or two had passed, and I was back on the bench, gripping the seat tightly. That was it, no drama, no murder or mayhem—just hands doing science stuff. Aidan's hands, I reasoned, which actually made me wonder if I'd somehow breached his mind from a distance and was simply seeing him hard at work, through his eyes.

I'd been thinking about him when the vision began— wanting to hear his voice, picturing him there in the chem lab doing his thing. I'd never before mistaken a mind-breaching incident for a vision, but then I'd never breached the mind of a vampire who wasn't sitting right in front of me. Maybe this was a sign that my *Sâbbat* powers were strengthening.

Why hadn't I been born a lycan slayer instead?

24 ~ What, No Tacos?

How's your friend Whitney doing?" Sophie asked. She was perched on the arm of the loveseat, flipping through a magazine while Cece and I got ready for dinner. Beside her, Marissa and Kate were both absorbed with their cell phones.

"Better," I said, running a brush through my wet hair. "I think I might have actually gotten through to her over Thanksgiving." At least, I hoped so.

Setting down the brush, I reached up to rub my shoulder. It was really bothering me. A cold front had swept through the Hudson Valley, the temperatures near freezing now—maybe that was to blame? Whatever the reason, it was bad timing, with the All-Ivy fencing tournament coming up. "Hey, Soph, would you mind taking a look at my shoulder?"

"Sure," she said, setting down the magazine and hopping down from the sofa's arm. "Let's see."

I held out my hand, and she took it firmly in hers and closed her eyes. A second or two later, she opened them and dropped my hand. "Not good," she said with a wince. "You've still got some inflammation in the joint."

I groaned. "Great. Just what I *don't* need right now."

"Hey, you want some Advil?" Cece offered.

"Yeah, maybe," I said.

Cece swiveled in her chair, toward the sitting area. "Hey, Kate, can you toss me my bag?"

"Sure." Kate smiled as the little pink messenger bag lifted from the floor by her feet and flew across the room, right into Cece's waiting arms.

God, I was happy to see them getting along again. The tension was finally gone, everything seemingly back to normal. Even Marissa was spending more time with us, probably because it was more comfortable to be around us now. I hoped that was the reason, and not because things were starting to cool off between her and Max. I knew how much she liked him, as crazy as it was to imagine someone like her with . . . well, someone like him.

I had to wonder what her conservative parents—an Ivy League professor and a fund-raiser—thought about Marissa dating a guy who played the electric guitar and wore eyeliner. Then again, that was the beauty of boarding school—it wasn't like their daughter's relationship was in their face. Besides, from what Marissa said, Max was a truly gifted musician. He'd auditioned for several prestigious conservatory programs, so it wasn't as if he was going to end up playing in subway stations or anything like that.

"C'mon, guys, hurry up," Marissa said, glancing up from her phone. "It's taco night."

"I thought you hated taco night," Cece said as she twisted her hair into a knot and pinned it at the back of her head.

Marissa stood, reaching for her own bag. "Only when I'm hanging out with Max after dinner. Nothing worse than taco breath."

"Someone needs to tell that to Jack," Kate said with a grimace. "I swear, it used to be like licking the floor at Taco Bell."

Cece rose, tucking her favorite tube of lip gloss into her pocket. "You've had a lot of experience licking the floor at Taco Bell?" she asked, raising her brows quizzically.

"Ha-ha. Very funny," Kate said with a smirk. "You know what I mean."

I let out a sigh. It was nice to have everything back to normal again.

Sophie stood by the door now, one hand on the knob. "You guys ready? I'm starving here."

"Yeah," I said with a grin. "Just let me grab—" I stopped short, reaching for the edge of my desk as I lowered myself to the chair. "Uh-oh."

My vision was tunneling, the telltale buzz in my ears growing louder.

"Grab what?" I heard Cece ask, her voice faint now. "Violet?"

But I was gone.

I was inside somewhere, my surroundings unfamiliar. There was carpeting—thick, patterned carpeting. I was crying, deep gulping sobs that made it difficult to catch my breath. "You have to do it, Vi," a voice pleaded. Aidan. I turned to face him, nearly blinded by tears. "Please, I beg of you," he continued. "It has to go into my heart. You can do it; I've taught you how. Don't let me down, not now. You promised."

"No," I said, my voice hoarse, my throat aching so badly I could barely stand it. "Please, no. Don't make me, Aidan. I can't do it."

"Yes, love. You can. Right here." He tapped his chest, above his heart. "There's no time to waste. You must do it now. Now," he repeated, his tone urgent.

"I can't," I cried. "I can't do it. How can you ask me to?"

"Because I love you, Vi. I love you, with all my heart. It has to be you—don't you see?"

I could feel the hot tears rolling down my cheeks as I nodded. He was right; I knew he was right. I had to—I'd promised. I raised my right arm, my fingers clutched tightly around something smooth. I took a step back, then lunged forward, my arm swinging in an arc that ended at Aidan's chest.

A scream escaped my lips as I hit my mark. I squeezed my eyes shut, refusing to look, unable to see what I'd done. Blindly, I stumbled back, my own heart aching as if it had been cleaved in two. This was it, I realized. I had to see, to make sure . . .

I opened my eyes just in time to see Aidan crumple to the floor, his eyes wide, staring, unseeing.

And then it was over, just like that. "No," I whimpered.

"Violet?" Cece wrapped her arms around my shoulders. "Geez, that was a long one. Are you okay?"

I shook my head. "No. I can't . . . I wouldn't."

"Someone get her some water," Cece called out. "Hey, it's not trying to pull you back under, is it?"

"N-no," I stammered, my whole body trembling. I couldn't possibly have seen what I thought I'd seen. Not again, damn it.

I needed to replay it, right away. "I've got to call Matth— Dr. Byrne," I muttered, rising on unsteady legs. "Right now."

* * *

"Wow, this must be serious," Matthew said as soon as I stepped into his office. "It's taco night."

I stopped short, covering my mouth with one hand. The thought of tacos—or any food at all—made my stomach lurch uncomfortably.

He reached for my shoulder, his brow furrowed as he led me to the chair opposite his desk. "I'm sorry, Violet. I shouldn't have been so flippant. What happened?"

My legs practically buckled beneath me as I lowered myself to the seat, draping my jacket over the back of the chair as I did so. "It's—I had a vision. A bad one. Really, really awful."

"You want to try and replay it?"

I nodded, my mouth so dry I could barely swallow. "Yeah, I . . . I didn't get many details. Nothing about where or when. This can't be happening. Not again."

Matthew leaned back against the front edge of his desk, peering down at me closely. "Are you okay? You're shaking all over. I have to admit, I'm pretty worried here."

Not half as worried as I am. "Yeah, I'm fine," I lied. "Just really unsettled by this one." How many times was I going to have to watch myself kill him? Over and over again, until I actually *did* it? I'd managed to thwart it before. Was this the universe righting itself, correcting the continuum that I'd somehow messed up? Because it was my destiny to kill him, or so the legend went.

No. I refused to believe that. I had free will. The ability to change the future was part of the gift of foresight—of precognition, or whatever the heck you wanted to call it. Otherwise, what was the point?

"Okay, Violet, you've got to tell me what's going on. Seriously, I don't like this." He raked both hands through his hair, looking suddenly as discomposed as I felt. "What did you see that's got you this freaked out?"

I felt my instincts rev at full throttle. I wanted to tell him. *Needed* to. I had to talk to someone; I needed someone to help me through it this time. I couldn't tell Aidan—not yet. Oh, he'd reached out to me telepathically right after the vision had ended, while I was walking over to Matthew's office. He always knew when I had a vision that frightened me, especially if he was involved. I couldn't say why, except that maybe it somehow triggered that psychic connection between us.

So I'd brushed it aside and told him it was a repeat of the vision in which Patsy got stung by a bee. I'd tell him the truth eventually, once I sorted out the details.

And why not tell Matthew the truth? He was a friend, a confidant. He already knew that Aidan was a vampire. The only thing he didn't know was that I was a *Sâbbat*, and considering the magnitude of what he *did* know, that detail seemed insignificant.

Besides, it was probably best that he understood the connection that Aidan and I shared. Maybe he would worry less about the danger once he realized that I was as much of a threat to Aidan as he was to me.

There was no reason *not* to tell him, as far as I could tell, and every instinct inside of me was telling me that I should.

I took a deep breath, in through my nose, out through my mouth, gathering my courage as best I could. "I just saw myself kill Aidan," I blurted out.

I held my breath, steeling myself for his reaction—shock, disbelief. Fear, maybe. Anything, except what happened next.

He nodded solemnly. "It's okay, Violet."

"What? No. No, it's not okay. You don't understand—"

"I *do* understand," he interrupted, kneeling down beside my chair. We were at eye level now, his dark gaze probing mine.

"No," I protested, shaking my head wildly now. "You really don't. Listen to me—I saw myself plunge something right into his heart. Saw him crumple . . ."

I couldn't go on. My chest ached; my throat burned. My eyes filled with tears, and I swiped at them with the back of one hand.

"It's what you're meant to do, Violet." He reached over to

brush back a stray lock of hair that had fallen across my cheek. "It's your destiny."

"Again with the 'destiny' crap?" And then it hit me. "You knew I was a *Sâbbat*?"

He didn't answer right away. He was rolling up one sleeve, exposing his right forearm. His tattoo.

Finally he looked up again, his gaze locking with mine. "Does this mean anything to you? This mark?"

"What?" I asked, shaking my head in confusion. The word "mark" spurred something in my mind—a memory. Something just beyond my grasp.

"Have you ever heard the word *Megvéd*?" he asked, his voice barely above a whisper. "The *Megvédio*?"

Holy crap. *No*.

"Don't," I said, closing my eyes, wanting to block out the image of his tattoo, the scripted letter *M* atop the dagger, an initial I'd assumed stood for "Matthew." "Please don't. You're not. You can't be."

He nodded. "It's *my* destiny. I've been waiting for you."

I rose from my chair, nearly knocking it over in the process. "I'm going to be sick," I said, bolting from the room, looking for the ladies' room.

I barely made it inside the stall before my stomach emptied

itself of its meager contents. Afterward, I sat there kneeling in front of the toilet. When my knees started to ache, I rose and went to the sink, splashing my face with cold water.

I cupped one hand under the faucet, letting the icy water collect in my palm before bringing it to my mouth. I rinsed and spit several times, wincing when I caught sight of my pale, pinched reflection in the mirror above the sink.

This was *not* happening.

I fully expected Matthew to barge in at any moment to check on me, but he didn't. I didn't want to talk to him right now, didn't want any more revelations. And I certainly didn't want any more assurances that it was *okay* for me to kill Aidan, because it wasn't okay, and it never would be.

When I stepped out of the ladies' room, he was there in the corridor, leaning against the wall, waiting for me. "We need to talk about it," he said.

I shook my head. "Not now. I just . . . can't, okay?" This was the way I always dealt with this kind of stuff, I realized. I ran. I needed time alone to sort things out.

He seemed to understand, because he nodded. "Just promise me one thing, Violet. For now, this has to stay between you and me, okay? I know that's a lot to ask, but if you can just trust me on this, I'd appreciate it."

"Okay," I agreed. I didn't want to tell Aidan anyway. Not yet. He would freak out for sure.

"Call me when you're ready to talk," he said, his voice gentle. "I swear it's not nearly as bad as you think it is."

I nodded, but I didn't believe him—not one bit.

25 ~ Dude . . .

Y ou're really not going to tell me what's wrong?"
Aidan asked as we slipped into our seats fifth
period. "You've been acting strange all day."

"I told you, it was just that stupid vision with the bee again.
It's got me on edge. Patsy's leaving on her trip soon, and I'm
just worried, that's all."

"Where's your friend?" He leaned forward, peering across
at Tyler's empty seat beside me. "He's usually so punctual."

"I don't know," I snapped. "I'm not his keeper." I let out my
breath in a rush. "I'm sorry. Like I said, I'm just on edge."

"It's okay. Just make sure you call Patsy each morning and

remind her about the EpiPens. That's pretty much all you can do, right?"

At the front of the room, Dr. Andrulis stood and cleared his throat. "Okay, folks, enough chitchat. Who's ready for a slide show? Jared, kill the lights." With one gloved hand, he gestured toward the switch by the door.

The tall, stocky guy in glasses whose desk was nearest the door stood and flicked the switch, and the room went dark except for the glowing light behind Dr. Andrulis's desk.

"Okay," he said as the first colorful slide flashed onto the screen behind him. "Let's start with some impressionists."

I settled back into my seat, glad for the distraction. We had a final coming up, so I couldn't allow my mind to wander into dangerous territory. I had to focus, no matter how exhausted I was.

And I *was* exhausted. I'd lain awake most of the night, staring at the ceiling as it had shifted from deep black to violet to the hazy lavender of dawn. I think I finally dozed off just before the sun came up.

When my alarm had gone off, I'd forced myself out of bed, as tempted as I was to tell Cece I was sick and lie there all day instead. But if I'd done that, I would have spent the entire day thinking about Matthew and the whole *Megvéd* thing. I didn't want to think about it, not now.

I'd worry about it later.

Right now, I just wanted to get through finals and the fencing tournament. I'd have the entire Christmas break to deal with Matthew and his revelations.

Forty-five minutes later the bells began to peal, signaling the end of class. Jared hopped up and flipped the lights back on.

I blinked hard, waiting for my eyes to adjust to the room's sudden brightness.

"Okay, class," Dr. Andrulis called out. "The second half of the final is going to involve identifying twenty of the paintings we just saw. Study, why don't you?"

"I was planning to," I muttered under my breath as I reached for my bag.

"You sure you're okay?" Aidan asked, standing beside my desk now.

I glared up at him. "Ask me that one more time, and see what happens."

He held up two hands in surrender. "Got it. I think I'll just head over to the lab now."

"You do that." I stood, hiking my bag up on my shoulder. Despite my crankiness, I couldn't help but smile. "See you at dinner?"

"Do you *want* to see me at dinner?" he asked with a wince. "Because I *have* grown rather fond of my limbs."

"Hey, I'm allowed to be in a bad mood every once in a while."

He grinned down at me. "Agreed. C'mon, we better get going or you're going to be late to fencing."

I followed him out, and my mood lightened a measure. I needed to just tell him, I realized. Get it over with fast—like pulling off a Band-Aid. Still, I was hesitant. Maybe over the weekend?

We parted ways by the fountain. I took the shortcut toward the gym, up the steep staircase. At the top, I paused to catch my breath.

"There you are," a voice called out, startling me.

It was Tyler. He reached for my arm. "I've got to talk to you, Violet. *Now.*"

"Can you talk while we walk? We're going to be late," I said, shrugging off his grasp as I hurried my step.

"Forget fencing—this is important. Is there somewhere we can go, somewhere private?"

What the heck was going on? "You want to skip fencing? Are you crazy? The tournament's next Friday."

He ran a hand through his hair. It was shaking, I realized. "This is more important than a tournament. Can we at least go over to the chapel or something?"

I sighed, shaking my head. "I can't believe I'm agreeing to

this. It better be important, Tyler. Seriously. If we get busted for skipping—"

"Trust me, once you hear what I have to say, getting busted will be the least of your worries. Hurry, we can cut across here."

We veered off the path and headed through a field that sloped down toward the edge of the woods separating the campus's neatly manicured grounds from the river. It was cold; my breath made white puffs in the air as I tried to match pace with his longer stride. "Hey, could you slow down a bit?" I called out testily, my mood going downhill fast. "And where were you during art history today? We went over the slides for the final."

He paused, waiting for me to catch up. "Whatever. C'mon, let's get inside before anyone sees us."

The chapel loomed before us, its stone mass blocking out the sun. We hurried down the shadowed path and slipped inside. My breath was coming fast, a combination of exertion and nerves, as I followed him through the vestibule and down the aisle.

Tyler stopped about halfway down, leaning against a pew. "This is good," he said with a nod.

I folded my arms across my chest. "Okay, are you going to tell me what this is all about? 'Cause this secret-agent stuff is starting to freak me out."

"You might want to sit down for this," he said, gesturing toward the pew.

"I'm fine standing. Go on."

"Okay, but don't say I didn't warn you. So, you know I've been working in the lab with Aidan this week, right?"

I nodded. "Yeah, he told me you've been really helpful. Thanks for that, by the way."

He began to pace. "All this talk about a blood-borne disease seemed strange because he doesn't look all that sick to me. Just pale. Anyway, I guess I'm a bit slow, but I finally figured it out." He stopped directly in front of me, his gaze meeting mine. "You've got to get away from him, Violet. He's dangerous."

I shook my head in confusion, unable to follow the train of his ramblings. "What are you talking about, Tyler?"

He glanced back toward the vestibule, then back at me, his eyes suddenly looking a bit wild. "Dude, your boyfriend? He's a fucking *vampire*."

"That's it?" I couldn't help but laugh. "That's what you dragged me in here to tell me?"

His eyes widened a fraction. "Did you hear what I just said? He's a vampire, Violet. A vampire. They're, like, dead creatures that go around sucking people's blood, in case you didn't know."

"Yeah, I know what a vampire is." I was hedging, trying to

figure out what I was supposed to say. Obviously Aidan and Dr. Byrne were being pretty open about it, even if they didn't come right out and say the word. They must have known he'd eventually figure it out.

"So that's it?" Tyler prodded. "He's a vampire, and that's all you've got to say?"

Oh my God, how many times was he going to say the word "vampire"? "I know what he is, Ty. You don't have to keep repeating it."

"You know?" he asked, his voice laced with disbelief. "What do you mean, you know?"

"I mean I've known for a long time, since last fall. Everyone knows—Cece and Sophie, Kate and Marissa, Jack and Joshua. Even Dr. Byrne," I added, hoping I hadn't forgotten anyone. "But listen to me, you can't tell anyone else, okay?"

"Are you kidding me? The hell I can't. In case you've forgotten, a dead body turned up on campus last week. Killed by the Vampire Stalker. You think that's just a coincidence?"

I sighed. Of course—I could see why someone might make that leap of logic, if they'd just learned the truth. "Aidan had nothing to do with it. And Jenna . . . Jenna wasn't even sure it was a real vampire. She didn't scent anything out of the ordinary in the woods."

"Jenna? Jenna Holley? What does she have to do with this?"

Uh-oh. "Just . . . you know, that's her gift. Heightened sensory something or other. Oh, and she knows, too."

"What the *hell*, Violet?"

I grabbed him by one arm, annoyed now. "Listen, everyone who knows the truth—who knows Aidan—realizes that they're perfectly safe with him. He's not a threat to anyone here at Winterhaven."

"Do you want to know where I was during fifth period, Violet? I was in the lab, snooping for clues."

I rolled my eyes. "Clues to *what?*"

"To prove that your boyfriend's the Stalker, that's what. To prove that he's a murderer."

"You're wrong," I said, forcefully now. This was getting ridiculous. Tyler could say whatever he wanted to say, but I *knew* Aidan. He was *not* a murderer. "For all I know, *you're* the Stalker. The attacks started happening right after *you* showed up, didn't they?"

He narrowed his eyes. "Yeah, that's bullshit and you know it."

I shrugged. "Not any more so than you accusing Aidan. He doesn't attack innocent people, Tyler. He only feeds from criminals—dangerous criminals. And even then, he doesn't kill them, not unless they're . . . they're . . . child molesters or serial killers," I sputtered. "He just, you know, takes them temporarily out of action. Thwarts crime. Besides, he would never leave visible bite marks the way the Stalker does. That's against their code, their rules."

"Oh, they've got rules, do they? The vampires?"

"Yeah, they do," I said with a nod. "Pretty strict ones, with some scary punishments to go along with them."

He didn't look convinced. "You actually want me to believe that he's like some sort of superhero, keeping Gotham safe from dangerous criminals? Seriously?"

"Pretty much," I agreed, realizing how dumb it sounded. Still, it was the truth. "It's *not* Aidan, Tyler. I know that you don't like him, that you somehow feel threatened by him or something—your stupid little macho 'I always win' thing and all. But you can't pin this on him, and you've got to keep your mouth shut about him being a vampire. If you're really my friend, if you care about me, you've got to trust me on this. Please?"

"Oh, so now you're going to play the 'if you care about me' card? You can't have it both ways, Violet."

I shook my head, confused. "Just drop it, okay? If it'll make you feel any better, I'll talk to him. I'll . . . I don't know . . . find proof that he wasn't anywhere near Manhattan when the Stalker attacked." *Was* he in Manhattan?

Crap. Now he'd planted a seed of doubt in my mind. It was going to stay there, gnawing at my brain, until I looked into it.

"Please, Tyler? Just . . . give me till after the break, and I'll show you proof. Until then, don't say anything to anyone, okay?"

"What if someone else turns up dead? How am I supposed to live with myself, wondering if I could have stopped it? How can you?"

"Because I'm *that* sure Aidan doesn't have anything to do with it, that's how. And you should be too."

"Just because you believe that?"

I clenched my hands into fists in frustration. "Look, I've got a better idea of where he's been—and when—than anyone else does. I was probably *with* him when most of the attacks happened."

"Okay, fine," he said at last. "If you say so."

I let my breath out in a rush. "Thank you, Tyler."

Now I just had to prove to him how crazy his theory was, and fast.

Easy, right?

26 ~ Angels and Demons

I shoved aside the piece of paper I'd scribbled on—a list of the dates of the Stalker's attacks—with a heavy heart. This did *not* look good. *Crap, crap, and double crap.* It *had* to be a coincidence.

"Hey, why so glum?" Cece asked. She was sitting on her bed, knitting, a hobby she'd picked up over Thanksgiving break.

Should I tell her? A battle waged inside my head. Ultimately, the desire for reassurance won out. "Okay," I said, "I know this is going to sound *really* crazy."

"Uh-oh." She froze, her two knitting needles pointing toward the ceiling. "Last time you started off like that, you ended up telling me that Aidan was a vampire. What is it this time? Someone's a demon? A fallen angel? Oh no, it's Tyler, isn't it? I knew there was something weird with that guy."

"Are you done?" I asked, reaching down to pick up the ball of pink yarn that had rolled off the bed and was sitting by her feet.

Her mouth curved into a smile as I set the yarn back beside her. "A demon, right? 'Cause that boy sure ain't no angel."

I shot her a glare. "Seriously, Cee."

"Sorry. Go on." With a flourish, she waved one of her needles in the air. "This is going to sound really crazy, but . . ."

"But yesterday Tyler dragged me off to the chapel to talk when we were supposed to be in fencing class."

"Wait, you skipped a class? That *is* crazy. You never skip."

"He's been working in the lab with Aidan and finally managed to put two and two together," I continued, ignoring her jests. "Anyway, now he's convinced that Aidan is the Stalker."

"He's *what*?" she shrieked. Dropping the needles to the bed, she unfolded her legs and scooted to the edge of the mattress. "He actually thinks Aidan's the one who attacked all those people in Manhattan? Who killed that lady?" She shook her head. "No way. Tyler must be smoking something, 'cause that's totally whacked."

"Tell me about it," I said. Relief washed over me, her vehement denial bolstering my confidence. Tyler didn't know what he was talking about; he didn't know Aidan like we did.

"The thing is"—I glanced down at the list of dates and my courage plummeted—"I checked online to see when the attacks happened." I paused, taking a deep breath before continuing. "And one of them was the night before Aidan turned up down by the river. You know, when he got sick. And didn't remember what happened the night before."

"Coincidence," Cece said with a shrug. "Has to be, right?"

"Right. Only . . ." I trailed off, shaking my head.

Cece's brow furrowed. "Only what? You don't really think he had anything to do with it? I mean, c'mon, this is Aidan we're talking about. He's one of the good guys. Even if he is . . . you know, a blood-sucking vampire. Wait, he really *does* suck blood, right?"

"Yeah, but he isn't a murderer. Besides, he would never flout the rules the way the Stalker does, leaving visible bite marks and all that."

"Well, there you have it," she said with a shrug. "Told you."

Oh, man . . . I was going to *kill* Tyler for putting this stupid idea into my head. "But on some of these dates—well, *all* of them, really—I'm not sure where Aidan was at the time. He wasn't with me. And the last one, when the woman was killed? That happened over Thanksgiving break. He'd injected himself with the serum then."

"Okay, so? I'm not following your logic here. What does the serum have to do with it?"

"It's just that he's had these really bad reactions to the serum, that's all," I said. "I wish I had a list of dates of when he injected it. I could compare *that* list to this one, and see if there's any overlap."

Cece shook her head. "Seriously, I'm still not following you."

"I don't know, Cee." I threw my hands up in frustration. "I guess I was just hoping that I'd look at these dates and be able to say, 'Nope, he was with me then. Couldn't have been him.' But I can't."

And then I saw it—the flicker of doubt that crossed her features. "Okay," she conceded with a sigh. "I guess I can see how Tyler could leap to his crazy-ass conclusion. But you know what? I don't believe it. These dates or whatever, it's just a circumstantial evidence kind of thing, you know?"

I nodded.

"And even this whole serum thing—I mean, he's injected it a lot this semester, hasn't he?"

Again, I nodded.

"So statistically there's a good chance that some of the dates are going to overlap anyway, right?"

"Right. God, I love you, Cee." I hurried over to her and

gave her a hug. "I knew you'd talk me down. So, what do we do now?"

She shook her head. "I dunno. Can you talk him out of injecting it for a little while? You know, like a control period?"

"That's a great idea! Only"—I shook my head—"he's not likely to agree to it. He thinks he's *so* close to perfecting it. I swear, he's in the lab working every spare minute these days. Matthew has really helped him with a breakthrough."

Matthew. My Megvéd.

"Okay, what's going on in that head of yours, Violet? You just went ten shades of pale."

"You want to hear more crazy?" I offered, deciding I might as well get it all out there.

So I told her about the whole *Megvéd* thing. Okay, technically, I read it to her, from the translated page.

She just sat there, blinking, absorbing it.

"And then a few days ago, when I had that vision that freaked me out? I had a vision where I saw myself kill Aidan."

"Not again!" Cece shivered. "Please tell me there aren't more Propagators on their way here."

I shook my head. "No, it was nothing like last time. All I saw really was the two of us—just me and Aidan—and he was begging me to do something. The same old 'you know how; it's got to go through the heart' crap. I was crying, telling him no, but eventually I felt myself raise my arm and bring it down, right on his chest."

"Your stake?"

"I guess it was my stake. I wasn't looking, but I felt something smooth in my hand. Anyway, it wasn't much and I didn't really get any details, so I went to see Matthew, to have him talk me through a replay."

"Yeah? I can't believe you didn't tell me about the vision, by the way. I mean, I can understand that you didn't want to alarm everyone else, but still."

"I was going to tell you, I swear. You know, after I replayed it. But anyway, Matthew somehow talked me into telling him about the vision, and then he was all like, 'Oh, don't worry about. It's your destiny.' So I totally freaked."

"He knew? About the *Sâbbat* stuff?"

I nodded. "And then he started rolling up his sleeve. Remember that tattoo I told you about? The dagger with the *M*?"

Her eyes grew as wide as saucers, her mouth forming an O of surprise. "No. Freaking. Way."

"Yup. Claims he's a *Megvéd*, and I guess that means he's mine, since as far as I know there aren't any other *Sâbbats* around here."

"Well, what else did he say?" she prodded, looking dumbstruck.

"Nothing," I said with a shrug. "I didn't stick around long enough for him to tell me anything else. I basically ran to the bathroom and puked, and I haven't spoken with him since."

"Wow. This is just un-freaking-believable. You and Dr. Hottie—"

"There is *no* me and Dr. Hottie," I interrupted. "Let's get that straight—I don't care what the stupid legend says." I dropped my head, cradling it with my hands.

Just as I suspected. If Cece's thoughts went right to that creepy "mate" thing, then Aidan's definitely would too. And how would he react to Matthew as the "mate" in question? *Probably not as well as Cece did*, I thought, waiting for her to break out into a rousing chorus of "Sitting in a Tree."

"I wish I wasn't going to New Orleans for break," she said, glancing over at the calendar on the wall. "I feel so bad leaving you to deal with all this. You really should talk to Matthew— Dr. Byrne, I mean. Whatever! Seriously," she added in response to my glare. "'Cause if what that book said is true, it's kind of his job to look out for you, right?"

"Maybe," I hedged.

"Just think about it, okay?" She stood and stretched, reaching her hands up toward the ceiling. "Man, I'm stiff. You want to go get some coffee? I don't know about you, but I've got to study."

"Yeah, me too. Coffee sounds good; it's going to be a long night." A long week and a half, actually.

And then . . . break.

Till then, I only had to win the fencing tournament, ace my finals, prevent my stepmother from getting a fatal bee sting, deal with Tyler's insistence that my boyfriend was the murderous Stalker, and . . . oh, yeah, face the possibility that one of my teachers was somehow fated to be my protector and mate.

Yeah, should be fun.

"You've been avoiding me," Aidan said, wrapping his arms around me from behind. His lips found my neck, and I shuddered.

Stupid Tyler.

I looked into my mail cubby. Empty. I wasn't even sure why I bothered checking anymore. "Just busy studying for finals, that's all. Besides, you barely left the lab all weekend." I turned to face him. "How'd it go?"

"Really well, even though your little friend ditched us. What's up with him? I swear, every time I see the little punk he looks like he wants to run me through. More so than before, I should say."

If he only knew the half of it. "He figured out what you're working on. I guess he doesn't much like vampires. Especially when there's a murderer running around here that they're calling the Vampire Stalker."

"Oh, I see. It figures he'd think me capable of something like that. Maybe he'll report me to Mrs. Girard," he mused. "That should be interesting. What are you doing after dinner?"

"The usual—staying in." It's not like we had much choice anymore. Gone were the days of hanging out with friends at the café and laughing over coffee after the sun had set. Anyway, finals started tomorrow and I had some last-minute cramming to do after my usual Sunday night phone calls to Patsy and Gran.

"Do you need any help with calculus?"

I shook my head. "Nah, Sophie's been working with me. I'm more worried about the French exam."

"Then let's work on it," he offered. Because he spoke French fluently, of course. "Here, after dinner."

"Not till after study hour is over and the underclassmen vacate. Oh, and Cece, too; I promised her we'd study together."

"Of course. I'll quiz you both." He looked around the mostly empty lounge. "Where is everybody now?"

"I don't know—at the movie, maybe? Marissa's probably somewhere with Max. I had practice all day, so I haven't seen anyone since breakfast."

"Except for Tyler, of course." A note of jealousy had crept into his voice.

"Yeah, except for him," I muttered. "I can't get away from him."

"Why do I get the feeling that he's just skulking around, waiting for me to screw up?" he asked, his jaw tense. "And when I do, he's going to swoop in and make his move."

"I don't know, but I kind of like it when you get all jealous like this. It's just so . . . human."

The effects of the serum, he claimed. It hadn't cured him, not yet, but it made him as close to human as he'd been in a century. Which was evidence that he wasn't the Stalker, as far as I was concerned. Maybe last year—when he'd go all vampiric on me while we were making out—maybe then I could have made the mental leap to Aidan-the-potential-killer. But not now, not when he seemed like a normal, human guy, for the most part. Now, it was impossible to believe.

Which is why I let him draw me close and kiss me this time.

"If a teacher comes in and sees us, we're busted," I murmured, drawing away. After all, there *were* some pretty strict PDA rules at Winterhaven, despite its progressivism.

"Then let's go somewhere we can be alone."

Oh, how I wanted to. I glanced down at my watch and reluctantly shook my head. "I can't. Not now; I'm supposed to meet everyone for dinner in fifteen minutes."

"Skip dinner," he urged, his lips brushing the spot where my chin curved down toward my throat.

As if on cue, my stomach growled loudly. "Unlike you, some of us *need* to eat," I reminded him. "Maybe later? After we're done studying?"

"How? With curfew, I mean. There's nowhere we can go to be alone, not if we're following the rules. Unless . . ." He had a wicked gleam in his eyes now.

"Unless what?" My heart accelerated, my skin flushing hotly in anticipation.

"Unless we do a jailbreak. After we're done studying, I'll come to your room and take you somewhere—anywhere you want to go. We could even go off campus; distance doesn't matter. I can have you back in minutes, if need be. Cece will have to be our lookout, that's all."

"Are you crazy?"

"About you, yes. It's been *so* long since we've been alone, Vi. Just think about it, okay? You don't have to decide now; you can let me know when we're done studying."

Which is how I found myself sitting on my bed several hours later waiting for him to come get me.

"Are you sure about this, Violet?" Cece asked, pacing back and forth in front of the door. "I just don't know, not after what you told me about the Stalker stuff."

"But you agreed with me that there's no way Aidan did it," I argued.

"I know, but still." She was wringing her hands now. "Where is he taking you?"

"I don't know. The chapel, maybe? I won't be out late, though, not with finals this week."

"I'm going to be a nervous wreck. Ugh, is this what parenting is going to feel like?"

I had to laugh at that. "Yeah, probably so. Hey, you haven't commented on my outfit yet. Do I look okay?"

I'd changed after our study session—out of my comfy jeans and sweater and into a miniskirt, tank top, thigh-high socks, and boots. I figured, why not? It's not like we'd be spending any time outside in the cold—traveling with Aidan from place to place was virtually instantaneous.

Besides, it had been a long time since we'd actually been alone together on anything resembling a date. I wanted to look cute.

"You changed into something easy-access, didn't you?" Cece's eyes narrowed as she took in my outfit.

Okay, so what if I had? Something about his kiss earlier had stoked a fire inside me, and I hadn't been able to stop thinking about him since. But I didn't want to admit it, not even to Cece.

Luckily, I was saved by Aidan's sudden appearance in the room.

"Hey," he said, ignoring Cece's gasp of surprise. "You ready?"

I just nodded, smoothing down my skirt with shaking hands.

He closed the distance between us in two easy strides, holding out a hand to me.

I took it, glancing back over my shoulder at Cece, who still stood there gaping. "Thanks, Cee," I said to her. "I've got my cell if you need to reach me, okay?"

"Okay," she answered, holding up her own cell phone. "Same here." With knitted brows, she turned toward the still-closed door, a look of pure wonderment on her face.

I could only imagine the look of surprise on her face when she turned around again and found us both gone.

27 ~ A Nip Here, a Tuck There

He took me to the chapel. We hadn't been in ages—not up to the loft, at least. Clearly, he'd come up beforehand and set everything up. Worn velvet blankets covered the floor, along with a half-dozen tasseled throw pillows. Colorful bunches of hothouse flowers were scattered about, scenting the air, which was warmed by a space heater in the corner. Above us tiny white twinkle lights were wound around the wooden rafters, and votives in paper bags lined the perimeter of the space, casting flickering light across Aidan's face as he sat facing me.

It felt as if we were all alone in our own tropical paradise, rather than up in a dusty loft on a cold December night. "How did you get this all set up so fast?" I asked, shaking my head in amazement. "I mean, the flowers and everything. You must have had to go into the city for them."

He glanced around the space. "You like it? I did most of it while you were at dinner."

"Before I'd even agreed to come? Wow, that was awfully confident of you," I said with a laugh.

His smiled widened into a grin. "Oh, that kiss in the lounge was answer enough. I knew you'd say yes."

I raised my brows. "Cocky much?"

He reached for my hand and placed it on his chest, directly over his heart. "I can always trust you to keep my ego in check."

Beneath my palm, his heart was racing, its rhythm matching mine. "I can't stay long," I said, almost breathless now. "But thank you. This is beautiful; it's just what I needed."

"Good." His head bent down toward mine, his lips just barely grazing my mouth. "I know I haven't been around much this semester. I just wanted to somehow make it up to you, to show you how much I've missed you."

I grabbed a fistful of his shirt, drawing him closer. "You've got the whole break to do that. Patsy won't be back till Christmas Eve, you know. That means we'll have almost a full week, all alone."

His mouth widened into a smile. "Trevors can do some

shopping, then. He'll be happy to cook for you."

"Sounds good. I loved that chicken thing he made last year. You know, with the asparagus and artichoke hearts?" My mouth watered at the memory.

"The capons? I'll tell him—he has to go to a special boutique butcher for those. Do you want to stay at my house? He can make up the rose room for you."

"I probably shouldn't. For all I know, Patsy's asked the doorman to spy on me. Which means you can't stay at my place, either."

He smiled wryly. "Just for the record, Vi, I can get you in and out of either place without the doorman noticing. Remember?"

I released his shirt, reclining back on my elbows. "Oh, yeah. Right." *Well, duh.*

"We don't have to decide now," he said, brushing my hair back from my forehead. "Let's get through finals first."

"And my tournament," I added.

"Right. And I've still got a lot of work to do between now and then. Byrne suggested something new today; we're going to work on it some this week, and then I'll give it a try over the weekend."

I shook my head, a feeling of unease settling into the pit of my stomach. I wanted to trust Matthew, but the fact that he was a *Megvéd* cast a whole new level of suspicion on him. Was he really as eager to help Aidan as he claimed?

I swallowed hard, forcing aside my doubts. "Not this weekend. Please? It's the beginning of break."

"Yes, perfect timing if it works."

I sat up sharply. "C'mon, you've got to promise me, Aidan. No tries with the serum till break's over. We're supposed to stick together, remember? I don't want you laid up in bed, all messed up from another bad reaction."

His jaw was set with determination. "I won't be. Not this time."

"You can't guarantee that, and I'm not willing to take the risk. Look, I don't ask all that much of you. I pretty much let you do your own thing and show up whenever it's convenient for you. You've got to give me this one. I've earned it."

"You feel that strongly about it?" he asked, his eyes troubled now.

"Yes. I mean, look, you've already been a vampire for more than a century. What's another two weeks?"

"Okay, then," he conceded. "Unless—"

"Unless nothing," I interrupted, shaking my head. "Got it?"

"Fine. Now that that's out of the way . . ." He leaned into me, pushing me down, pressing me back against the pillows. "You said something about not being able to stay long?"

"Right," I murmured. "School night and all that. Plus we're breaking curfew."

He combed his fingers through my hair. "Do you want me to take you back now?"

I let out my breath in a rush. "No way."

His mouth covered mine, his hands on either side of my rib cage now.

Almost involuntarily, I raised up, arching myself against him as he deepened the kiss. It felt as if little sparks of electricity were racing across my skin, down my spine, all the way to my toes. His fingers clutched at the thin fabric of my tank top, his knuckles rough against the sensitive skin at my waist.

I kissed him greedily, hungrily, whispering his name each time his lips left mine.

"Oh God, Violet," he said hoarsely. "I don't know if I can stop."

"Then don't, not yet." I hooked one leg around his hips, trapping him against me.

His hands were under my top now, his fingers—so, so cold—skimming my belly, drawing gooseflesh in their wake. My skirt rode up; my thigh-high socks slipped down to my knees. And I didn't care, not even when his fingers found the bottom edge of my bra.

With a groan, I tipped my head to one side, offering him

my neck. I couldn't help it; I craved it with an inexplicable desperation. As if sensing my need, his lips left my mouth and slid down the column of my neck, his breath far warmer than his flesh. The electric current between us crackled, every cell in my body humming with it as his mouth found my throat.

And there it was, at last—a piercing pinch, just below my left ear. I cried out, even as the twinge was immediately replaced by a soothing warmth that seemed to fill my veins all at once, sending waves of pleasure across every inch of my body.

Oh no. Dazedly, I tried to call out his name, but all that came out was a strangled sound. Somehow I managed to get my hands between our bodies, my palms flat against his chest as I pushed at him with all my might.

In a matter of seconds, he had flung himself across the room. Okay, not just across the room, but all the way up into the rafters.

Oh my freaking God.

I sat up in a panic, reaching a trembling hand to my neck. It was warm and sticky, slightly wet. *No. Just . . . no.* I stared in utter disbelief at the crimson smudge staining my fingers.

Swallowing hard, I wiped it off on my skirt. And then I looked up, my eyes straining to find him above the twinkling lights in the rafters. "Aidan?"

No reply.

"Answer me, Aidan. I need you to stop the bleeding."

"I can't, not yet," came his disembodied voice.

"You're . . . hungry?" I ventured, wondering just how long it would take me to get down those stairs and out of the chapel if I didn't stop to put my boots on first.

He didn't reply, and for a moment I wondered if he'd left. But then I heard something that sounded like a ragged sob.

I sat up on my knees. "It's okay, Aidan. You didn't hurt me. Really, I'm fine." I put my hand back up to my neck and brought it away again. "Look, it's not even bleeding anymore. You barely broke the skin, just scratched it, really." God, I hoped I was right.

Several minutes passed in silence. My heart was beating loudly, a deafening din in my ears as I waited, waited.

And then he was beside me, his face filled with anguish. "How bad is it?"

I pushed aside my hair, exposing my neck. "See? It's nothing."

He inhaled sharply. "Don't lessen what I've done, just to protect me, Violet. Dear God, I actually bit you." His voice was laced with a mixture of horror and disbelief.

"It's fine," I said. "Seriously, I don't even feel it."

He shook his head. "It's not fine. It will *never* be fine."

He was starting to panic, I realized. I needed to bring him

down a notch, to reassure him that he hadn't committed some unforgivable crime. "I really think it's just a scratch," I insisted, my voice slightly wobbly.

"It's not a scratch." He raked a hand through his hair, his eyes slightly wild now. "How did this happen? I was kissing you, that's all, and the next thing I remember is you shoving me away!"

I *had* to ask. "You didn't inject the serum this weekend, did you?"

"No, and I took the elixir just this morning, which should have prevented this. But . . . I don't know, we've made some changes to it, something that follows the same protocol as the changes we've made to the serum."

A frisson of fear shot through me. Could that explain it? And if it did . . .

No, I didn't want to think about the implications. "Can you fix it now?" I asked instead, forcing my voice to steady. "It's getting late, and I can't go back to the dorm with two puncture marks on my neck."

"There's . . . it's just one. But yeah, let me fix it." He reached for my neck, then hesitated, his eyes suddenly blank now. "I won't hurt you, I swear."

"I know you won't." I tipped my head to one side and waited.

One lick, then two. Again, waves of pleasure seemed to wash over me. There was something in his saliva, something that did far more than anesthetize a wound, I realized. I couldn't describe it, not exactly, but it was . . . pleasant. More than pleasant. Not exactly like sexual pleasure—at least, I didn't think so. But probably pretty similar.

"There." He swallowed hard. "It's gone."

"Thanks." I reached up to feel it, my fingertips searching for some indication of where the wound had been. There was nothing—my skin was perfectly smooth now. My gaze met his. "Wow, that's amazing."

"I am so sorry, Violet. Sorrier than I've ever been about anything in all the years I've walked the earth."

Wow, that was a lot of sorry. "Please tell me you're not going to freak out about this. We'll be more careful from now on, that's all, okay? It's not that big a deal."

"How can you even say that?" He sounded angry now. "It's an enormous deal. A monumental one. I've done something so terrible, so unspeakable . . ." He trailed off, shaking his head. "And I can't undo it, no matter how badly I want to."

"Will you stop blaming yourself? You're a vampire, okay? It's just your nature. If I'm stupid enough to put myself in situations like this, then I bear as much responsibility as you, right?"

"Wrong," he said, his voice clipped. "Completely, unequivocally wrong. It's my responsibility to keep people safe from me, and I failed you in the most spectacular fashion possible." As it always did when his emotions ran high, his British accent became far more apparent than usual. His Lord Brompton voice, I liked to call it. It was never a good sign when he slipped into it. It usually meant there was no arguing with him.

The campus bells began to peal, marking the hour.

"I'll take you back," he said. One by one, the candles extinguished themselves. The space heater hissed as it shut down. Above us, the twinkle lights flickered out. Only the light of the moon illuminated the loft as Aidan held out a hand to me.

I took his hand with a sigh. *Well, that went badly.*

"Ready?" he asked.

"Ready." I squeezed my eyes shut and braced for the weird sensations.

In a matter of seconds, I was back in my dorm room. Cece stood by her bed in her pink robe and bunny slippers, her mouth open in surprise.

And Aidan? He was gone.

28 ~ The Gloaming

Aidan really *was* gone. He missed all his finals and didn't even show up for the tournament on Friday night. Tyler claimed to have seen him once in the lab with Matthew, so I supposed he was still around somewhere. But he wasn't going to class and he wasn't responding to me telepathically.

Somehow, I managed to get through my finals. I was pretty sure I'd aced them—but then, I'd been studying like crazy for weeks. With a sigh, I ran a finger over the new golden trophy sitting in front of me on my desk. I'd done well in the tournament, retaining my title as All-Ivy girls' champion.

I knew Aidan was scared; I knew he was totally freaked out

and hating himself right now. He needed time, that's all. A few days to sort things out in his head. I would give him that. But I'd promised Mrs. Girard that we'd stick together over break. He'd just have to get over it, and quickly. School got out on Monday at noon, and when it did, I was going to find him, and he was going to talk to me.

Cece could track him down, astrally speaking. And she would, if I asked her to. I wasn't going to let him brood, hating himself, forever.

Beside me, my cell rang. *Patsy.* With a sigh, I connected the call. "Hey, you all packed and ready to go?" I asked. Her flight to the Caribbean left first thing in the morning.

"I think so. I just feel terrible, though, leaving you. Are you sure you're going to be okay?"

"I'm going to be fine." *And much better with you far away while I sort things out with Aidan.* "You've packed your EpiPens?"

"Yes, I've got them." I could hear the frustration in her voice. "All six of them."

"One in each bag? And one in with your golf clubs, just in case?"

"Yes, and yes. Paul even bought himself this little clip-on pouch, so that he can carry one around for me, too. Seriously, though, when did you become such a worrywart?"

Gee, maybe when terrorists executed my father and I had the pleasure of seeing it happen before it actually did? "I don't know," I said instead. "But I wish you'd take it more seriously. You're all I've got, you know." My eyes were suddenly damp.

I heard her sniffle. "I know, hon. I'm sorry. Seriously, just say the word and I'll tell Paul I've changed my mind."

"No, I want you to go. I want you to have fun with Paul. He sounds like a really nice guy, and you deserve this. Okay?"

"Okay." She was crying now. "I know I don't call or e-mail enough. But I love you, Violet, as if you were my own flesh and blood."

"I know you do," I said hoarsely. "And I love you, too."

"Oh my God, listen to us." She laughed, a snuffling noise. "I swear, you'd think I was going away for good instead of just eight days."

My blood turned cold. What if this was it; what if I never saw her again? "Just promise me that you'll be careful—that you'll make sure you have an EpiPen with you all the time. Especially on the golf course," I added. "I'll text you and remind you, okay?"

"Okay, if it'll make you feel better."

"It'll definitely make me feel better." What was I going to do? It's not like I could follow the woman around for the rest of her life, making sure she did what she was supposed to do—what my visions told me she needed to do.

"I'm glad you suggested I tell Paul. If I'm going to be spending a lot of time with him, he needs to know what to do if I'm stung. Anyway"—she sighed loudly—"I should let you go."

I swallowed the lump in my throat. "Have fun, and don't worry about me. I'll be fine, I promise."

"I know you will, sweetie. Okay, then. Bye."

"Bye." I hit the end button and set the phone back on my desk, plugging it back into the charger that attached to my laptop. Only then did I realize that she hadn't even asked me about the tournament—the one she'd missed so that she could stay home and pack for her trip.

I shook my head in amazement. I'd never understand her, not really. But that didn't change the fact that she was the closest thing I had to a parent, and as selfish and self-absorbed as she was, I knew that she *did* love me.

What will I do if I lose her, too?

Forcing away the thought, I reached for a tissue and blew my nose. I needed to go and find my friends. Otherwise, I was just going to sit here worrying—about Aidan, about Patsy. Definitely *not* the healthy choice, mentally speaking.

But before I had a chance to go looking for them, they found me. At least, Kate and Sophie did. The door was flung open, seemingly on its own, just seconds before the two of them strode in. "Guess who's looking for you?" Kate called out in an annoying singsong voice.

"Would it kill you to knock?" I muttered.

"We were in a hurry," she said with a shrug. "After all, we've got an important message to convey from none other than Dr. Hottie."

Uh-oh. I had skipped our coaching session this morning. I kind of figured he'd gotten the message that I didn't want to meet with him anymore after I'd stormed out of our last session. Guess not.

"We've got"—she nudged Sophie in the ribs, and Sophie held up a piece of paper—"his cell number. Which we're supposed to give to you, and tell you to call."

"When you're ready to talk," Sophie added, handing me the paper.

I took it, folding it into fourths before tossing it onto my desk. "Is that all, Tweedledee and Tweedledum?"

Kate shrugged. "I don't know. Can we stand around and listen while you talk to him?"

I shook my head. "I'm not calling him now."

"Maybe later, then?" Sophie suggested.

"Weren't you the one who was all like, 'Eww, he's a teacher'?" I asked her, waving my hands in the air for emphasis.

She shrugged. "Maybe. He's still hotness personified."

"Yeah, *Byrne*-ing hot," Kate added.

I leveled them a glare. "You finished?"

Sophie nodded, looking solemn. "What's the deal with Aidan? Is he still MIA?"

"Yep, and I'm going to kill him when he shows up again." I glanced over at my cell, hoping to find that I'd missed a call or a text. There was nothing.

Kate sat down on Cece's bed. "Uh-oh, someone better hide her stake. Otherwise, there might be a case of vampiricide. How's that for a word?"

"Very impressive," I said. "Your parents should be proud."

Kate reached down to zip up her hoodie, a pale blue the exact same shade as her eyes. "It's cold in here," she said with a sigh. "And I'm bored. I don't understand why they insist on keeping us here through the weekend. The final assembly is always so lame."

Sophie nodded. "Yeah, but I kind of like that we have a couple of days here to decompress after finals. You know, to hang out with our friends. I'd just be sitting around at home, doing nothing."

"Yeah, I guess," Kate conceded. "So, are you gonna tell me what's up with you and Tyler?"

That suspicious tone had crept into her voice again. "There's nothing up with me and Tyler. Why?"

"I don't know." She shrugged, fiddling with the hem of one sleeve. "It's just that the two of you were acting all weird at the tournament last night. Did he even congratulate you? It looked like he just took his trophy and stalked off."

"His *second*-place trophy," I said, unable to hide my glee. Some kid from Riverdale took first. Whoever he was, I wanted to hug him.

Kate winced. "Yeah, he's pretty upset about that, by the way."

I couldn't stanch my curiosity. "Are you and Tyler still . . . you know, doing whatever it is you're doing together?" I wasn't quite sure what they were calling it at this point.

"That's an awfully personal question, isn't it?" she asked coyly. "I don't hear you dishing up particulars about you and Aidan."

"You never had any problem giving us the play-by-play with Jack," Sophie argued. "Even if we didn't want to hear it."

"Oh, you know you wanted to hear it." Kate's eyes were twinkling with mischief now. "Every naughty detail."

"You *do* realize that you sound just like him, don't you?" I said with a groan.

And then it hit me—she and Tyler really *were* perfect for each other. I don't know why I hadn't recognized it before now. Maybe she didn't want to dish about the details because she really *did* like him. Maybe even more than she'd liked Jack.

"Hey, you guys want to go to the café?" Sophie asked, hooking a thumb toward the door. "Cece's headed over there after her student council meeting, and I think Marissa's already there with Max."

Kate nodded. "I'm in."

I reached for my sweater. "Yeah, me too." I wasn't going to let Aidan's disappearance ruin this time with my friends.

After all, I had the entire break to work things out with him. And we *would* work things out; I was sure of it.

Two days later, I took one last look around my room, making sure I wasn't forgetting anything. Patsy had arranged for a car service to pick me up—it should be out front any minute now. My big rolling suitcase stood by the door, my coat draped over it. My bag and laptop case sat beside it.

My phone. I'd left it sitting on my desk, just in case Aidan tried to call. I hurried over and grabbed it, pausing when I noticed a folded square of paper shoved into the desk's corner.

I picked it up and unfolded it, smoothing out the creases. It was a phone number scrawled in an unfamiliar hand, with the word "Matthew" beneath it.

His cell number, of course. I wasn't planning on calling him, but I shoved it into my jeans pocket anyway.

It took me a good quarter hour to maneuver my suitcase through the corridors and down the curved marble staircase that led to the admin building. I waved good-bye to the statue of Washington Irving in the rotunda as I passed by, and awkwardly rolled my bag through the double doors that led outside.

I paused, sweaty now. The sun had just set, the sky a pale silvery gray tinged with orangey pink. The gloaming, Aidan called this time of day.

A cold breeze blew through the valley, lifting my hair and cooling my overheated skin. Unzipping my coat, I scanned the drive below, looking for my ride. There were a few cars lined up in the gravel drive—mostly SUVs and minivans. Family cars. I was looking for a Town Car, the vehicle of choice for the cast-off kid.

The driver was running late, I guessed.

The campus had pretty much emptied since the all-school assembly had ended at noon. I'd taken the afternoon to pack, telling my friends good-bye one by one as their families arrived to retrieve them. I wasn't in any rush. Unlike them, I was going home to an empty apartment.

Tomorrow I'd find Aidan and get him to talk, convince him

that I was none the worse for wear following the "nip incident," as I was now calling it—in my mind, at least.

But tonight . . . tonight I just wanted to curl up with a good book and some Chinese takeout, maybe take a hot bath, and go to bed early. Actually, that sounded perfect.

"Hey, Violet," a familiar male voice called out. I looked over to see Tyler jogging toward me. "What are you still doing here?" he asked.

"I could ask the same of you," I countered.

"My mom got the pickup time confused. She's on her way now. What about you? Where's Patsy? She wasn't at the tournament Friday night, was she?"

"She's out of town." I avoided the question, since Patsy hadn't actually left till Sunday, but it was close enough. "I'm waiting for a car service."

He looked over his shoulder, scanning the drive. "Not here yet, I guess." For a moment, neither of us spoke. He scratched one cheek; I scuffed the toe of my right boot on the stone steps. Above us, a raven arced across the sky, its wings beating loudly in the quiet stillness of dusk.

"So," Tyler said at last, breaking the uncomfortable silence. "You got any big plans over the break?"

I shook my head. "Just hanging out. How 'bout you?"

"We're flying to Austin on Friday."

"Oh. Well, have fun." This was *so* awkward.

Just then, a sleek black limo pulled up. A placard in its side window had "McKenna" written in black Sharpie. Wow, either Patsy was feeling *really* guilty about leaving me or there had been a mix-up at the car company.

"Someone's traveling in style," Tyler said with a grin. "Here, let me help you with your stuff." He reached for my rolling suitcase and started bouncing it down the steps.

"Thanks." I hefted my remaining bags up on my shoulder and followed him toward the waiting car.

A minute or two later, all my stuff was stowed. The driver had retreated to his seat up front, offering Tyler and me privacy, I guess.

Tyler stood by the open door, waiting to help me inside.

"Well, thanks again," I said lamely. "Have a great trip, okay? I know it's going to be hard . . . you know, without your dad and all. If you need to call . . ." I trailed off, feeling stupid.

"Thanks, Violet," he said softly, reaching out to wrap me in a hug. "I really do appreciate it."

I nodded, my cheek pressed against his chest.

"Just be careful, okay?" There it was—the elephant in the room.

"I will, I swear. Trust me, there's nothing to worry about."

"Yeah, uh-huh," he muttered as I extricated myself from his

embrace and slipped inside, settling against the limo's smooth leather interior.

He reached for the door. "See ya, Vi," he said, offering me a salute with his free hand.

"See ya, Ty," I echoed as the door slammed shut.

As crazy as it sounded, I was going to miss him.

29 ~ Broken

Forty-five minutes later, we were sitting in snarled crosstown traffic, going nowhere fast.

The window separating me from the driver slid down. "Sorry about the delay, Miss McKenna. Apparently the president's in town."

"Hey, it's not your fault," I called back. And here I thought I'd been smart, avoiding rush hour.

From the depths of my bag, my cell phone rang. *Whitney's ring.* I dug around for it as the glass divider slid shut.

"Hey, what's up?" I said, shoving the headset's earbuds into my ears.

"Where are you?" she asked, sounding impatient.

"On my way home—I mean, to Patsy's apartment. Stuck in traffic. Why?"

"Oh, no reason. Wait, never mind, I can't hold it in any longer." She sounded all excited now.

"Hold *what* in?"

"Guess where I am!" She sounded like a kid on Christmas morning. Wherever she was, it must be somewhere good.

"I don't know, where?" I played along, laughing.

"Here's a hint: Park Avenue."

I sat up straight in my seat. "Wait, what?"

"I'm at Patsy's place! Waiting for *you*—you were supposed to be here thirty minutes ago!"

"Oh my God, what? Are you kidding?"

"Nope. It was supposed to be a surprise. I've got an audition at Juilliard this week. I flew into Newark this afternoon, and Patsy arranged to have me picked up. The driver was holding a sign with my name on it and everything!" She paused for a breath. "Anyway, Patsy left keys for me with the doorman, and I've just been sitting around, waiting for you!"

I was smiling from ear to ear now. "Wow, this is so cool! How long are you staying?"

"Not long, just till Friday. My audition's on Wednesday. I promised my parents you'd come with me. They're totally freaked out about me walking the streets of New York by myself.

You know, with the Stalker on the loose. I didn't tell them that Patsy was going to be out of town."

"Good call," I said, nodding. There was an uncomfortable feeling in my gut, though. Probably because she'd mentioned the Stalker, I mused.

"Anyway, I hope I can meet some of your friends while I'm here. The girl who can move stuff with her mind and the one who can leave her body and all that."

I laughed at her descriptions of Kate and Cece, relieved that it was all out in the open now.

"And I'm dying to meet Aidan," she added. "Just a little worried that he'll read my mind."

"Don't worry, I'll make him promise to behave." My call waiting beeped, and I glanced down at my phone's screen. It displayed an unfamiliar Manhattan number.

"Hey, Whit, can you hold on a sec? I've got another call."

"Sure, I'm not going anywhere. Just waiting on you."

"Okay, I'll be right back." I hit the button to switch calls. "Hello?"

"Oh, I'm so glad I reached you, Miss McKenna. This is Trevors, by the way," he added unnecessarily. I'd recognized his voice right away. "Are you at home?"

"No, I'm in a car headed there now. Is everything okay?"

"I'm . . . not certain," he answered hesitantly. "I think we need to sit down and talk, but until then . . . well, right now I must insist that you do me a favor and stay away from Aidan for the time being. Until sunrise, at least. I don't have time to explain at present, but I think he might be headed to your home. Is there anywhere else you can go, somewhere you can stay tonight?"

"Not really. I've got company, and—" Again, my call waiting beeped. I looked down at the screen with a scowl. Whitney. She must have accidentally hung up and then called me back. "Wait, can you hold on, Trevors?"

"Of course," he said.

I connected the call with Whitney. "Hey, what happened? Where'd you go?"

"Sorry. There's a weird buzzing sound in the apartment. Do you hear it? It's really loud."

I heard it then, in the background. "That's the intercom," I told her. "Over by the door. Press the button—it's just the doorman."

"Oh, okay. Hold on a sec." I could hear her shuffling across the room. "Hello?" Her voice sounded far away now, as if she'd set down her phone. "Really? No, that's fine. Go ahead and send him up."

Him? My stomach did an uncomfortable flip, my pulse racing dangerously fast.

"Whitney?" I called out, yelling into the phone now. "What's going on?"

I heard a clunk, and then she was back on the line. "Sorry, I dropped my cell. Anyway, you're not going to believe this, but Aidan's here. I told the doorman to send him right up."

It was wintertime; Whitney was there at Patsy's apartment.

Oh God, no. Please. I took several deep, gulping breaths. "Whit, I know this sounds crazy, but what are you wearing right now?"

"What am I wearing? What difference does it—"

"Just answer, okay?" *Please don't say a pink sweater and jeans. Please, please, please.*

"A pink sweater and jeans. Why?"

My stomach dropped. *No.* This wasn't happening—it *couldn't* be. With a horrible sense of clarity, I knew that the dream must have been a vision, after all. Even if I was wrong, too much was at stake to risk it.

And then I remembered Trevors on the other line. Trevors, telling me to stay away from Aidan tonight. He was warning me; he must have known something was wrong, that Aidan was coming to find me. Instead, he was going to find Whitney there, all alone . . .

Holy crap. My hands were shaking so badly now that I nearly dropped my phone; one of the earbuds slipped out of my ear and it took me several tries to shove it back in.

I took a deep breath, trying to calm myself. I had to do something. Now, for God's sake!

"Whitney, listen to me," I said, trying unsuccessfully to keep the hysteria out of my voice. "This is important, okay? Get out of the apartment. I can't explain it, not now, but Aidan . . ." I shook my head. "You've got to get out of there. Don't worry about locking up—just leave. Get downstairs and wait with the doorman."

Would she be safe there? I didn't know, but I had to chance it.

"What are you talking about?" she asked, sounding incredulous. "It's only Aidan. You know, your boyfriend?"

"Just go, Whitney. Now! I'll explain later. Seriously, this is life or death, okay? I'll be there as fast as I can!"

"Are you crazy, Violet? I'm not—"

"Go, Whitney." I was crying now. This was my fault—all my fault. "Please!"

"Fine! You're scaring me, you know."

I heard the door slam, heard the elevator ping.

And then I realized what I'd done. "Wait, don't go near the park!" I screamed.

There was a beep on my phone as it dropped the call. Which meant she was in the elevator now, stabbing at that *L* button, her hair slipping from its ponytail, just as I'd seen.

Damn it, I should have told her to stay *inside* the apartment. Stupid, stupid. But it was too late now—the vision was in motion.

Frantically, I pressed buttons on my phone's screen, trying to get back to Trevors, but he was gone. I pulled up the number he'd called from and hit redial. Tapping my foot against the divider in front of my seat, I waited while the phone rang—and rang and rang.

Crap. What was I supposed to do now? There was no one else to turn to, no one to ask for help. Except . . .

Matthew.

Of course! I dug in my pocket and pulled out the crumpled slip of paper. I misdialed twice, completely unable to make my fingers work properly. After the third try, it started to ring.

"Violet?" he said, sounding breathless. "Where are you?"

"Stuck in traffic, trying to get home." I was nearly blubbering now. "You've got to help me—it's Aidan! My friend Whitney . . . a vision . . . he's going to attack her!" I couldn't even string together a coherent sentence.

"Take a deep breath, okay?" It sounded like he was on the street, walking. Running, maybe. "I think I had the same vision—blond girl, pink sweater, ponytail? In Central Park?"

"Yes! It's all happening, right now."

"Shit. I think Aidan injected the new serum this morning." He sounded slightly stunned.

"He *what?*" I asked, my voice rising. *No!* He'd promised me that he wouldn't.

"I'm on my way, okay? Meet me in the park, at the foot tunnel. Do you know which one?"

Of course I did—the image was burned into my brain. I glanced out the window, surprised to find that we'd finally made it across the park. We were halfway down the block between Fifth and Madison, waiting for the light. It wouldn't take me long to get there on foot.

"Yeah, I know where it is," I told him. "I'm going to get out of the car now and run."

"And, Violet . . . bring your stake."

My stake?

"Go," he yelled into the phone. "Now!"

I ended the call and banged on the glass, trying to get the driver's attention. Slowly, it slid down.

"I'm getting out here."

"What about your luggage?" he asked, his puzzled gaze meeting mine in the rearview mirror.

"Just take it to my apartment—the address you've got. Leave it with the doorman." I was already opening the door and reaching for my bag—the one that held my stake. *This can't be happening.*

I stepped out, lifting my bag over my head and draping it across my body as I prepared to run.

I took off at a sprint. My panic rose with each slap of my shoes against the sidewalk. I was nearly hyperventilating, blinded by tears as I ran, picking my way through the crowds of pedestrians. I missed a curb and tripped, twisting my ankle. Ignoring the pain, I continued on, running as fast as I could into the streetlamp-lit park.

Please, oh please. Just let me get there in time.

Or, even better, let me be wrong. Let Whitney be safe with the doorman right now, Aidan standing at the apartment door, shaking his head and wondering what is going on.

At last I found the path toward the foot tunnel. It was strangely empty, the landscape as bare and brittle as it had been in my vision. I picked up my pace, ignoring the painful stitch in my side and the twinge in my ankle. At last the tunnel came into view, the yellow light illuminating it as eerily as I'd remembered.

I paused, listening for footsteps as I caught my breath. I heard them up ahead on the footpath to the left, a dirt track that led slightly uphill under a canopy of barren, spindly branches.

"Whitney?" I called out as I dashed up the path. In seconds,

I crested the rise, and there she was, just up ahead, directly beneath a streetlamp.

"Violet?" She stumbled, half turning in my direction as she fell to her knees, her eyes widening with terror as Aidan appeared—*poof*—just like that, midway between where I stood and where Whitney cowered. "No!" she cried out.

He was seemingly unaware of my presence as he bore down on his prey. He was in some sort of a trance, I realized.

He could have struck in an instant, his movements a blur to the human eye. Instead he moved slowly, deliberately. It was almost as if . . . as if he were toying with her.

"He kept appearing out of nowhere," Whitney sobbed, her terrified gaze meeting mine. "I didn't know where to go. I just . . . kept running."

I watched, frozen in fear as he reached out and grabbed her arm, pulling her to her feet.

"Aidan!" I screamed. "Stop!"

Still clutching Whitney by the arm, he turned, his eyes a horrifying red. He lifted his lips in a sneer, exposing his fangs.

Holy hell and God in heaven. Whatever this creature was, it wasn't Aidan. It was a shell of him, a horror-movie imitation. He wasn't in his right mind. Something was wrong—really, really wrong.

I heard pounding footsteps, and then Matthew drew up

beside me. I realized then how vulnerable he was, how vulnerable we all were. Aidan didn't recognize me, didn't know me. He could very well kill us all.

"Get your stake, Violet," Matthew said breathlessly. "Now!"

Dazed, I nodded, unzipping my bag and reaching inside. I let out a gasp of surprise as my fingers closed around the smooth, satiny shaft. Instantly my mind was flooded with thoughts—Aidan's thoughts. A single thought, actually: *Feed*.

I tightened my grip, choking on a sob. *This isn't right!* a voice screamed in my head. No, I'd had another vision where I'd seen myself plunge something directly into Aidan's heart, but it hadn't been here, in the middle of Central Park on a cold December night. We'd been inside, on plush, thick carpeting. And he'd been lucid, arguing with me, urging me to do it. I could still change this. I *had* to.

"Aidan, please!" I tried again, taking two steps toward him. "Let her go. You don't want to do this."

Matthew grabbed me by the wrist and dragged me back to him. "Listen to me," he whispered harshly, his mouth beside my ear. "You've got to do this—he's not himself, don't you see? He's going to kill us if you don't."

"No," I said, struggling from his grasp. "I can get through to him; you've got to let me try."

He shook his head. "I can't let you do this."

But I *could* do it. Like Jenna in the vision with Julius last year, *I* was the different element this time—the element that could set the chain of events off onto a different course.

With some of my visions, it was clear that I wasn't actually there. I was like a fly on the wall, watching the action unfold. But with others, I *was* there, an integral part of the action. Matthew had helped me learn to distinguish between the two.

In this dream that was really a vision, I hadn't been there. I hadn't been able to interact, just watch. Which meant my very presence—here, now—could change things, could alter the outcome.

"Look at me, Aidan," I called out, my voice deceptively calm as I moved toward him, holding my stake close. *Please, God, don't make me have to use it.*

I switched to telepathic mode. *You don't want to hurt her,* I said. *You don't want to hurt anybody.*

Still clutching a whimpering Whitney, Aidan blinked several times, shaking his head, as if he were trying to rid it of my voice.

Aidan, please. I took another tentative step in his direction. *Look at me—look into my eyes.*

He did.

30 ~ . . . Beyond Repair

My gaze locked onto Aidan's bloodred one, and suddenly all I could think about was driving my stake through his heart.

The urge was overwhelming, my fingers itching, the adrenaline surging through my veins like a drug.

No. I forced it back, commanded myself to ignore it. *Not yet.*

"Christ, Violet, why are you hesitating?" came Matthew's panicked voice behind me.

I ignored him.

Just listen to me, I commanded, my gaze never leaving Aidan's. *I love you, with all my heart. You're not yourself; you don't know what you're doing.*

Violet? His voice was weak, just a whisper in my mind. But it was there—I could hear it, I swore I could.

"Violet, you've got to do it," Matthew shouted. "I know you don't want to, that you—"

"I've got this, Matthew—just trust me," I called out, refusing to turn around, to break the visual connection.

"Please, Violet," Whitney whimpered. "Do something."

Aidan, are you listening to me? You're going to cure yourself, and we're going to be together, always. But you've got to wake up from this; you've got to let her go.

Something weird was happening with his eyes. The red receded, then flooded back in again. Once, twice.

Aidan? I prodded. *Come on, Aidan. Please. Just let her go.*

He released Whitney then, just like that. She fell to the ground and scrabbled away, half running, half crawling. Matthew reached for her and pulled her back behind me.

"Are you okay?" I asked her. "Please tell me that you're okay!"

She nodded vigorously, her eyes wide with shock. "I think so."

"Thank God," I mumbled.

"Go!" Matthew told her, his voice urgent. "Back to Violet's apartment, okay? We'll come for you as soon as we can. Can you find your way?"

She nodded, and I turned back toward Aidan as she dashed away to safety.

Aidan?

Violet? He took a step toward me. Again, the red washed from his eyes, revealing the familiar blue-gray.

I'm here. I shifted my stake into my left hand, and reached my empty one out toward him. *Take my hand. Come back to me.*

"Violet, no!" came Matthew's voice behind me. "What the hell are you doing?"

"Shh. It's working."

"*What's* working? You're not doing anything!"

"I'm talking to him in my head," I said, still holding out my hand to Aidan, willing him to take it. "And it's working; he's listening."

"You're . . . what? How?"

I love you, Aidan. Somehow it just seemed like the right thing to say, over and over again. *Wake up. Please?*

This time he spoke aloud. "Violet?" He took my hand, clasping it tightly in his. The moment he did, his features slipped back to normal. The color returned to his eyes and stayed there; his fangs retracted. He blinked several times, shaking his head.

He was himself again, just like that.

"Oh, thank God," I said. I unclenched my left fist, allowing the stake to clatter to the ground.

He glanced around, taking in his surroundings. "Dr. Byrne? What are you doing here? What's going on?"

"You don't remember?" I asked.

His gaze landed on the stake by my feet, his face a mask of confusion. "Violet, what . . . why?"

I swallowed hard, unable to speak. What was I going to tell him? Wordlessly, I turned toward Matthew.

He stepped up beside me. "You were attacking her friend, Aidan. You could have killed her."

"I . . . what?" He looked as if Matthew had slapped him.

"What's the last thing you remember?" he pressed. "C'mon, think back. How did you get here?"

Aidan's brow furrowed in concentration. "I was at school, at the lab. I injected the serum. I'm so sorry, Violet," he said quickly. "I know I promised I wouldn't, and I meant to keep that promise. But, damn it, I was *so* sure this time, positive that I'd finally perfected it. I couldn't wait another minute, not if it meant I could be with you over break without worrying about biting you again."

Beside me, Matthew groaned. "Again? What does he mean, again?"

I ignored him, raising a hand to massage my now-throbbing

temple. "Oh, Aidan," I said with a sigh. "I really wish you hadn't."

"I took a blood sample afterward, to check," he continued. "I knew then that I was wrong, that it hadn't worked. Still, I felt fine. I needed to see you, to apologize for breaking my promise, to talk about"—he glanced over at Matthew, then shifted his gaze guiltily back to mine—"what happened in the loft. I had some things to do first, some notes to enter into the computer. I went home, just before nightfall, and then I set out for Patsy's apartment. That's the last thing I remember."

Matthew glanced up at the inky sky. "Maybe it has something to do with night falling, then," he speculated. "Maybe you're fine during the day, but as soon as the sun goes down, something happens inside you? Like . . . Jekyll and Hyde."

I shivered violently, suddenly cold. My hands were like ice, my cheeks numb.

"She's freezing," Matthew said, shaking his head. "We've got to get her inside."

"M-Matthew," I stuttered, my teeth chattering now. "C-can you call a c-cab or something? I've got to check on Whitney."

"Whitney?" Aidan asked. "Your friend in Atlanta?"

"She was here," Matthew explained. "She's the one you attacked."

"I . . . what?" He raked a hand through his hair. "Please tell me that I didn't hurt her, that I didn't—"

"You didn't," I said, shaking my head. "She's fine."

Matthew nodded. "She was luckier than that woman they found in the woods at Winterhaven."

Aidan's gaze snapped up at once. "You think that I . . . that I'm responsible for that woman's death? That I'm the Stalker?"

"After seeing you tonight, Aidan, what else can I think? If Violet hadn't been here, if she hadn't managed to get through to you . . ." He shook his head. "Christ, I don't even want to think about it."

A shudder worked its way down my spine. Oh my God. Aidan had *killed* that woman. I clapped one hand over my mouth, afraid I might vomit.

"We've got to get her out of the cold." Matthew wrapped his arms around my shoulders. He was warm, *so* warm. I leaned into him, my legs suddenly weak, my twisted ankle throbbing.

"I'll go get a cab," Aidan said, his voice flat and lifeless. "I'll take Violet with me."

Matthew tightened his grip on me. "Oh, no, you won't."

"It's the fastest way," Aidan argued, "and she's clearly in no shape to walk."

"There's no way I'm leaving her alone with you." His tone

was firm, resolute. "Go, hail us a cab. We'll meet you by the street."

I closed my eyes, taking a deep breath. When I opened them, Aidan was gone.

"You okay to walk?" Matthew released me, leaning down to retrieve my stake.

"I . . . yeah, I think so." But as soon as I took a few steps, my ankle buckled. I winced, crying out in pain.

"You're not okay," he said, stepping in front of me and bending down. "Go on, hop on my back."

I shook my head. "You're crazy. You can't carry me out of here like that."

"Of course I can. Now hop on."

With a groan, I followed his command. He straightened, hiking me up higher on his back, and then set off. I wrapped my arms around his neck, laying my cheek flat on his back, absorbing his heat.

We continued on in silence, past the tunnel, back down the winding walk that led to the park's edge. I could hear the sounds of traffic now, a siren blaring in the distance, a horn honking.

When we reached the street, Aidan was there, standing beside a yellow cab. "I gave him a hundred to wait," he called out, meeting us on the walk, "so there's no rush."

Matthew stopped, bending his knees so I could slide down. I bit my lip, trying not to cry out in pain as my right foot made contact with the ground.

"Aidan? Master Gray? Oh, thank God, I'm not too late."

We all turned in unison to see Trevors move out of the darkness toward us.

"Trevors?" Aidan took a step toward him. "What are you doing here?"

Trevors looked from Aidan to me, and back to Aidan again. "Has anyone been harmed?"

"No, we're fine," I said. "Well, except my ankle."

"What's going on?" Aidan asked.

Trevors swallowed hard, indecision written all over his face.

"C'mon, Trevors," Aidan pressed. "You've got to tell me why you're here."

"Perhaps later," he hedged. "In private."

"No, now. You can speak freely in front of them." He tipped his head in our direction.

The elderly man nodded. "Very well. You came by the town house today and told me that you planned to go to Miss McKenna's apartment this evening. But when you set out, I could see that you . . . well, that you were slipping away from yourself. I've seen it before; I know the signs. Normally I don't interfere, but in this case it seemed prudent."

He nodded in my direction before continuing. "So I called her and warned her, just to be safe. I've been trying to track you ever since, afraid I was too late."

"What do you mean, you've seen it before?" Aidan asked.

Trevors shook his head. "You, in some sort of altered state. It's as if you don't see me, don't see anyone except perhaps your prey."

Aidan visibly flinched. "My prey?"

"They're not my concern—you are," Trevors said with a shrug. "And when you come home, disheveled and disoriented, it's not my place to ask where you've been or what you've been doing. It's my job to clean you up, to see to your care and comfort, that's all."

"What the hell?" Matthew shook his head. "Are you saying that you've known all along that he was the Stalker, and you've been covering for him?"

Trevors shot him a glare. "I had suspicions, nothing more. No proof. All I knew for certain was that if he *was* the one they were calling the Stalker, he had no idea, no memories of the attacks. I had to protect him."

Holy hell. This was a nightmare—an un-freaking-believable nightmare—and it just kept getting worse.

Aidan turned toward Matthew, his face seemingly blank now. "Can you see her safely home? Her stepmother's out of town. You should stay with her tonight and make sure she and Whitney are okay."

"What? No," I protested. "Aren't you coming with us?"

He shook his head, his eyes full of such sadness that I could barely stand to look at them. "I'm going back to Winterhaven. To Mrs. Girard. I'm turning myself in to the Tribunal, Violet."

"No," I cried, reaching for his arm. "Just . . . come home with me. You need to see Whitney, to see that she's okay. And then . . . I don't know, maybe we can figure out why this happened. It's not your fault; you didn't mean to hurt anyone. You can't just turn yourself over to them." Bile rose in my throat at the thought of what the Tribunal would do to him. "Not now, not till we can explain what happened and why."

And there *would* have to be an explanation.

I took a deep, ragged breath. And then I remembered the vision I'd had—the one in the lab, the one that hadn't made any sense to me. It had been so brief, just a quick series of images. I'd thought I'd seen Aidan using a dropper to take something from a vial and drop it into a test tube. It had been just a flash, my vantage showing me nothing more than a pair of hands and what they held.

I hadn't really thought about it much, mostly because it had seemed so harmless at the time. I'd even considered the possibility that it hadn't been a vision—that I'd simply breached Aidan's mind and seen him working in the lab.

But now . . . now I realized there was another possibility. Maybe someone had tampered with his work, and I'd seen it happen. But who? It had to be someone who had access to the labs, someone who understood the science behind the work, and who had the means to effect whatever disastrous outcome they'd planned.

I looked over at Matthew—my protector. Could he possibly have done something so terrible, so cruel? Or Jack? Jack had changed this year, seemingly pulling away from all of us. Was *he* somehow capable of something like this? And then there was Tyler. Tyler, who didn't much like Aidan, who always wanted to win. The Stalker's attacks had only begun *after* Tyler's arrival at Winterhaven. A coincidence?

"Violet?" Aidan said, drawing me from my thoughts. He reached for my face, cradling it with both his hands. "Look at me. I am so very sorry. For everything. For breaking my promise, for hurting you, for hurting your friend. I love you; I'll always love you. Just remember that, okay? But I have to do this; I have to turn myself over to them. I always said I was a monster, didn't I? Now you have proof." His voice broke, and I looked away.

I couldn't bear it, couldn't stand to look at him while he told me good-bye. Because that's what this was—a good-bye. God only knew what they were going to do him. According to Trevors, he'd gotten twenty years of confinement just for destroying a murderous vampire. This was so much worse—innocent people hurt, a woman killed, their rules flouted. He'd risked exposing the very existence of vampires, even if he hadn't known he was doing any of it.

Whatever the penalty was, it would be harsh. I wouldn't see him again, not in this lifetime.

"Don't, Aidan," I pleaded, reaching up to grip his wrists. "Please, you can't do this."

"I have to, don't you see? How can I look at you, touch you, without remembering what I've done? You deserve better. Remember, you're a *Sâbbat*. Find your *Megvéd*. You're meant to be with him, not me."

With a start, I turned toward Matthew. He was leaning against the cab now, watching us intently.

Aidan's gaze followed mine. A split second later I saw a flicker of understanding in his eyes. "Ah, I see you've found him already."

I felt it then—his pain. Exquisite pain, radiating from inside him in rippling waves of utter devastation and hopelessness. With a gasp, I blocked my mind, unable to bear it.

When he raised his gaze to meet mine, his eyes were shuttered, his expression wiped clean. "It's okay, love. You need to go. Whitney's all alone, and you've got a lot to explain to her."

I nodded, choking back a sob.

He glanced back at Matthew, his expression grave. "Dr. Byrne?" he said, taking a step away from the curb. Away from *me*. "Take care of her, okay?"

Matthew nodded. "Of course."

Aidan turned back toward me. He raised a hand to his lips and kissed his fingers, then pressed them against my chest. *I'll always be yours*, came his voice in my head. *Heart and soul.*

And then he simply turned and walked away, falling into step beside Trevors.

Matthew reached for me, steadying me. Wordlessly, he helped me into the cab. As soon as the door shut, he called out my address to the cabbie. I had no idea how he knew it; I didn't care.

The car lurched forward, and I twisted in the seat, looking out the rear window, hoping for one last glimpse of Aidan—just one.

But he and Trevors had vanished, swallowed up into the night.

"It'll be okay, Violet," Matthew murmured beside me. "It has to be this way; deep in your heart, you know it. There's no other way."

Oh, but there is.

Straightening my spine, I turned to face forward, my jaw

set with determination. There *was* another way, and I was going to find it. If they thought I was going to sit by idly and let them take Aidan, let them torture him or whatever else the Tribunal did to their prisoners, they were wrong. *Dead* wrong.

I wasn't sure what my next move was, but I knew I needed to find Mrs. Girard, and fast. I needed to talk to her. If she wasn't still at Winterhaven, Cece could help me track her down. In the meantime, I'd get Matthew to help me replay the vision that I believed showed the sabotage. There must be some small clue that I'd missed, not realizing its importance. Some identifying mark on the hands I'd seen, maybe. A blemish. A watch. *Something.*

I glanced up, the city lights reduced to a colorful blur outside the cab's window. My resolve strengthened with every block, my certainty increasing.

Mrs. Girard would listen to me. After all, Aidan was her greatest creation, her crown jewel. She needed him for *something*, and whatever it was, it was important to her. She didn't realize that I knew about his royal lineage or that I'd told Aidan about it. I would use that to my advantage, somehow.

And Aidan, well . . . at some point he'd have to forgive himself. I knew it wasn't going to be easy, but maybe proof that someone had sabotaged his work would make it more so.

At least, I hoped it would.

"Right over here, at the end of the block," Matthew called out. As the cab slid in front of Patsy's building, he gently touched my hand. "Hey, you okay?"

I took a deep breath, and then looked him in the eye, my *Megvéd*. "I'm going to be," I said with a nod. We were *all* going to be okay—even Aidan. I would make sure of it.

Because despite it all, I still loved him. I *knew* him, recognized the kindred heart that beat inside his immortal body, desperate to be set free.

I was going to set him free.

There was at least one part of the *Sâbbat*/vampire legend that was correct: He was meant for me, and I for him.

Just not quite the way it was intended.

ACKNOWLEDGMENTS

I'm always amazed when I realize how many people play a role in turning an idea into a real, actual book. What seems at first glance a solitary effort is really a collaboration, and I have so many people to thank.

First, my wonderful critique partners and beta readers. Carey Corp, I couldn't have done this one without you! Your notes, ideas, and brainstorming sessions—all priceless. Thank you! An equally enthusiastic thank-you to Cindy Thomas and Amalie Howard. I owe you all some *serious* chocolate!

Thanks also to my supersupportive writer peeps—the ones who listen to me whine and help keep me sane on a daily basis: Ann Christopher, Lori Devoti, Laura Drewry, Caroline Linden, Sally MacKenzie, and Eve Silver. You all are the bestest.

As always, a giant thank-you to my amazing agent, Marcy Posner, and equally fab editor, Jennifer Klonsky. I'm so lucky to work with the awesome team at Simon Pulse—Michael Strother, Lydia Finn, Carolyn Swerdloff, Dawn Ryan, and so many others. Cupcakes one day. I promise.

Thank you to the readers and bloggers who embraced

Haven and who dedicate so much time and effort to the YA community. Special thanks to the lovely ladies at Good Choice Reading: Damaris, Wanda, and Maria. You rock!

And last, a huge, sloppy thank-you to my wonderful family—Dan, Vivian, and Eleanor. Love you guys!